This is a work of fiction. Names, characters, places, and incidents either are the product of the author's imagination or are used fictitiously, and any resemblance to actual persons, living or dead, business establishments, events, or locales are entirely coincidental.

Wahida Clark Presents Publishing
60 Evergreen Place
Suite 904
East Orange, New Jersey 07018
973-678-9982
www.wclarkpublishing.com

Butterfly by Michael A. Robinson
ISBN 13-digit 978-19366496-8-6
ISBN 10-digit 1936649683

Library of Congress Cataloging-In-Publication Data:
LCCN 2014904049
   1. transvestite  2. Thug Life  3. Thugs
   4. Check Fraud  5. Life Sentence Years
   6. Transgender    7. Drug dealers    8. Black
   Romance Novels  9. Sexual Abuse

Cover design and layout by Nuance Art LLC
Book design by Nuance Art LLC
Proofreader Rosalind Hamilton
Sr. Editor Linda Wilson

# Acknowledgements

I was in deep waters when it came down to writing this manuscript. So I want to give a shout out to Damien Amin Meadows, who not only inspired me to write Butterfly, but gave me the blueprint with his masterful and exciteful Convict's Candy. Big Homie – you know you lit the torch for people enjoying books dealing with subject matters that people deem taboo. I just hope I have the skills to keep 'Convict Candy's legend alive. We spent hours hitting the yard and screaming door-to-door in the SHU at Loretto, PA with always one goal: how to pencil a good book and gracefully depict the raunchy details. Keep ya head up Amin.

I have to give a shout out to my sister's Neshay (Neehigh), Faith (Dookey), and Joy (Green Booty). Without ya'll three's love and support, I would have fallen apart. Ya'll show me that blood is thicker than water, stronger than concrete, and more durable than eternity.

You know I can't forget about my spring-chicken Lachez & Tyshea. Lachez, we are bonded by that unique thing called love. You remember what I told you: "You cannot humble vanity!" You know I'll never say that at you, but at those forces that are behind my incarceration. You know what I have endured and the people who tried to step on me. But it's the samething: They can't humble me. Love you Golden' Girl.

To my Big Brothers, Omar Kadafi & Arron. I owe ya'll two everything; Omar- for making me sharp intellectually; and Arron- for making me tough. Real talk, ya'll are like demigods in my eyes. Ain't nothing we can't make happen together.

What about my cousins EJ & Joey! You two are more than extended family: we brothers. You know what it is. What up RaRa! We go back to Midtown Ave. in Carson CA. what up DGAF! What up Delamo! The Feds only took me out physically, but my heart is always there, AAAAh!

To my two seeds- - sons its about strategizing success. Chill-out and watch your Pops pluck this chicken. Erica, we just had a bad start. But the race is measured by its finish, and we're nowhere close to the finishline. You remember what my moms said.

John Cornelious, T-Bone, Blue, Meeko, J, Joe Red, Barima what's up Carson's Finest. Yeah- when I touch down, let the Revolution begin. Jaban & Big Suge, ya'll real niggas in my book.

To Wahida Clark [WC]! The embodiment of Auset, [Isis] bringing together the dismemberment of the Blackman [Ausar Osiris] by creating a Movement that empowers them financially & intellectually.

I'll never begin to describe my appreciation for when you welcomed me to the fam 'WCP' and was there for me during my darkest hours. Let's make history, because you gave me the best editor Maxine Thompson.

Daddy, it wouldn't be right if I wasn't your spittenimage. "I'll always love my momma." Momma, I was your worst but your favorite. I miss you more. To my G-moms who's always believed in me. Last but not least- to Phil and G-pops. R.I.P.

This wouldn't be right without a shot-out to the LGBT Community! Dudes incarcerated are praying earnestly peradventure a Butterfly would pop up – so they could turn it up a notch in here. Let them know—

Don't front. Because the Butterflies I've seen come

# CONELY BRANCH

thru here done turned these fools out. Who am I to judge? Enjoy!

# BUTTERFLY

## Prologue

W ho's counterfeiting these checks?" the detective asked, sitting in a room filled with cigarette smoke.

"I don't know, I don't know." Peyton's whimpers worsened as the interview continued.

"Aw, give me a break with the sad girl act. You could be facing some serious charges that we could easily drop if you give up your source."

A smile appeared on Peyton's face once the detective said that. "You can drop the charges?"

"That's on the condition that you give us your source. We want to know who's making these counterfeit checks."

Peyton stopped her tears from falling. This was the hardest decision she'd ever have to make. But once made, she had to make sure that everything fell into place.

"Okay . . . Okay . . . I'll give you my source."

"When?" the detective asked.

"Please, can you give me a couple of days?"

The detective looked up at his partner who had just lit up another Marlboro. His partner nodded. "Sure, you got a week."

That's all she'd ever need.

\* \* \* \* \* \*

Summer almost missed the call she should have been expecting. It was no one other than her best friend.

She rushed to answer the phone. "Peyton?"

"Where are you? You should have been here."

"Hold your horses, bitch. I'm on my way." Summer hung up and washed her face after she finished brushing her teeth. She listened to Rihanna on her iPod, mouthing along to the song "Diamonds." Summer threw on a red spencer dress and some easy going flip-flops. One look in the mirror was all she needed to kick-start her day.

Breathtaking . . .

She flashed her porcelain smile, and she couldn't believe there was so much resemblance between her and her favorite artist Rihanna, except that she had more luscious measurements: 36-22-40; but lacked the colored eyes. The other thing she shared with Rihanna was the sex appeal.

It hadn't always been that way.

Summer hopped in her Range Rover truck that her uncle Kevin had bought her, and bee-lined it to Peyton's apartment across town.

Washington, DC at this time of the day had the worst traffic.

Peyton came out on the first honk of the horn wearing Michael Kors sandals with highlights of lime that went well with the lime green Bongo watch. She carried an {insert color here} Aldo bag. Candies' sunglasses hid her eyes. Summer's little white friend was fly. The graphic design Mill dress accentuated the soft touches of her curves.

"Come on, girl! We're running late," Peyton said.

"You need to hurry up and get your car out of the shop," Summer replied.

# BUTTERFLY

Peyton rolled her eyes. Their friendship had seen better days. Summer had, had a tragic breakup with Peyton's cousin, Clayton, who had beaten her nearly to death. Afterward, they just never had the same connection as friends.

Their photo shoot was in Hyattsville, Maryland. When they pulled up to the warehouse, a dark van swerved alongside Summer's truck as she parked, and three guys hopped out waving shotguns.

"Get out the truck, bitch!" one of the masked gunmen said as he leveled the double barrel shotgun in Summer's face.

It took everything in Summer's power not to faint, and she immediately started to sob. "I don't wanna die! Please don't kill me! I have some money in my purse!"

One of the other masked gunmen who was pulling Peyton around from the other side of the truck said, "Bitch, do you have eighty thousand dollars in your purse?"

"I'm gonna die!" Summer cried, realizing she only had $800 in her purse.

"Shut the fuck up!" the masked gunman yelled.

It only took seconds before Summer heard Peyton being smacked to the ground.

"Where's Ellis' money? You think you can play with somebody like Ellis? Bitch, you'll watch all your friends die first."

"I'm gonna get it," Peyton managed to say. But before she could finish, one of the masked gunmen was already flinging stuff out of Summer's purse. That was until he found Summer's ID.

"By midnight, if you don't have that eighty grand, I'm going to kill your girlfriend, and then tomorrow

3

we'll find somebody else close to you to kill. Maybe your cousin, Clayton."

"No! Don't kill my friend."

"Well then, get that money!"

The masked man showed Sumner her own ID, as if she didn't believe he had it. With one last shove to the ground where Summer nearly lost her porcelain smile, the three armed gunmen hopped in the van and skirted off.

"I'm gonna die!" Summer kept saying through sobs. There was no way in hell that she could go through with her photo shoot. If those guys were telling the truth, they'd never have to worry about a photo shoot ever again.

Everything dawned on Summer as Peyton tried to hug her. She pushed her away but then tried to claw her eyes out. "They're gonna kill me because of you!"

Peyton was quicker than she looked. She jumped back and held her hands out in complete submission.

"Summer, wait! We can get the money. You know how to get the money. We can have it by nightfall." Peyton kept a fair distance as Summer neared her.

"I can't ask my uncle? I told you the situation between us."

"You know what I mean, Summer. We only have a little while left."

"You want me to cash some checks? Are you crazy! I nearly died the last time when I almost got caught."

"You're my only chance."

"It's your own fault; all you do is gamble. I can't believe you went to a loan shark like Ellis. He would rather clean his books with bullets than to be owed."

"Help me please!" Peyton begged.

# BUTTERFLY

Summer went back to her Range Rover and sat down. She couldn't believe she was getting pulled into something she promised herself she'd never do again: bank fraud. But the more she saw the tears sprouting from her friend's eyes, and the promise of death lingering overhead, her decision was easy to make.

"Get in the car."

\* \* \* \* \* \*

*Damn . . . Damn . . . Damn . . .* Summer thought as she bee-lined it back to her apartment. She made one quick stop at Office Depot to get the specific set of checks she needed: payroll checks. She had been doing the scam for years until her tumultuous relationship with the love of her life, Clayton had come to an end, and she moved back to town.

But Summer didn't have any of her fraud ware on hand, and she'd have to go and get everything together.

She couldn't even look at Peyton as she got back in the truck after leaving Office Depot. The most she ever made cashing checks was eight to ten G's in one day. It was impossible in her mind to pull off ten times that much. But only if she could get enough good paper.

Summer stared ahead, but she told Peyton, "I'm gonna drop you off at your apartment. Put on a nice, classy business suit and break out a briefcase. In about an hour, I'll come back and pick you up."

Peyton still had a shimmer of tears and a dash of fear in her eyes that lightened once she realized Summer would help her. "Thank you."

Summer took a deep breath. She couldn't be mad at her friend. "Don't worry. We'll have it by nightfall."

After leaving Peyton's apartment, she had to kick everything into gear. She had to get the account numbers from a guy she hadn't spoken to in six months, then go back to her apartment, make the checks, and then go and cash them. But there was a big glitch in her program. She didn't know if Glen, whom she hadn't spoken to in six months, would give her the account numbers. And that's why she was headed to her house instead of the bank.

She went into the house and quickly dressed in the sluttiest mini-dress in her closet. Then she put on foundation and the reddest lipstick she could find. Black eyeliner darkened her eyelids, and she pulled her hair into a neat ponytail. Damn, she needed her stylist, but this would have to do.

She kicked her flip flops off for a more seductive pair of Narcisco Rodriguez wedges that stuck her fine ass up for display, and then she headed straight for the door as she made the phone call she said she'd never make again.

Glen picked up on the second ring.

Summer was already hightailing it to his office, and it didn't matter what he said because by the end of the phone call she would have those much needed account numbers.

"What do you need, Butterfly?" His voice was flat, but after six months he didn't need her to ask or say anything to know she needed something.

"Glen . . . Hey. I wanted to call you because I haven't heard from you."

Glen smirked as he looked off to the side. He still wondered about Butterfly, who had all but pushed him away after he expressed his love for her.

"Are you still having nightmares?" Glen asked.

# BUTTERFLY

His inquiry was like a punch in Summer's gut. She figured he'd forgotten that. She'd been having them for as long as she could remember.

"I need to see you," she said, ignoring his question.

"Not now. I'm very busy." He couldn't have known that Summer was pulling up outside his law practice. She slid into the vacant parking spot next to his BMW and blatantly honked the horn. "Who the hell is that?" Glen asked.

"It's me," Summer said, putting the truck in park. She exited the vehicle and stood there so he could see her from his office window.

"I'll be out in just a second." They hung up as Summer laughed to herself.

"I thought so . . ." she said in an even voice.

It's true that Glen looked like a version of Eddie Murphy who had a serious bout with weight gain. He could dress nice, but the flopping love handles on his bad body threw everything off.

"I haven't heard from you in quite some time," Glen said, subdued by the lust egging at every ounce of his core.

"Glen, I'm really, really needing a really big favor," Summer said as she ran her fingers along his neckline and got closer and closer.

"I knew you needed something." He was almost about to break into a sweat. Summer was damn near breathing down his neck.

"I only need a dozen," she said as she slid her hand over his crotch area and gripped his dick.

"A dozen!" Even with her hand on his dick massaging it so pleasurably, the request was way beyond his limits. "I'll give you three."

7

# MICHAEL A. ROBINSON

"No!" Summer whined like a spoiled child. She pushed him on her truck and stuck her tongue down his throat.

"Okay, I'll give you five."

That still wasn't enough. She had calculated that the account numbers' figures would make a bit over eighty grand after she cashed them. But that would mean she'd need twelve checks to arrive at that amount. She knew what she'd have to do.

"Get in the backseat of the truck," she said.

Glen couldn't believe his ears. She briefly gave him some a year ago, but he had begged and begged for some more, but she never relented, using it as a carrot for a chasing horse.

He got in the back of the truck, and she followed him as she shut the door. Glen felt the pressure of his stiffened penis as she zipped his pants down and slammed his dick in her mouth.

"Oh God yes, Butterfly!" He sounded pathetic. It wasn't cries of pleasure, but admission of the love he still had for her.

Summer sucked on his dick as she looked at her watch. Fuck! It was nearly 12:00 p.m., and she still had to print the checks, get dressed, and pick up Peyton. She started to hum on his dick until he shot a wad down her throat that she gladly swallowed.

"Oh my god! I'm in love with you!" He kissed Summer's soft lips. How much longer would this have to take! It was unbelievable, but he was trying to undress her and his dick was still hard!

"Glen, I'm gonna give you some more tonight," Summer said in her most seductive way.

8

# BUTTERFLY

"I know, baby, but we're only at eight if you leave now."

Summer could have cursed under her breath, but she had to hurry and get twelve account numbers and skedaddle the fuck out of there.

"I ain't going nowhere until you fuck me in the ass and give me twelve."

"Oh baby, you're gonna give me some ass?" His lips were almost quivering with excitement.

"That's what I said I had for you." Summer didn't waste a moment. She spit amply on his dick and again in her hand as she pulled her mini-dress up and lubed up her ass. He was already groping away on her tits as she put her back to him and guided his medium size dick into her asshole.

"Oh fuck, Cla—" She almost slipped and said Clayton, but she corrected herself gracefully and said, "Glen. You feel so good." She hadn't fucked around in a minute, and it didn't feel good at all—it hurt like hell. But she slammed her hips back faster and faster until he was grunting and panting.

"Ahh—yes!" he uttered as he exploded. That time around, Summer had drained him completely. "Twelve . . . no—I'm gonna give you twenty." And that was that.

\* \* \* \* \* \*

Summer was back home in a flash. She looked at her watch. She had eighteen minutes left before she'd have to pick up Peyton. Her computer already had the software she needed to make the checks, so she entered the account numbers she had gotten from Glen, who in turn had gotten the account numbers from the accountant who worked at his firm. Summer pressed twenty copies each for all twenty account numbers.

While that was hatching, she ran to the shower and washed Glen off her and out of her and then dressed in a business skirt suit.

Time was ticking away.

She had to make the transactions during lunch hours, which was the busiest time of day. It would give her a higher chance that the bank wouldn't call on the checks to see if the people had written the checks out to her. But she knew if she didn't get a hold of herself, she would later regret it.

Summer took her medicine for her bipolar disorder and popped two Molly pills behind it. It was her favorite forbidden mix. After she made sure she looked decent, she grabbed the payroll checks off the laser printer and was out the door.

* * * * * *

Peyton was outside awaiting Summer's arrival. Peyton looked the part well enough. Since Summer had taken her meds and got fucked fast and hard in the ass, she didn't feel so hateful toward her friend.

"No time to waste. We have to cash these checks at their home branch. If they call on the check, leave immediately. We can go to the same banks and cash them together, but we have to hurry up and do this while it's lunch time." Summer explained every detail of the process.

Peyton flipped her eyes because she didn't need the pep talk. She had done this a thousand times, but she never learned how Summer got the paper. She still didn't know Summer's source.

Bank of America on M Street was their first stop. Each check was made out for eight G's, and if everything went according to plan, they'd be finished by the end of the lunch hour.

"You ready?" Summer asked.

"Yeah, I'm ready. I'm going to wait three minutes, and then I'll come in behind you."

"Okay. I'll see you then."

Summer went straight into the bank. Everything was going smooth. The guard standing at the door smiled at her and that always was a good sign.

As the line dwindled down to her, she noticed that Peyton still hadn't come in yet. Gosh, the bitch had to be faster on her feet, or they would never be finished by her timetable.

It was her turn . . .

Summer went to the bank teller, who was a female. That was always a bad sign. She should have allowed herself to be skipped until a male bank teller's counter became available.

*Damn, shit wasn't adding up.* And just then Summer remembered: she had forgotten to put super glue on her fingertips to cover up her fingerprints. *Shit!*

Everything in her mind told her to abandon this mission. But she couldn't just walk out with the threat of death hanging overhead. And shit! She didn't even have her ID anymore.

"Can I help you?" the easy-going bank teller asked.

Summer smiled kindly, and all her tension and uneasiness came off naturally.

"Yes. I'd like to cash this check."

"I'll just need your ID."

*Of course*, Summer thought. She fumbled through her purse and her wallet and lucky enough, her driver's

# MICHAEL A. ROBINSON

license wasn't taken by the masked gunman. She always kept it behind her ID.

But still no Peyton anywhere in sight. *What the fuck!*

Summer laid her driver's license on the table to hear words that anybody who cashed checks illegally would hate to hear: "I'm going to have to check something real quick." If the bank teller called on the check, the owner of the check would say they never made the check out to Summer, and she would be arrested on the spot.

Summer had to control this situation. "I'm really in a rush—my lunch break's almost up."

The bank teller studied Summer for a second. "Oh, forget about it. How would you like it?"

"Large bills," Summer said, and she could have kissed the lady as she cashed the check for eight thousand dollars. It brought back good memories of survival and making it finally out of the mud. "Thank you."

When Summer left out the bank, guns were drawn on her, and she fainted.

\* \* \* \* \* \*

"Bobby Moore, wake up," the detective said.

Summer awoke from her peaceful sleep. But when she saw the same detective who had put the gun to her head, she knew she wasn't having one of her recurring nightmares.

"Bobby Moore . . ." the detective chanted again and again, and Summer whose alias was Bobby Moore, couldn't believe the detective knew her real name.

Born a man, Bobby Moore had gone under the knife to add more bust to her bra-size, and had her ribs removed to make her waist seem slender. By taking butt shots, she tailored her figure until she had her desired

12

# BUTTERFLY

results. The only thing left was to go all the way and have the sex change, which she put on hold after her break up with Clayton.

"I'll just die if I go to jail! They'll kill me in there!" Summer whose nickname was Butterfly, couldn't contain her worst fears coming to life.

"Oh, you won't die. You have too much going for you," said the unkempt, fat detective, who smelled of deli pickles, bacon, and raw onions. Mustard stained his shirt and tie. Dark rings under his eyes didn't cover up the scattered moles, and his lips were too loose and gummy. Butterfly just hated him!

"You're going down!" the other detective said, who looked like a ridiculous version of ex-NBA baller, Jason Kidd, with his bushy eyebrows and slit lips.

"I can't. I'll die! I'll kill myself. Please don't take me to jail!" Butterfly begged, placing her hands in front of her face and noticing the handcuffs around her wrists. "Take these off, take these off! I promise I'll tell you everything."

The detectives smiled at one another. Why couldn't everybody be this easy?

"We have you on bank fraud, identity theft, counterfeiting and manufacturing—"

"Uttering forged documents," the other detective aided his partner's statement.

"You're going to get an enhanced sentence for sophisticated skills and a far lengthier sentence for the dollar amount," the Jason Kidd look alike said.

Butterfly heard nothing but her own sobs. How could her life continuously go deeper into a ditch? Wasn't it enough that she was born a man for crying out loud! There was no way she'd make it in a male prison. She'd be raped and passed around like reefer in a group of Rastafarians.

"Where did you get the account numbers from?" the detectives asked, and before the words were off his lips, Butterfly said, "Glen! He gave them to me after I gave him some head and some butt!"

Notwithstanding Butterfly's distraught conditions, the detectives both broke down and laughed.

"It ain't funny!" Butterfly couldn't think of anything worse than being killed in prison by somebody who looked like Big Bubba on *Money Talks*. "I had stopped doing fraud, but my friend Peyton came to me because she owed Ellis, the loan shark, eighty grand, and I was only helping her out."

It all became clear to the detectives. They knew Peyton had set Butterfly up. But when they thought about Ellis the loan shark they laughed hysterically, because Ellis wouldn't loan money for gambling debts. From their investigation of that individual, he funded Black Market enterprises, not gambling debts.

"Get her the fuck out of here," the unkempt detective told the one that looked like Jason Kidd.

"I'm gonna kill myself," Butterfly said to the detectives.

"Get her, her medicine or tranquilize her ass."

She was being escorted to her cell at the DC jail, when she was sat down momentarily before being dressed out to don her prison garb. Moments later, Peyton came out of a room near Butterfly.

Peyton stopped right in front of Butterfly, and Butterfly wouldn't have noticed her through the lens of tears in her eyes until Peyton said sweetly, "Summer . . ." When Butterfly looked up, Peyton blinded her with a searing slap across her face. "Fuck you, you faggot bitch!"

\* \* \* \* \* \*

The following six months were a blur. Butterfly was heavily sedated during the whole ordeal in the DC jail. All she remembered was the frightening nightmares that tackled her in her sleep, and she'd scream herself into a corner of her cell and hug her knees to her breasts. She couldn't even remember her lawyer, or how he or the judge looked. The only thing she remembered was the judge finding mitigating circumstances to give her eighteen months in a medium security federal prison. She was being sent to FCI Schuylkill, PA.

During those six months, Butterfly only received one letter in the mail because she wouldn't tell anybody in her family that she was in jail.

Butterfly opened the letter to read the following:

*Summer, Bobby, Butterfly, or whoever you think you are.*

*I finally was able to get you back for turning my family against me. You broke up our whole family because you never told me you were a "MAN" before I hooked you up with Clayton. Just know – Faggot . . . You TWISTED FREAK– that I got you in there. I set you up, sissy!*

*I hope you kill yourself in there, and if you don't have the courage to rid the world of one more fag, then I hope you get killed.*

*Just know, bitch, blood is thicker than water, and just because your family rightfully hates you for being a punk doesn't mean you have to [pervert] everybody else's. And since you're not even punk enough to own up to being a twisted man, you done got yourself*

*tangled up in one of your twisted frauds. LOL. Get it:
You faggot fraud.*

*If I ever see you again, I'm going to try to stick my
6" YSL's up your ass. Fuck, you'd probably like it,
faggot! TWISTED-FREAK!*

Butterfly was leveled. She ripped up the letter and
flushed it down the toilet. Her inner shell was so weak,
brittle, insecure and unsafe, that the smallest test could
throw everything out of whack.

She grabbed the nearest razor, took out the blade,
and deeply sliced both her wrists. The pain and the fear
of death felt better than the pain from her life and the
fear of going to prison. She climbed under her bunk
until she fainted again.

Her cellmate found her and hit the panic button.
Without that, Butterfly would have bled to death. She
was placed on suicide watch until she made a full
recovery, and then sent to FCI Schuylkill.

# BUTTERFLY

## Chapter One |
### *How Would She Survive!*

Six months and a day and Butterfly was finally leaving DC jail. She was little more than a semblance of her former self. She had lost ten pounds and couldn't weigh more than a hundred and thirty pounds. Butterfly had lost her cinnamon color, and now she was high-yellow from not being exposed to the sun all that time in DC jail.

The US Marshals did all the transporting for the Feds. So after fifty or more inmates were cuffed and shackled, they were loaded on the transportation bus that everybody called the grey goose. The wee hours of Monday morning brought a cold breeze that left everybody shivering until they were on the heated bus.

"What you in for?" a Mexican asked Butterfly as he took the seat next to her. He wore dark D&G glasses that had to be corrective wear, or the DC jail wouldn't have let him have them. His mustache was perfectly trimmed, and his hair was slicked back.

Butterfly studied him for a few seconds, and she decided she wanted to talk. "Bank fraud."

"What are you? Dominican?" The more the Mexican talked the more Butterfly could tell that he had a sexy, heavy accent that was surprisingly easy to understand.

"No, I'm Black," Butterfly said. Notwithstanding the fact that she felt she looked like hell. But by the way she was being stared at because she could see nothing but raw hunger, and it told her she still looked good.

17

"Everybody calls me Sosa."

Despite Butterfly being filled with the fear of going to jail and having tried to kill herself not even three months ago, as well as her conflicting feelings about Peyton, Clayton, her uncle, and her family, it felt good speaking to Sosa.

"My name is Butterfly." A hint of a smile spread across her face.

"Mariposa," he seductively chanted in Spanish while licking his bottom lip. "Damn, I wish you were Mexican, or at least Spanish."

"What for?"

"Because I could have asked for you to be my cellmate. I just came from Schuylkill a year ago. I went back to Mexico, and the Feds came back and got me. Now I have a thirty year sentence." They were silent. Butterfly didn't know that he was the under boss of the biggest drug lord in Mexico, Chapo Guzman.

"But I own this pinche pais. You see, when I get back to Schuylkill, they're gonna make me shot-caller again. Ever since I've been locked down I've always called shots for my people. They got some nice names for shot-callers: they call us Reps or Representatives. Like we're running for Congress." They laughed. "But I spend lots of money every month." If Butterfly didn't know any better she would have thought he was over-exaggerating in the animated and excited way that he spoke. But she was so charmed by his charisma that she didn't notice it. "Every month," he continued, "I put $500 on ten different commissary accounts. I spend the shit like it's water."

Butterfly looked around to see if anybody was looking. It was still dark outside, being that it couldn't

# BUTTERFLY

be any later than 5:45 a.m. Most everybody on the bus was asleep. "You must be rich."

"Listen to me." Sosa's accent was heavy and forceful. "I'm from Sinaloa. I know a lot of mero-mero. I think you call them Bosses. But listen, I want you to give me your name and register number."

"Register number?" Butterfly asked as she interrupted him.

"Yeah, it's the number everybody has in the federal prison system. Excuse my English; I think I'm saying it right." He organized the sequence of words in his head. "Yes, Federal prison system." He was pleased with himself, almost forgetting his train-of-thought. "Yes, I want your information."

"For what?" Butterfly was somewhat defensive, but elated that Sosa was so into her.

"I swear I gonna send you some money!"

Butterfly never had to accept money in exchange for sex. She had been kicked out of her father's house when she was seventeen years old, because her uppity father couldn't accept the fact that Butterfly was a pre-op transgender who was going to have the operation to make Butterfly fully a woman once she turned eighteen. Her father lived under a pretense, being that he had a political career to uphold. He started off as a county commissioner in neighboring Hyattsville, Maryland, where he was eventually elected a seat in the state's legislation. All the annual banquets, monthly outings, balls, galas, and his fraternity conventions, and he never ever once brought Butterfly along—not once! She was always shuffled off neatly to her uncle Kevin, who had been molesting her ever since she was seven. And that's why she always associated the unfortunate

19

# MICHAEL A. ROBINSON

sequence of words: Kevin-seven-heaven. Yes, Uncle Kevin was the pastor of one of the biggest Protestant churches in Maryland.

When Butterfly's father kicked her out, she was forced to live with her uncle, Kevin, who doled out money and lavish presents on Butterfly in exchange that she remain quiet about their daily sexual rendezvous. Uncle Kevin was sick to say the least, and insanely in love with Butterfly. He attributed his overzealous love to some farcical explanation of her being the "son" he never had—or couldn't have because his wife was infertile.

Butterfly could have told her father, but she knew 100% that her father would have killed Kevin, who was her mother Sandra's younger brother. So Butterfly always kept the fact that her uncle molested her a secret, and for the most part she kept the fact that she was a man a secret. Secrets . . . Secrets . . . Secrets.

Butterfly knew she had to leave her uncle's house. He was becoming so increasingly in love with Butterfly that he became blatant with his affections toward her in front of his wife, Debra. He even kissed Butterfly on the lips once in front of Debra and would stay up in the furnished attic with Butterfly until the wee hours of the night.

Debra had been the owner of the franchise of women's clothing that she sold out of several different warehouses across the country called Debra's. She taught Butterfly the ins-and-outs of running a multi-million dollar franchise, but most importantly she taught Butterfly how to do payroll. It wasn't too long after that, that Butterfly used common sense to figure out how to counterfeit checks. And when she met her ex, Clayton, he had all the connection she'd ever need to obtain fake identification. At first, it was for the express purpose of identifying her as a woman, and secondly to cash checks!

"Why you haven't said anything? Did I offend you?" Sosa brought Butterfly out of her brief reverie. She had been crushed by the legal system, her family and friends, and depressed for as long as she could remember. So Sosa's smiling face was the least offending.

"No, I'm not offended," she said innocently.

"Then I send you money. I scared, 'cus you being morena."

"Morena?" Butterfly asked quizzically.

"Yeah." He laughed, not believing himself for going against all odds because he wanted to fuck Butterfly so much it hurt. "Morena means Black in Spanish. We also say Negra or Negro, but we don't say it because we think it will offend you."

"I'm not offended."

"I know, 'cus I not call you Negra. I say Morena. Morena deliciosa." They laughed. "See, I know you gonna cause mucho problema," Sosa said with charming and squinted eyes. It was a threatening foreboding prophecy that Butterfly couldn't exactly place, and it only exemplified what she had already feared.

"Why you say that?"

"You're gonna see, morena deliciosa. When those guys get one look at you, they're gonna get so hungry, they'll do anything to get some of you. I'd be able to smell you from the other side of that big compound. You smell so sweet I wanna fuck you right here."

They laughed again. Sosa couldn't be older than forty-five years old, but he still had a lot of youth.

"You're playing." She was hoping that was not the case, because she was non-confrontational. She wouldn't stand a chance if otherwise.

He laughed. "I no lie. I tell you this; those morenos from DC marry each other."

"Marry?"

He excitedly shook his head. "Once you get married, you married wherever you go."

*Married! Good grief!* Butterfly thought. She didn't know that it was a binding non-legal process equivalent to slaves hopping the broom. If she got married, wherever she would go, she'd be "whoever's" Mrs.

"I can protect you, morena deliciosa." Sosa's youthful and charming face was replaced by stern eyes that read: stone-cold killer. And his expression said the same. But no matter what he said in his last statement, there was only one thing Butterfly heard.

"I'ma need protection?" Butterfly asked, now visibly shaken as the sun finally cracked the horizon outside of the bus.

This time all the charisma and charm was all the way gone as Sosa looked over at her and nodded yes.

# BUTTERFLY

## Chapter Two |
### *The Arrival*

S end them in!" a man from the gun tower yelled. He hung out of the gun tower holding an automatic weapon.

The bus pulled into an enclosure of gates, so the prison COs, who were in the shack at the entrance, could inspect the bus to make sure that no contraband was in or under the bus. COs entered the bus and counted the fresh bloods who had newly arrived. "Protection from what?" Butterfly asked as her anxiety mounted.

"You see soon enough mi morena deliciosa. You see very soon."

Sosa said, and they sat quiet. Butterfly didn't belong to this scene. Just the sight of her soft and delicate being amongst the ruffians who sat around her was awkward.

What a sight Butterfly was amongst the ruffians who sat around her. As the bus was being inspected, Butterfly looked over at Sosa, who looked as if he was preparing himself for whatever awaited his arrival. As Butterfly observed the other passengers on the bus, everybody's expression was the same. All the looks had anticipation, readiness and anxiety in them. All it did was confirm Butterfly's worse fears. Contradictory to how she felt within herself, her soft features against her light complexion gave off a sort of awkwardness that even made the COs feel uneasy. Her soft and fluffy lips cast against her features could only be described as very beautiful yet exotic, and it could not fit with the rough necks around her.

23

# MICHAEL A. ROBINSON

Once outside the bus, a team of COs removed the handcuffs, belly chains, and ankle braces as the inmates descended the bus. They were marched inside the R&D (Receiving and Discharge), and they sat for what seemed like endless hours waiting to be processed inside of the system.

There, Butterfly felt how humiliating and humbling the whole ordeal of Intake and Screening was upon entry to the institution. It was a timely task of being strip-searched, dressed with unwashed and smelly garbs that almost made her puke. She held the disgusting underwear away from her body because they had shit stains in the part where the ass crack was supposed to go. She opted to wear the jailhouse khaki pants without underwear.

She then was shoved into having to take a mug-shot, and that was the first time she noticed how terrible her hair looked. The perm was completely worn out, replaced by what appeared to be the making of a natural. The sight made her feel how she truly felt: nasty, dirty, and disgusting.

Butterfly went to the health department where she was asked very personal questions by a tall, white male nurse who had a shit-eating grin on his face the whole time she was interviewed.

"When was the last time you had sex?" the nurse asked with a hinting smile.

"Let's see: none of your business," Butterfly answered. There was nothing about the nurse that made her afraid.

The nurse, whose badge read: RN Eddings, enjoyed the exchange. "When was the last time you had an HIV test?"

# BUTTERFLY

"DC jail, when I almost bled to death."

"Let me see . . . Oh yeah, you're negative. Let's hope it stays that way." Nurse Eddings held the paper in his hand out to Butterfly. The paper was an authorization that she had been medically cleared to go to the compound.

Butterfly was ushered into Case Manager Attenberger's office. He would assign her to a unit, and he would have the final say-so as to if she would go to the compound. Or not.

"Are you going to be a problem?" Attenberger asked, and it can't be said that the question wasn't asked rudely.

"Excuse me?" Butterfly asked, and not without an attitude.

"You heard me. Are you going to be a problem?"

"Why would I be a problem?"

Attenberger smirked. "Let's just say you're obviously gay, and you don't look like a man at all. I'm impressed myself. But do you know what's out there?"

"Men." Butterfly smiled wanly.

"You know what. You're going to the SHU till the Captain signs off on you," Attenberger said sullenly.

"The SHU? What's that?" Butterfly said, as if the fear in her voice could keep her from going.

"Oh, you are all woman," Attenberger added, referring to what was written in her pre-sentence investigation report, which was prepared by the probation officer. The report was a far intrusive history file about Butterfly's life, and all Butterfly could remember from the interview was she hated it!

Attenberger continued. "The SHU stands for

25

# MICHAEL A. ROBINSON

Special Housing Unit, or the hole, or a disciplinary confinement."

"But I didn't do nothing."

"You can't go to the compound anyways, not today. There are no available cells. But in case you do go, if you're so much as found kissing or obscenely touching anybody, I promise you we'll ship you to that underground joint in Colorado. Have you heard of ADX?"

"No."

"I didn't think so. That's where we send our incorrigible inmates. Let's just say, you wouldn't last five minutes."

There was no doubt in Butterfly's mind that she couldn't last two minutes, let alone five. "I'm not going to do nothing."

"You better not. Now get out of my office," Attenberger said. But before she left, he had almost forgotten to ask some key questions. "One last thing: do you have any separatees at this joint?"

He might as well had been speaking a foreign language because Butterfly didn't know what he was talking about. "What's that?"

"Boy, you are green. This has to be your first time in jail. What are you in for?" Attenberger asked. He didn't want to waste time fingering through her file in his hands.

"Bank fraud and identity theft," Butterfly answered sheepishly.

"Did you testify against anybody? Or did anybody testify against you?"

"No," Butterfly lied. Well, she didn't technically "testify," but she did cooperate.

# BUTTERFLY

"Are you in a gang?"

"No." Butterfly snickered.

"I had to ask. This is what determines if you'll go to the compound or not. You can leave now."

As Butterfly walked through the door to leave, Attenberger yelled for the next candidate to enter. Butterfly went to a holding tank that was crammed to the max, and everybody made a way for her as if she had a disease. Many didn't want to be seen with a homosexual or gay or fag or gump or sissy. To be seen with one, most guys thought, would cast a sweet-spell around them, so the best thing was to stay as far away as possible.

At least that's what Butterfly thought. And remembering her awful experience at the DC jail, she knew that homophobia was something that all gay guys had to face while in prison. From Butterfly's point of view, it usually left them to deal with loneliness and isolation. And she knew that if one wasn't strong, he'd lose his sense of balance; because as Butterfly had read in an article, nine out of every ten gay men in prison took psych meds to help them cope with the loneliness and open hostility coming from inmates and Correctional Officers.

The COs put lunch bags through the trap in the door of the holding tank. It was a wet bag of low-quality lunch meat, a rotten apple, molded bread, and milk so spoiled that it had lumps in it.

Butterfly held the lunch bag away from her body to offer it to anybody because she couldn't stomach, let alone bear the awful, foul-smelling meat. But it seemed that nobody would take anything from a gay's hand, at least not in public. But moments later, a big, dark-skinned

27

guy arrived, and he was the biggest, by far, in the holding tank. Once he saw Butterfly, he headed straight for her, and his voice was strong, aggressive and inconsiderate. "You're not going to eat that?" he asked her.

"No, you can have it," Butterfly said as she scooted over so he wouldn't sit on her.

"Where you from?"

"DC," Butterfly answered, thinking that where Sosa's presence was warm and welcoming, this guy's was coarse and unsettling.

"I'm from Northeast, and when I seen you, shorty, I kind of figured you were from DC," he said, because the majority of pre-op transgender in this area were from DC.

"What part you from?" he asked.

"Southeast," Butterfly answered, still unsure of who the guy was or what he really wanted. He seemed as if he had an ulterior motive.

"My name is Black, and I've already been to this joint for three years. I had to go back to court on a state case. "Now, it's a rack of homies here, so you ain't gonna have no problems. But if you do, come and holler at me." His eyes glimmered until their conversation was cut short when the COs opened the door and yelled out the inmate's names.

Once the inmates exited the door, they were given bedrolls, which consisted of a comb, toothbrush, toothpaste, shampoo and soap that were stuffed inside a plastic cup. All the contents was wrapped inside two bed sheets and a cover. And some were off to the compound, while others were off to the deserted SHU, which was not deserted at all, but only seemed that way. The more

# BUTTERFLY

Butterfly was shoveled through this crazy and unnerving process, the more she understood what it felt like to be an animal in a slaughter house.

Butterfly was ushered to her cell in handcuffs with two COs by her side. They took her through the small maze of halls to a cell, which from the rectangular window in the door, looked dirty, cold, and empty.

They closed the door behind Butterfly and took her handcuffs off through the trap in the door. She looked around at the cell and there was a toilet off to the side with an attached sink, a table, a shower, and a bunk bed.

Butterfly was so exhausted from the four-hour bus ride, and depressed from how her life had turned into a nightmare, that she collapsed on the bed without making it up. She wrapped herself in the covers, discarding the toiletries that were inside the bedroll.

She had fallen asleep for what seemed to be two minutes when the COs opened the trap to the door and told her to cuff-up. When Butterfly went to the door, she heard somebody who seemed outrageous and obnoxious.

"You bet not put me in the cell with just anybody! I don't play that shit, and I ain't scared of you crackas," said a gay guy. He didn't have any feminine features like Butterfly. But he was a ball of fire, sassy and pretentious, as any diva would be.

"Adams, shut the hell up. It's one of your kind in there. You should be happy," one of the white COs said, who didn't give a fuck about being politically correct.

"What do you mean 'one of my kind'? You bet not be talking about because I'm Black?"

"Not 'cause you're black—because you're gay," the same CO added as the other handcuffed Butterfly through the trap.

# MICHAEL A. ROBINSON

"Okay. I'm all right with that." He smacked his lips as he looked at Butterfly through the window.

"By the way, you're kind of cute."

"Not a chance in a lifetime, Adams," the CO responded, realizing the inmate, Adams, was speaking to him.

The COs waited impatiently for the control center, which was a command center that opened the automatic cell doors. They controlled the SHU through the surveillance cameras, and when the COs in front of Butterfly's cell waved at the camera, they opened the door. And to the COs statement, the inmate said, "I don't blame you 'cause if you seen how I'm packing, you'd probably doubt your sexuality."

"Get your ass in there!" the CO said brusquely. "Shut cell #118," he said into his walkie-talkie.

The COs took the handcuffs off both Butterfly and the other inmate and left. Once they were gone, the new inmate didn't even introduce himself.

"Gurl, how can you lay down on that nasty bed without cleaning it first?"

"Clean it for what?" Butterfly sat back down on the bed.

"So you won't get staph infection, scabies, crabs, or you can take your pick."

"I don't care."

Butterfly's new cellie looked at her with understanding eyes. "What is it? Heart broken? The judge gave you too much time, or your first time being locked up?"

"All of the above."

"How much time did they give you?"

"Eighteen months."

30

# BUTTERFLY

Butterfly's cellmate laughed in her face. "Are you crazy? That's nothing! I know it may seem like the end of the world, but it's nothing. You probably did twelve months at DC jail and should already be ready to go home. Gurl, you can't be no older than nineteen."

"I'm twenty."

"Did you cooperate?" The new cellie knew the question had to be asked.

"What do you mean?"

"Duh! Did you *snitch* on anybody—hello?"

Butterfly's eyes became as big as an owl's, and knowing that snitching was bad she didn't want to answer.

"Bitch, don't get all weird on me all of a sudden, because the fool that didn't tell wish he had, let me tell you. But make sure you keep whatever you did on the down low because they'd love to fuck you around with that."

"Am I in danger?"

"You don't have nothing at all to worry about. Gurl, please. Nuh-uh, we're in heaven. There's a lot of guys perpetrating like they ain't going, but when they with you by themselves, it's completely different . . . *trust*.

"My name is Buffy Da Body, and if you ain't already got a nickname, they'll give you one."

"My name's Mariposa. It means butterfly in Spanish." That was the only thing Butterfly could think to say. She didn't know why, but she liked the sound of the Spanish version rolling off Sosa's lips.

"Excuse me, bitch, but around here we're going to call you Butterfly. You don't want nobody to confuse you as being Spanish, because the Spanish boys will have you in a world of trouble."

# MICHAEL A. ROBINSON

*Damn*, Butterfly thought. *How am I ever going to make it out of here?* It was bad enough she was gay, and it was even worse that everything had a shade of racial tension with it.

"But Sosa said he'd protect me," Butterfly said to herself but aloud.

"Sosa?" Buffy asked, and it jolted Butterfly out of her inner-cognition.

"Sosa, he said he used to be here and was a shot-caller."

"Sosa! Gurl, he came back?" Buffy asked with added amazement. "My God, they're gonna tear the compound up because of you, let me tell you."

# BUTTERFLY

## Chapter Three |
*He had to conquer the world...*

To touch the weights, and feel the steel in his hands. The power his body produced to lift 405 lbs. went through Atwaters' mind as he unracked the weight and took it slowly down on his chest. The weight felt good, and he was getting his mind and body right because he was preparing to go home . . .

18 long ass years . . . Imagine that. Not hour glasses pouring sand through a moderated hole . . . but years, draining the life out of him. And he pushed the steel and the 405 lbs. came up with ease and it was money and payback that his heart and soul craved! To prove his worth, value, mettle!

He was so focused that he could not hear the raucus round 'about of other guys lifting weights. His future, was again, on the chopping block, and he was going to have the opportunity to put it down. Shit . . . Somebody had to pay for robbing him of 18 years . . . 18 precious years that he could never ever get back! And he racked the weights and hopped up and curled 135 lbs. on his arms until he felt them swell and he threw them down and he could see something of a visible future where the stakes were high and he'd have his foot on the fuckers necks who buried him alive for 18 precious ones.

And his mind was intent on delivering that justice . . . but something was missing from the picture. And it was an intrical part. And his mind was searching it for what it was when his concentration was interrupted.

"Atwater, come here," Old School said once he had

# MICHAEL A. ROBINSON

gotten Atwater's attention.

Old School was an old-timer from Chicago, who was well-respected, and he had a life sentence to serve. No matter the life sentence or the time he had already served, he looked considerably good for his age.

Atwater went over to him and they shook hands and embraced as only gangsters do.

"Islam – Moor." Old School paid Atwater the greetings of the Moorish Americans. A religious group who were like the Nation of Islam, but who followed the teachings of Noble Drew Ali, and Atwater was not only a lowly member, but he held rank as the Assistant Grand Sheik.

"That's my Atwater," Old School said proudly. "How's your wife Shonda?"

"She's doing well. She's been riding out with a brother for these eighteen years, which seem like eighteen different lifetimes."

"It hasn't been wasted, young blood. You understand that it's direction that gives vision and mismanagement that leads to collision."

Atwater looked admiringly at Old School. "You still speak in riddles, old man."

"It's not the riddle that's spoken, but the decipherment once it's broken. I can place wisdom kike a dessert before your face, but what you choose is according to your taste.

"I've helped you elevate your game. Your wife is now an accountant of a reputable accounting firm. And she has you to thank for that."

"Islam; and I have you to thank."

It was music to Old School's ears. For one to be grateful and appreciative when somebody taught him

34

# BUTTERFLY

something said a lot about his character.

"Game's to be sold, not told," Old School said. "I'll life out in here. I just want you to pass the game on to those who are receptive, selective, and a little deceptive. What I teach you ten years back about your right to choose who you walk with, be it friend or foe?"

"To always exercise that right and to keep from allowing no-gooders to get under me." Atwater answered by rote.

"Right. Because lames are always looking for some protection. That's what they make gangs, organizations, and armies for. It's a sort of protection program, because real men stand on their own two feet. But they use the gangs, organizations, and armies to make themselves feel like real men; and it's because they can't think outside of the box. When a gang begins to exceed it's usefulness, then cut it loose."

Atwater could never fully digest that teaching. "I feel you, Old School, but what about loyalty?"

"You are loyal: loyal to ya'self, your ambition, and your success. Those fools are on autopilot to crash. You'd get run over trying to stop them. The only loyalty they understand is a face you put on to deal with them. You're in a whole other class. And what I teach you about classism?"

"The Haves and the Have-nots."

Old School had to smile at his pupil; he had learned his lessons well. And without showing his true satisfaction, Old School asked, "And at what time do you tie your fate with the Have-nots? "

"At no time. Pimping ain't tender – dick and kindheartedness. The mack has to accumulate funds at the expense of a woman's virtue. But along with her

35

virtue goes his own sense of humanity."

"Don't tell me you still pray?" Old School tested Atwater more.

Never that, Old School. I don't pray, I prey."

"Calculation, misinformation, and mass manipulation is what rules the nation. You can never pluck a flower till after you've given her a mental orgasm.

What you wear, drive, and speak does all of that."

One of Atwater's friends who was working out interrupted Old School. "Atwater, come on, man. You still gonna do squats?"

Old School and Atwater ignored him as Old School said, "You see how a Have-not thinks? He thinks everything is brute force and physical strength. All these fools out here lifting crude instruments when the master chess players have aircraft carriers posted in front of a new victim's shores. New countries with new slaves to play to the master's tunes. But game's to be sold, not told.

"I told you, Atwater, to elevate your pimping, and I'm, quite impressed at what you've accomplished. But I want you take it one step further. Remember that a tender dick ain't got the apple sauce to pimp.

"I'm about to continue upon my journey. I entrust I'll be seeing you."

Atwater laughed from the trance Old School had him in, the trance he was already in when he was plotting his future.

"All right, Old Man. Much love, and I'm gonna take this pimping to a whole other level – that's my word."

"Your access has been granted."

# Chapter Four |
## *The SHU Had Its Way Of Offering Solace*

Butterfly felt like more of an animal trapped inside a cage than a beautiful insect. As she looked around the cell, she felt she was going to be a victim of a degenerative disease or worse. Her skin crawled now that she had woken and realized this prison wasn't a nightmare but a living reality.

The cell itself was suffocating, with minor accommodations of a metal shower, a washbowl, and toilet that was some sort of hybrid stuck together. The two-bed bunk was as comfortable as sleeping on a concrete slab.

Butterfly had spent one day in the SHU with Buffy, and after they did their best to clean everything, the cell didn't seem as nasty.

Plus, Buffy was so fun, funny, and adorable with his big lips and Buck Roger's teeth that the time flew by. Butterfly had taken an instant liking to him, and Buffy spent the majority of time telling Butterfly what to expect once she was released to the compound in his overly pretentious and feminine manner.

"Let me tell you," Buffy said as he smacked his lips and spoke with a pronounced and unnecessary lisp that made him sound as if he was sucking on a lollipop. "I don't care what anybody tells you about Schuylkill. It's the bomb out there. It's a rack of fine ass niggas who are most definitely going. I had to come here to take a break."

"You never told me why you're back here," Butterfly asked, excited from the stories Buffy told.

"Gurl," Buffy said, and as always, it was followed by a smack of his lips. "It would be easier to say why I ain't back here. Let's just say I got caught in a compromising position. I was hunched over getting stuffed like a bell pepper with a yard of dick in the recreation bathroom." They laughed.

"You got caught?"

"Yeah and that ain't it." He smacked his lips again. "Lieutenant Muncy who usually never gives a fuck, got all saintly, and he got the nerve to call me a black faggot, so I smacked that asshole in the face. They about snatched a bitch out her panties and dragged me here."

"You're crazy!" Butterfly laughed.

"These scrapes on my legs look like rug burns, as if I slept with King Mandingo himself."

Butterfly had to hold her stomach because she was laughing so hard.

"Gurl." Buffy smacked. "Let me tell you. From the other jails I've been to, this place is okay, let me tell you. There's some fine ass niggas out there, like T Roy, Banks, Eddie, Milk, Atwater, and Lazy Eyes. That's just to name a few, let me tell you. Don't sleep with nobody that's been with Britney Spears 'cus that bitch got the hee-bee-gee-bees."

"The what?"

She smacked her lips. "HIV. Hello!"

"Oh my god!" Butterfly said, thinking how horrible it would be to have HIV, or worst, AIDS. And she would have thought she had one or the other if her DC jail results didn't come back negative for both.

"Don't sound so shocked, bitch. You better be EXTRA careful, or you'll get more than a sore ass."

"How do you protect yourself?" Butterfly asked.

Buffy looked as if he'd been asked the dumbest question in the universe. "Go to the chapel, make a wooden cross, and get a spray bottle full of holy water, let me tell you, because ain't nothing under God's green earth gonna keep me from getting some dick."

Butterfly laughed all the more. "You've completely lost your mind!"

"Other than that"—She smacked—"you can try and use latex gloves and a lot of prayer. Because most of the time ya ain't gonna wanna mess with a wee-wee that can fit in a finger of a glove, let me tell ya. Sometimes I like it when I can't sit down for a couple of days."

"I know what you mean . . . something that lingers!" Butterfly couldn't agree more, as they slapped hands in full accord. All she could think about was Clayton, because he was well-endowed.

"What?" Buffy smacked. "Listen to me, little sister," Buffy said on a serious note. "Be careful out there. Not only with your health, but with your heart, let me tell you. Don't get ya head involved 'cus some guys are too pussy to be seen with you in public. They won't even acknowledge you. But it's the life we have in here and in the free world, let me tell you. Don't even mess with nobody if you can't control your emotions, because it will get you messed up. Plus, that's how a lot of people be getting stabbed. And you look psycho-ish."

Buffy said seriously, because he could sense that Butterfly was unstable just by looking at her.

Butterfly laughed. "What! No I don't!"

"Please. What kind of medicine they have you on?" Butterfly didn't answer. "That's what I thought. How many times have you tried to kill ya'self?" Buffy asked, seeing scars on Butterfly's wrist.

"Too many to count," Butterfly answered matter-of-factly.

"Gurl, what is it? You hate the isolation, the ridicule, or the fact that you're always a secret in your lover's life? I already know, let me tell you. But ya's a crazy bitch because you tried to kill ya'self."

Butterfly laughed as Buffy continued. "I ain't never went that far. I love dick too much, let me tell you."

They were interrupted when they heard the COs bringing somebody down the hall, which was announced by the CO's tolling keys.

Buffy ran to the door to see if he could peep down the hall through the crack in the door, and he could barely make out the image of Fats, who was coming down the hall.

"Stephens, make sure my cellie packs me out. I don't know if I'm going back to the compound," Fats said to the guard who brought him to the back and he was hoping his cellmate would send all his property to him in the SHU.

Somebody in another cell screamed, "Ya bet not go to the pound again, ya hot bitch!'

Fats ignored the guy screaming and said to the CO, "You see what I mean? I need all my property."

"Fats, is that you?" Buffy screamed, because he loved him some Fats. Not only was Fats funny and fun to be around, Fats smuggled drugs into the prison.

"Hey, Buffy," Fats said warmly.

"What the hell you doing back here? Don't answer that; I already know."

"Did you see Bad Breath Britney out there?" Buffy asked.

"Hold up. Let me get in my cell first."

The COs put Fats into an empty cell as they kicked his bedroll in, closed the door, and uncuffed him through the trap. He waited till the COs left before he resumed his conversation with Buffy. It required talking over other inmates' conversations, who screamed from cell to cell as they trafficked property

# BUTTERFLY

underneath the doors by using strings torn from bedsheets, and they used toothpaste tubes to launch the line.

The whole time the COs were putting Fats in his cell, Buffy was telling Butterfly who he was.

"Gurl, we done came up! Fats is my baby. He be having wine, cigarettes, cocaine, heroin, and whatever else you like."

"What! That's what I need right now, something to calm my nerves."

"Oh, I hope he brought something back with him. Anything."

"How would he bring anything back here? They stripped searched me," Butterfly asked.

Buffy looked at Butterfly, green as could be. "You don't know who Leester-Keester is?"

Butterfly looked confused. "No, who's he?"

Buffy shook his head. "It's when you hide something in ya ass."

"My God!" Butterfly said as Buffy laughed.

"Buffy!" Fats called.

Buffy ran back to the door.

"Fats?" Buffy called him for the fifth time, and he was getting agitated because Fats ignored him.

"Buffy, I got something for you. You have a car?"

"Of course I do," Buffy said, running over to his bed and ripping his bed sheet. He tied a small toothpaste tube to one end of the string. And to Butterfly he said, "Baby, I told you we're going to Venus tonight." He danced with glee.

"What he got?" Butterfly asked.

"Bitch, how the hell do I know?" Buffy said sarcastically and laughed.

MICHAEL A. ROBINSON

"Fats, I'm sending the car down," Buffy yelled.

Fats went to the door to steer the line in. Buffy had to try and try again to get the toothpaste to land in front of his cell door, but the shit seemed nearly impossible after more than six tries.

"Damn, bitch, take your time, ya non-driving muthafucka." Fats laughed.

"Fuck you Fats!" Buffy fumed. "Dammit, I'm gonna chip my nails. Ya damn near gotta be Danica Patrick to drive this shit down the hallway."

"Right there! It's in front of my cell. Hold up!"

Buffy looked over at Butterfly because they were about to get higher than kites.

"Pull the line!" Fats hollered back.

Buffy pulled the line in till the small package of goodies had arrived.

Butterfly ran to the door to see what it was. It was two pin-sized cigarettes with a striking match.

"What is that?" Butterfly asked.

"Let me see," Buffy said as he unraveled it to see a mixture of marijuana, heroin, or crack. Who knew?

"We know there's weed in there. But we'll figure out the rest once we're high." He laughed.

"Damn, bitch, you didn't even thank me!" Fats yelled.

And with much affection, Buffy yelled, "Thanks Fats!" And then he turned his attention back to the items at hand.

He turned the shower on and put a towel under the door to trap the smell from going outside the room. And when they blazed, it became a puff-puff-pass rhythm between the two of them until their faces and heads felt heady and numb and good!

42

# BUTTERFLY

They both wanted to get fucked, but they resolved to crawl into Butterfly's bed and hold each other, wishing the other was a man, or at least a real one.

But Butterfly's dreams took her deeper into a trance. And as her head started to spin, she coughed and ran to the toilet because she thought she would vomit. She felt truly high! But when she got to the toilet to vomit, nothing came out, and Buffy laughed all the more.

Butterfly's mind was drug-induced, and her vision was watery, dreamy, and languid. And while sitting on the ground next to the toilet, Buffy's laughing sounded distorted and heinous, and his face seemed almost sinister. Butterfly leaned back onto the toilet and the high felt good and mesmerizing. She crawled back into the bed and after a second, she felt her mind drift back to when she was a child in elementary.

*"You're a sissy: nanny nanny nanny . . . you're a faggot and you act like a girl," a group of kids teased, but it had the rhythm of a song, and Butterfly was the innocent kid who was backed against a wall and she felt trapped!*

*"I'm not, I'm not. Stop it!"*

*But they wouldn't, no matter how much she screamed. And she didn't know if she was fighting to free herself from the corner that the kids had backed her into, or if she was struggling to be freed from the nightmare she had collapsed into. Once she realized that she couldn't escape from the corner, she covered her ears. She noticed she wasn't the beautiful woman that she had grown to be, but she was a boy with pants, tennis shoes, and a T-shirt on, and she hated the feeling of being in that body! It was nauseating, and she fought against the teasing, the kids, the dream itself.*

*In the watery vision, Butterfly could still sense Buffy walking around the cell, and she could hear Fats muzzy*

# MICHAEL A. ROBINSON

*screams to Buffy.*

*But Butterfly was still stuck in the dream or trance that seemed almost nightmarish. She was in her parent's car, and they were dropping her off at her uncle's house, and she felt like she was ten years old. She couldn't help but feel her father's accusing eyes looking at her with disgust, and if that wasn't hurtful enough, her brother had had the same accusing eyes!*

*They were in her father's car, and they were going on vacation, but they were going to leave Butterfly behind because of what she was!*

*"I don't want to stay, Momma! I wanna go with you! Why are you gonna leave me behind?" Butterfly was too young to understand, too young to comprehend, that he/she didn't fit into his family's picture of a perfect family. He/she was a freak, an accident that should have never been born to tarnish their family's name, or his father's honor, as his father saw it.*

*Butterfly's father looked at him with disgust written in his eyes as Butterfly's brother juggled a football between his hands in the back of the car, impatient to rid himself of his gay brother!*

*"You can't come to the political convention with us this year. Wait till next year, I promise," her mother Sandra said.*

*"But, Mama!"*

*"Get out the car. We have to go!" Butterfly's father screamed at her. He couldn't take any more of the weakling he had as a son. It made him feel as if he was weak for being Butterfly's father. And all it did was confirm the word's belching forth from Peyton's letter: "I hope you kill yourself in there."*

*Butterfly's mother had tears in her eyes, and she was just*

44

# BUTTERFLY

*too afraid of what her husband would think of her if she were to brush the tears from her youngest son's eyes. She hated the fact that Butterfly was gay, and she knew her youngest son would never be accepted by his own family. It was as if he was a stepchild or a foster kid, as if he wasn't flesh of their flesh and blood of their blood.*

*It was all the crying Butterfly could do. He was quickly whisked out of the car into his uncle's arms.*

*"Bye, baby," Butterfly's mother, Sandra said. "Be good, Bobby. Bye Kevin."*

*Kevin was Sandra's brother, a pastor of a famous and prosperous church, and he understood that Butterfly would never fit into his family's picturesque frame.*

*Kevin waved to the car as they sped off, and for each yard they drove away, a tear had fallen from Butterfly's eyes.*

Butterfly fought to wake from the dream, but she couldn't break the trance! She was still a child, and she was still in the nightmare of the past. She couldn't break free, and she and her uncle floated to her room. Before long, her uncle was naked and bent over her as she felt him thrusting inside her. It felt so wrong and so unfair, but no one cared!

And as with all the other times that she had been molested, it was as if she wasn't there. Her mind drifted away from the experience, and she had fled to a field of orchards where dozens of enchanting butterflies floated around in the pollen infested pastures. It was so beautiful and breathtaking and Butterfly finally felt free, as if she had wings with pretty patterns of lively colors! Butterfly felt as free as a butterfly and as a butterfly only. And before her dream had faded to total darkness she had seen herself as a teenager dressed in drag for the very first time. And then and only then did she finally feel like a butterfly, as the beautiful woman in the mirror stared back at her. She had found herself.

# BUTTERFLY

## Chapter Five |
### *To The Compound But Of Course*

Butterfly still could feel the sun on her skin where she had been lying in the orchard during her dream, and when she thought she would see more butterflies, she awoke to the alarming sound of the trap on the door having been yanked open.

"Bobby Moore, get up!" an irritated CO yelled.

Butterfly had to try harder to pull from her sleep.

"Bobby More, get up now!" the CO screamed again. He didn't have time for this shit! He had other inmates to wake up, and he didn't want to stand there all day.

Butterfly turned over in the bed to acknowledge him.

"What?"

"You have Team. And Adams, you know I have to cuff you up too. Get up!" the CO yelled.

"Buffy, get up," Butterfly said as she shook him.

"What, gurl? They need to learn how to talk to a lady," Buffy said, completely frustrated and feeling cranky. "Waking me up with that bullshit! Hold your horses, cracker!" Buffy said to the CO.

"They said I'm going to Team. What's that?"

"Don't worry. It's your counselors, so you might be going to the compound today."

Butterfly was handcuffed through the trap in the cell door and taken to a room where her counselors were. One was a fat white lady with a short hairstyle, and the other was a buff white guy who looked as if he had chewing tobacco in his mouth.

47

# MICHAEL A. ROBINSON

"Mr. Moore," the buff man whose name was Scandal said.

"Miss," Butterfly said as a normal response when referred to as a man.

"We have room on the compound, and we're going to let you out, but the Captain sent us down here to browbeat you on our strict policy against any sexual activity between inmates. If you think that's going to be a problem you should let us know now."

"No, it won't be a problem," Butterfly said, sounding surly.

"You don't sound too sure," Ms. Mires said with a marked attitude. Ms. Mires was, of course, the rotund and amorphous-shaped lady with the short hair, and it took everything in Butterfly's power not to quack like a duck in response to how Ms. Mires looked and spoke.

"I'm sure!" Butterfly resolved to say as she rolled her eyes.

"There's no need to get angry with us; we're just doing our job."

*Sure*, Butterfly thought. *That's if being an asshole is your job.* "I'm not angry at you. I'm just tired of everybody making a big deal out of who I am," Butterfly exclaimed to Ms. Mires.

"This is jail! You do what we say and what we want. You're going to be assigned to Unit 2A, and you better be on your best behavior. If you have any further questions, they'll have to wait until your initial team or open house every day during mainline."

*My God*, Butterfly thought, *you have to be a rocket scientist to be an inmate—initial team, open house, mainline.* But she was too pissed off to ask the two

# BUTTERFLY

people in front of her what any of it meant, especially considering it was their job to be assholes!

"Bye," Butterfly said smugly.

The COs took Butterfly back to her cell to pack her things. On the way, they passed a closet where inmates were getting their hair cut. The barber, Atwater, who cut their hair, met eyes with Butterfly, and they held each other's gaze until she passed the door. When she returned back to her cell, Buffy was brushing her teeth.

"Gurl, you was on some weird shit last night, let me tell you. You got in the bed with me and curled up and you was holding ya hands against your ears. I thought I was going to have to press the panic button."

"Just had a bad trip," Butterfly said.

"What unit are you going to?" Buffy asked.

"I think they said 2A."

"Damn, they're sending you over there with Bad Breath Britney. She's okay. She'll steal ya man as fast as you can blink your eyes. So watch her. And make sure all my property got packed out. I'll be out in three weeks or more."

"There was this guy out there cutting hair. Who's that?"

Buffy had to think for a second, and then he knew instantly. "Atwater? He act like he's all that. He's the Assistant Grand Sheik of the Moors, with his bourgeois ass. Why? Did he say something to you?"

"No, I was just asking."

The COs had returned to get Butterfly. And after asking if she was ready, they popped the trap to put them in handcuffs.

Buffy hugged Butterfly before they were placed in handcuffs. "Give me a hug because I won't see you for a few weeks. But you be careful out there. And I forgot to tell you last night, but don't even think about messing around with Sosa if you don't want a race riot on your hands."

Butterfly looked frightened. She didn't know what awaited her, and she was scared shitless.

When Butterfly walked out the SHU, her eyes had to adjust to the bright and gleaming sun. It was sunny and hot and her mind, body, and bones felt relaxed in the sunrays, despite the fact she was trembling with fear.

She had to carry the little belongings she had, and she walked with about six other inmates who had been released with her. And all eyes were on her because she was the only irresistible gay amongst the guys who surrounded her.

They walked down the compound, which seemed like, if she had to compare it to anything, a college campus. The whole compound was outside with buildings, and corrugated barb-wire toppled the gates that surrounded the prison. You couldn't see the trees on the outside of the prison for the buildings that were in different portions of the prison.

Butterfly walked down the walkway, amazed at how big the prison seemed.

Other inmates ogled her, and she heard all types of stuff: "Damn baby, you need help with that?" and "Just what we need: more fags on the compound." Someone sighed.

Butterfly knew that she had to be strong, despite her harrowing fears, because she had already felt the negativity coming from so many guys as they stared at her, as if she could change who she was! She walked to the unit, and when she had finally gotten inside, everybody there, which were 120 or more men, got up to look at her. She didn't know if to feel like a star or a fly on a wall. But she noticed immediately that Sosa was in the same unit, which was very reassuring.

The CO came out of his office. "Who are you?"

"Bobby Moore."

"You're assigned to cell #208 on the top range. Let me know immediately if you need a pillow or a mat."

Butterfly waited to see if the CO had anything else to say.

"Is that it?"

"Yes," he answered curtly.

Butterfly looked over at Sosa, who was sitting at one of the tables that was in the unit. He was sitting with three other Mexicans, and he didn't hide when he winked at Butterfly and gave a welcoming smile.

Butterfly smiled back and almost tripped over her bed roll as she picked it up and headed to her cell. When she got there, she noticed the cell was smaller than the cell in the SHU and lacked a shower, but had everything else like the SHU cell, in addition to lockers.

There were pictures of her cellmate with his family on the bulletin board. Her cellmate was white and most definitely gay.

After she arranged her bed, she was startled to see Sosa standing at the door looking at her with a genuine smile on his face. But whatever fear she felt went away immediately as she heard him say, "Morena deliciosa, you are all mine."

She couldn't help but laugh as he entered the cell. She said, "And what makes you so sure I'm yours?"

He sat on the toilet as Butterfly put the finishing

touches on her bed. "I was hoping and praying that you would come to this unit. And here you are. It's a sign for me, you know?"

She turned and noticed he had a commissary bag full of stuff. She squinted as a smile spread across her face.

"Sosa, I don't want to cause no problems. I've been told about some racial stuff, and I don't want to be in the middle of it, so there's no way I can take anything from you." Butterfly didn't know what made her say what she said next. "But I do think you are so adorable!" What she said was ironic because it was discouraging and encouraging.

"Listen, morena deliciosa, I got these things because I want you to have them. What they say?" He searched his mind for the limited English words he had. "No strings attached." Sosa got up and gave Butterfly the bag that fell to the floor because of how full it was. He smiled as he held Butterfly's gaze until they both walked out of the cell, and he was about to leave until they both turned to somebody speaking to Butterfly.

"Home girl, what's up?"

Butterfly was on guard at the unfamiliar short, acne-faced guy who approached her carrying another commissary bag of goods in his hands. He appeared to be in his mid-thirties, but she couldn't really tell his age. This guy who Butterfly had never met, walked up to Sosa as he set the bag down on the ground and said, "Sosa, you know how this or any place is run. You know the rules, man. She's from DC, and you respect it or get your people ready."

Sosa stood tall and bristled under the affront. "Fraze, when I left a year ago, I didn't even know you had a voice without Black, E, and Berry with you."

# BUTTERFLY

It was clear Fraze didn't want to start anything right here, so he held up the bag to Sosa. "This bag here is from Black."

Sosa waved him off, seeing that he didn't want any drama. So he looked at Butterfly as he said, "I'll see you later, Morena, but don't forget what I told you on the bus."

Butterfly was momentarily speechless because this was the time she needed his guidance and protection, and here he was walking away to leave her with whatever his name was.

"Fraze," he said to Butterfly as if reading her mind. "Black told the homies that you were here, and he gave me this to give to you. It's a care package."

"What's this for?" Butterfly asked, somewhat defensive.

"Nothing," Fraze said. "Nothing at all. Whenever a homie from DC comes in, we give them something: zoom zooms and wham whams, and a radio. We's DC, and we gotta look out for each other. If you wanna catch up with Black, he works in the barbershop. He'll be there tonight after count."

"Catch up with him for what?" Butterfly was still apprehensive.

"Check this out, champ. A lot of fools are gonna be hounding you around here. Black is good protection. Everybody respects his gangsta; keep that in mind. So swing by and say what's up to him. And now is a good time to start looking for a job before they put you in the kitchen or CMS."

"I ain't working for nobody in the kitchen or whatever CMS is."

"Chill out, home girl. Tomorrow, all you have to do

# MICHAEL A. ROBINSON

is talk to Ms. Mires and tell her to hold down on giving you a job assignment until you find the job you want. Because, trust me, they'll stick you wherever they want. But I gotta run to make a phone call before everybody comes back on recall. I'll holler at you later."

*Shit*, Butterfly thought, *some more language I don't understand.* But if her memory served her right, Buffy explained that recall meant when everybody had to return to their units in order to be counted at 4:00 p.m. And whatever he said about CMS had something to do with Compound Maintenance Services, which she read on a wall outside the officer's office upon entering the unit. She knew for a fact that she wasn't working for anybody. Lucky enough, her modeling agent had cut her a check for her last gigs, totaling a whopping $6,000, of which, in DC jail, she had only spent $600. She was cool on funds. Butterfly dragged the care package in the cell and tried her best to fit two commissary bags full of commissary into her 4X3 locker. She was hoping to God Sosa wouldn't put any money on her inmate account, and people would stop bringing her bags of commissary. It all extremely frightened her.

## Chapter Six |
### *Gay Bash*

A twater Has His Wife In The Palm Of His Hand Atwater wore his prison garbs, which were the same as everybody else's, either a khaki suit or sweat pants. But due to the unexpected heat outside, he had on shorts and a wife-beater. He was speaking with his wife in the telephone room, and he hated the fact that whenever somebody else spoke in the room, there was an echo that bounced off the walls and made it hard for him to hear his wife over the phone.

"What? Stop worrying and calm down. Tyler should be over there to speak to you in a second. Everything's under control," he said to his wife Shonda. She didn't fit the description of a woman riding out with her man while he was incarcerated. She was very attractive; no matter the fact that she was in her early 40s and had two children who were twenty-one and eighteen with Atwater before he was arrested eighteen years ago. At the beginning of his bit, things were a little rocky. But eventually he started to listen to the older guys around him, who gave him advice on how to get his wife back like he had her on the streets. And most of the advice consisted of him being understanding that he wasn't there with her anymore.

"I don't like Tyler coming over here. He ain't ya friend, and I hate when you regard him as one. If he was ya friend, you wouldn't be in jail—he would."

Atwater heard the attitude in her voice. "What I tell you about speaking reckless over this horn? That's too much information. Baby, to be with a boss you have to think bossy without letting your emotions cloud your judgment. So boss up."

"Mace"—She called him by his first name—"I don't want to hear that or anything about the Prophet Noble Drew Ali. I'm the one out here with these kids. I've raised them all by myself."

That took Atwater by surprise. "I'm going to act as if I didn't even hear that. No—matter of fact, I'm going to address it, so we won't ever have to cross this bridge again.

"When I met you, you didn't have dreams and aspirations. All you wanted to be was a housewife. Everything about going to school to become an accountant was my idea." Atwater could hear Shonda slamming pots and pans down in the background, but he continued. "It was an idea within a bigger idea. Remember when the kids were young and I suggested that we put them in private school and I paid the tuition? Yes, I know you remember. Everything up till this point we've done together. I know you're stressing, but I got ya, baby."

Shonda sighed, and at that moment, she didn't even know why she had been mad in the first place. She wasn't mad at him, per se—she was simply mad at the fact that she was tired of waiting for him to come home.

"I didn't mean to say that. I'm sorry."

"Don't worry about it." Atwater understood her to the tee. "I know you're just anxious to get me home."

"That is so true." She laughed, and when she did, the phone beeped to mark that the fifteen minutes allowed for each call had come to an end.

"The phone's about to hang up, but rest assured

knowing I'm on my way home and we're going to be together like I always promised you."

"I love you, Mace."

"I love you more."

"I'm going to write you and e-mail you tonight. I got some things on my mind that need to be put on paper." She sounded morose.

"I'm going to write you too. I'm romancing you though. I have to get your mind and body ready for when I get out."

"Yeah." She smiled. "What are we going to do when you get out?"

"We're gonna make this hunger disappear."

"I can't wai—" The phone cut off in the middle of their conversation.

After Atwater hung up the phone, he went to his friend Jeffrey Bey's cell, who was cleaning when Atwater walked up to him.

"Islam Moor," Atwater greeted.

"Islam. What's going good with you?"

"Same ole same ole. It never ceases to amaze me how shortsighted some people can be. I just hung up with Shonda, and she hit me with: I've raised the kids all by myself."

"She knows that ain't right," Jeffrey Bey added.

"I know," Atwater replied.

"Moor, you're a hustler. You're one of the few that can still send gees home and take care of ya kids and family. You're a percent of a percent in federal prison that can do that. Most of us have been washed up by the Feds."

"Real talk, Atwater said and he told Jeffery Bey about the conversation he had with Shonda and about how much she hated his best friend Tyler."

"What's that about?" Jeffrey Bey asked as they walked into his cell. He had placed the trashcan under the sink, and they sat in opposite chairs once inside. The room smelled like prayer oil, and there were pictures everywhere of when Jeffrey Bey was on the streets. Now he, like many, was serving a 30-year sentence.

"When she went to college, she got all brand new and who knows. She knows that Tyler should have got this beef, but I took the rap for him. And she's been tripping ever since." Tyler had been the cause of Atwater getting busted. Atwater was selling drugs too, but he told Tyler to move the drugs from the house that they were staying in because he felt like the spot was hot. Tyler told him he had for whatever reasons, but when the Feds kicked in the door and searched the house, they found the drugs. Atwater was charged with the dope which he wouldn't have had, had Tyler done as he was told. But one lives and learns.

Jeffrey Bey sighed, knowing how hard it was for anybody to keep it real and be a stand up man while the government hung time over their head.

"Atwater Bey, there ain't too many brother's out there like you no more. To stand up when you could have easily never came to jail, but you didn't do that—you kept it real, which speaks volumes for you. When you go back out there, you're not only going to be a leader of your family, but you're going to be a leader of the community. You have to catch brothers up to your pedigree."

"Real talk. I wish I felt as confident as you sound. I don't know what the world is like anymore. I've been down practically my whole adult life."

"Trust, you are more than able."

They were momentarily interrupted when they heard the CO yelling mail call. They walked out of the cell to see if they had received some snail-mail.

The CO called off a list of names, and individuals received their mail and returned to what they were doing.

Atwater heard his name called, and he called down for Craze-zo to get it.

Craze-zo was twenty years old and far away from home. He didn't have many homeboys from Los Angeles, but he had gotten real close to Atwater. After Craze-zo had gathered the mail, he walked over to Atwater.

"Islam, cuz. I see you have the pony-express crack-a-lacking."

Atwater laughed. "For sure. The love you get from without, demonstrates the love you have within."

"I would get on some die-hard Cali time and express that I don't love them hoes, but I feel like it wouldn't fit in this demonstration we're having."

"It's not that." Atwater laughed. "You're elevating ya game. And what's up with ya fade? I'm used to seeing you look dapper than that."

Craze-zo was high yella with freckles and curly hair. Overly conscientious about his pretty boy looks, he felt he had to balance his look out by being an over-the-top gangster.

"I'm waiting on you," Craze-zo said as a matter of fact.

"You know where I'm at. Meet me at the barbershop this evening after count."

"You heard they got a new punk on the compound they say looks like Rihanna?" Craze-zo asked.

"No," Atwater said, not really feeling like discussing the fact that he had seen Butterfly in the SHU while he was cutting hair.

"Cuz, on Crip, I can almost guarantee on all my dead homies that that punk is gonna have these niggas fucked up like that Puerto Rican punk J-Lo did. Remember how that fag who looked like Jennifer Lopez had those fools? Atwater just shook his head affirmatively to Craze-zo's question. "But on Crip, if I see one of those fags out of pocket, cuz, I'm trippin' on sight." Craze-zo said as he showed Atwater the handle of his eight-inch steel homemade knife that he always carried with him.

# BUTTERFLY

## Chapter Seven |
*That's When He Found Out Where True Power Lies*

It was funny and grotesque at the same time how Nathan had the name Britney Spears when he looked more like Adam Lambert. When Britney Spears came into the cell, the CO slammed the door behind him.

"Hey, my name is Nathan Howard, but everybody calls me Britney."

They shook hands, and for the first time, Butterfly understood why everybody called him Bad Breath Britney. One whiff of his breath was enough to make Butterfly nauseous, but soon the feeling had passed as Butterfly sat down on his bed, which was the bottom bunk.

Once Britney had taken off his uniform and put on his sweat suit, he rearranged the medicine cabinet to make room for Butterfly's things.

"My name is Mariposa—I mean Butterfly." Butterfly remembered what Buffy told her.

"Mariposa is the same as Butterfly in Spanish."

"You know?"

"Of course. I'm from San Fran, a very diverse place and the capital of gays or whatever you want to call it: Adam and Steve or Sodom and Gomorrah. I know everything you should and shouldn't do with guys in here. If you want to learn, we can play trivia, or I can give you the encyclopedic description." Britney spoke a mile a minute and Butterfly couldn't help but laugh.

"This cabinet over here is yours. I'll move all those

# MICHAEL A. ROBINSON

cosmetics on my side. I hope you don't snore or fart in your sleep, because I do. I don't have any grippers left, and if the both of us are farting at night, this room will smell worse than *Dante's Inferno* come morning. And we're ladies, so windows always stay cracked come winter, spring, or fall."

Butterfly kept laughing. Buffy never prepared her for Britney being so funny.

"Do you ever breathe when you talk?"

"Nostrils baby. Inhale . . . breathe . . . suck . . . breathe . . . suck . . . inhale." Britney rocked his head as if performing oral sex on somebody.

"Top range, stand up count!" the CO screamed as two COs counted the inmates.

"Stand up or they'll shake our cell down and take all our stuff." Britney and Butterfly had to stand up quickly before they passed.

After the COs passed, they relaxed and Britney took the time to run everything down to Butterfly.

"I work at Unicor. My job includes boosting the factory manager's confidence. I literally sit behind a desk and tell Mrs. Bowers how beautiful she is and that her husband's a jerk for banging the pretty little secretary in Unit 3B. And the first chance you get, you need to find a job."

"I know. Somebody named Fraze told me already."

"Fraze is all right. But I can help you get a job at Unicor as a production clerk. Mrs. Bowers will hire anybody I suggest. That is, if that's what you want."

"I don't know where I want to work, or if I want to work at all."

"Believe me, you don't want to work in the kitchen. They'll have you serving 1,200 inmates,

# BUTTERFLY

sometimes twice a day. Talk about draconian measures . . . this is a real Gulag Archipelago."

"What?"

Britney waved her off. "Don't worry about it. At Catholic school you get a good education on literature and priests." Britney winked.

"Nuh-hum, Buffy said you were crazy, but I couldn't have imagined that you were this crazy."

"You met Buffy the Vampire?"

Butterfly looked confused. "I thought his name was Buffy da Body?"

"Not with all the guys he's shredded around here with those horse teeth."

Butterfly laughed. "You're crazy!"

"You don't have to lie. I know he was back there talking about me. Let me guess: Bad Breath Britney. But he doesn't know that Ray Ray doesn't think my breath stinks, and you bet not say anything."

"I won't." Butterfly laughed.

"Come on, let's go to chow. They're opening the doors."

"Besides, that's hardly my business, and a closed mouth never tells."

"Hopefully not."

# Chapter Eight |
## *Sosa*

H ey fool, get up," Michoacan said to Sosa, who was on the bottom bunk fast asleep. "Tis time to eat."

"I can't eat right now. I'm in love with the pinche Morena deliciosa," Sosa said as he sat up. It was better now to tell his partner, who was a part of the "Paisas," which was a Spanish word loosely translated to mean "countrymen," how he felt about Butterfly.

Paisas were probably the biggest prison organization or cartel in federal prison. Their shot callers were called Reps or Representatives, and because they controlled all the illegal immigrants from Mexico, they generally always had numbers on their side. In federal prison, their numbers toppled more than 50% of the overall number of those incarcerated. And to be somebody as connected as Sosa was back at home with money carried great weight.

Michoacan, who was 5-feet 5-inches tall, dark-skinned with long hair was somebody Sosa knew he could depend on if he ever needed to make a hit in jail. Michoacan just laughed about Sosa being in love with Butterfly. "Un culo al ano no hace dano."

They both laughed at their familiar saying. It was a saying they used to say getting a piece of ass a year couldn't hurt.

"Yeah, but the pinche ruka is a Morena. But I want to fuck her so bad I couldn't sleep for two nights. Fuck the pinche myates. I'm going to get some of that sweet ass if I have to cause a riot." Sosa was in a tunnel vision and nothing to the contrary could pull him from it.

"No vale la pena," Michoacan said, who loved Sosa because he was the boss, and he put plenty of money on his inmate account.

"Fuck it—I don't care. I got to have morena deliciosa."

# MICHAEL A. ROBINSON

## Chapter Nine |
### *She Just Couldn't Keep Her Eyes Off Him*

**B**utterfly was scared to death as she followed close behind Britney as they walked to the kitchen once their unit was called for chow. It took them a minute to get to the serving line, and once they got there, they regretted they had come.

The line server plopped a scoop of runny mashed potatoes on their tray and a beef fritter that hardly looked edible and was hard and crusty.

"Eat up, baby girl," the server said to Butterfly, hoping he could get her alone one day.

"Shut up, Terrence," Britney said.

"Why you putting my government all on front street like that? It's T-Wire."

"Whatever!" Britney said.

They sat down at the table where guys from DC sat, and a couple of guys came over to meet Butterfly. They were all cool. Buffy had explained to Butterfly that DC guys were open-minded to having gay home boys.

Butterfly couldn't eat the food because it looked disgusting and tasted bland. But Britney ate it as if nothing was wrong.

"What?" Britney asked as Butterfly looked at him.

"I can't eat this."

"It takes some getting used to. But if you want to skip it, I have some food in my locker. Wait—you just got here. You can go to commissary tonight, even though it's not your shopping day. You can get first time shopper. You have money on your account?"

"Yeah."

# BUTTERFLY

"Let's go see if you can shop tonight," Britney said. Unbeknownst to him, Butterfly had a locker that was already semi-full.

They went directly to the commissary, and when they got there it was crowded. Britney went to the head of the line, and he could hear all the sneers and shit-talking going on as they passed.

Britney asked the CO at commissary if Butterfly could shop and he said yes. So they filled out a commissary list of all the things she wanted and handed it in. They had to wait a long time before Butterfly's number came over the display, and then they filled two laundry bags full of food. It was then that Butterfly knew she wasn't going to have anywhere to store all the stuff.

"What kind of ice cream you want?" the CO asked Butterfly. She wasn't that big on ice cream, so she asked Britney if he wanted one.

"Cherry Garcia," Britney responded. Butterfly went ahead and ordered two.

Slim stood in the door waiting to be called for his commissary. He was dressed fly and his clothes were ironed to a crisp and his braids were twisted. He stood tall, and he always stayed clean and fresh with new shoes and new clothes that were purchased from the commissary. That's what he was known for, flossing, even though all the sweat suits & uniforms were the same.

"Punk, ya betta stop looking at me for I give you a black eye," Slim said to Britney.

But Britney walked over to him, set the commissary bag on the ground, and got in his face.

"You haven't heard what happened to Run when he

tried to give me a black eye?"

Slim didn't say anything; he turned his lips to the side of his face as if he wasn't hearing it.

"FYI, I dislocated his jaw and broke his arm. Just let me know when you're ready to give me a black eye, because I love the spousal abuse. Break up to make up."

Everybody laughed, but Butterfly was scared out her mind with everybody gathering around to see if they were about to fight. She could only think what if Britney hit him in the mouth, or if Slim hit Britney in the mouth. Butterfly looked to see if there was anywhere she could hide. There wasn't. But it was a stroke of luck they didn't fight, because if they did, she wouldn't know what to do. Butterfly sighed as she grabbed the receipt, signed it, and they exited the same door that Big Franco was entering.

Franco waited till Butterfly and Britney went through and he looked at Butterfly's fine ass on the down low and was mad at himself that he had. *I ain't no fag*, he thought.

When they walked out, Butterfly saw the barbershop on the side of Commissary, and she wanted to say thanks to Black before heading to the unit. She didn't know how all these political factions in jail would play out, but she was sure she didn't want to be on his bad side.

"Is that the barbershop Black works at?"

"Yeah, and he should be in there," Britney answered.

They went into the barbershop. It was about eight to nine people in there, and for the most part, everybody was getting their hair cut. But in one of the chairs, somebody was braiding another person's hair. Butterfly

# BUTTERFLY

didn't pay attention to anybody after she saw Atwater through the mirror where he had his back to her. And after a second, she remembered she had come to say thanks to Black.

"What's up, home girl? What you been up to?" Black asked.

He looked different from how she had remembered him from the other day when they both were in the holding tank. His matted afro was now laid down in braids, and he wore a gold chain, but he still looked as big as ever.

"I'm okay. I just wanted to say thanks for looking out and to see how you were doing?" Butterfly spoke to Black, but her eyes were glued on Atwater, who tried to act as if he didn't notice her.

"Don't worry about that, you can thank me later. I want you to meet the homies over there. That's E and Berry."

Butterfly turned to see the two young brothers behind her, who looked like stone cold killers. Besides E having braids, and Berry having a short haircut, they appeared to be twins. They nodded. "Whenever you have a problem, holler at one of us."

Black turned and faced Britney. "Damn, what's up, Britney? You act like you can't talk."

"I can talk, Black. I just didn't want to say nothing because you have his hairline pushed behind his back. That's why I can't let anybody cut my hair."

"Bad Breath Britney always got something slick to say," Berry said as they laughed.

"Ain't nobody going to cut your hair anyways, white boy. I don't even know how to cut white people's hair," Black said as they laughed.

# MICHAEL A. ROBINSON

"Those clippers cut my hair like they cut everybody else's, so stop it."

"You a sexy-momma, but all that shit you talking is gonna get your ass kicked," E said playfully as they laughed.

While they were clowning with Britney, Butterfly kept her eyes on Atwater. He was an item worth mentioning, brown-skinned with a Caesar haircut and smooth, creamy skin. It all looked rich and satisfying, and he had the look like he always smelled good. He was average height and in perfect shape.

After a moment of the initial shock of seeing Butterfly and how he/she looked exactly like a girl, Atwater stole another glance at her and couldn't help but feel his blood rise. But he had to keep his eyes on Craze-zo's haircut.

"Britney can back her shit up though," Berry said.

"I'd whip Britney's ass," E said as they laughed.

"Hey, homie, I'm with you. But I seen Britney in action. Believe you me—you don't want to have to live with the reputation of getting beat up by home girl," Black said as they laughed.

"You mean: faggot," Craze-zo interrupted them, tired of hearing all the gay shit being spoken in his presence. He was ready for whatever with his knife with him. Everybody looked at him questioningly as Britney let the commissary bag fall to the ground again.

"Islam Moor," Atwater said, trying to keep everybody's temper calm. "Sometimes foolishness goes faster than wisdom and sound judgment. Excuse us."

"What! That fool don't want no wax with me!" Craze-zo said as he snatched his barber bib off his neck.

"You disrespecting my friend, Cali?" Black said as he placed the clippers down.

# BUTTERFLY

Craze-zo looked confused for a second, and Atwater came to his aid. "He straight, Black. He's with me. I just need to have a word with him. He's like family to me."

Black was reluctant as he said, "Islam."

Britney picked up the commissary bag, and they walked out as Butterfly followed.

Black was about to follow them when he stopped and said, "Don't be mad, Britney. Shit! See you later, Butterfly."

"Bye, Black," Butterfly said as they left.

Black looked at Craze-zo, who stood there still heated. But Atwater shook his head at Black to suggest that he understood his frustrations with Craze-zo.

"I said I got him, Black. Don't trip off that shit."

"What was the disrespect for?" Black still couldn't understand. E and Berry were ready to put in some work anyways, especially on this nigga who didn't have any homeboys from Cali and was a thousand miles away from home.

"Moor, let that die down. Islam," Atwater bid him.

"Islam, but hey, champ, don't be so quick to judge the next man till you've walked a mile in his shoes."

Black recommenced cutting hair, but you could tell he was thirsty for blood, as well as E and Berry. And to cool everything down, Atwater took Craze-zo outside, and they walked to the other side of the Commissary.

"Craze-zo, what kind of idiot shit was that?" Atwater asked once they were by themselves.

"Homie, I ain't tripping or worried about no fag or no fag-lovers. I hate faggots!" And I told you I'm waiting for one of those fags to jump out there."

"It wasn't that fag you would have had to worry about. You would have had to worry about E and Berry, who

71

# MICHAEL A. ROBINSON

were strapped to the teeth waiting for you to jump out there. They would have butchered us in there."

"Us?" Craze-zo asked.

"Yes-us, because I wouldn't have let them do anything to you. You were with me. Just like Black couldn't allow you to disrespect his people, because they were with him. You gotta step your game up if you're kicking it with me. I can't have you jeopardizing my life with that 'I don't give a fuck' attitude. I've built too much shit in my life to have it torn apart on some bullshit. You could have fucked up all the shit I have going on, my plans for the future, in a couple of seconds of being out of control of yourself.

"Now go back in there and apologize to Black."

"What for? I didn't call him a faggot?"

"Craze-zo." Atwater realized it was going to take longer than he thought to make him understand. "It's called finesse. Never ever allow yourself to use disrespectful words, not even to your enemy—not even if you're going to kill him. If you compliment the man you're going to kill, he'll never put his guard up to you. And trust me, you don't want the likes of Black, E, and Berry sitting around with unresolved issues with you."

It took a minute for Craze-zo to capitulate, and it was largely out of the respect he had for Atwater, whom he saw as an older brother, or better yet, a father.

They went back into the barbershop and Craze-zo said, "Black, I didn't mean to disrespect you. I just called it how I seen it. My bad. I was out of pocket."

"Apology accepted, Cali." And Black meant it. "They throw us all together in here, and we have to learn to have respect for people who are different, that's all."

Craze-zo finally understood. "That's real talk."

# BUTTERFLY

Atwater looked at Craze-zo through the mirror and smiled on some big brother shit. But he knew the feeling was only temporary because Craze-zo was hot headed.

# Chapter Ten |
### *The Making Of Greatness*

W ould you like to share the meat and mead of an old man, young black scholar?" Old School asked Atwater as he was heading to his unit after leaving the barbershop at 7:30 p.m.

It was obvious that Old School referred to Atwater as the young black scholar, and Atwater would never pass an opportunity of sharing meat and mead with Old School. Although he was on his way to shit, shower, shave, and then put in a call to Shonda, those things could wait.

"You're going to break bread with me?"

"The breaking of bread is for Lords and disciples, while the sharing of meat and mead is for friends and family. Come on and take a lap with me."

On their way to the yard, Atwater told Old School about his conversation with Shonda when she told him she had been raising the kids all by herself. Old School laughed and attributed Shonda's statement to the unique station of a woman, their frailty. Atwater couldn't help but laugh at how Old School summed matters in a few words, and although Old School was fifty-seven years old, he seemed far beyond his years.

They got to the yard and walked the track. It was nice out and very few people were out and about. This was usually the time when Old School took advantage of the peace and tranquility of the yard. He'd come out every night around this time and walk and think and plan. He was always planning and plotting.

"Do I see a worry crook in your forehead?" Old

# BUTTERFLY

School asked.

"What?"

"That wasn't there when I saw you yesterday. You're letting Shonda stress you out?"

"No, Old School." Atwater laughed.

"You know the youngster I'm always with? Craze-zo? He got into it with the homosexual, Britney Spears. He called him a faggot, and Black, E, and Berry were going to back Britney up."

Old School assessed the situation before he would speak. People usually gave bad advice, not because they couldn't have given good advice, but because they didn't fully appraise a situation by first listening and getting an understanding.

"Why would Black back the homosexual?"

"Because he came to see Black, and Craze-zo butted in their conversation and called him a faggot."

"I see. Being a young man is very hard. We both were there, and it always seemed like we had to prove ourselves in an effort to become our own men. Being Black and young and in jail, we think the only way to prove ourselves is by hitting or stabbing somebody. How many of these brothers do you remember has written a National Best-seller or did some Don King moves once he got out of jail? You see, it's hard to think of that, but I'm sure you can think of more than enough examples of when somebody stabbed or hit somebody upside the head."

"You're right about that."

"You're about to go home, Atwater. I don't want you to go to the streets and get drowned in the sea of the economic crisis. But to leave here and go out there with no plans or saving grace would mean that the eighteen years you've just put behind you were all for naught. And when you go back, remember this: a man who fails to plan plans to fail."

"I got some plans, Old School, but they're scattered in my head."

"I know you have that partner of yours out there and he's still selling drugs and he's probably knee deep in the streets. So do you know what that means for you?"

"No."

"It means that that's all he can offer you, a spot in his dope territory. And believe me, he'll share it reluctantly. It's cool to send some funds and take care of your wife, but he's been out there practically surviving by keeping people out of the game. And friendships are easily broken when you have to be a real friend.

"But it means more for you too. If you go back out there and get in that game, it means that if you come back here, your sentence is going to jump from doing another eighteen years to something harsher like thirty years or more. The crackers have set this game up for us to lose, and the more we try to get-over, the deeper the shit gets.

"Riddle me this: the President, a terrorist, and a wise man; what do they have in common?"

"That's a trick question, Old School. They don't have nothing in common."

"You're very wrong, pupil. All three of them want to persuade an overall theatre full of a certain audience—an audience they intend to control to make a decision, action, or to behave a certain way; one through wisdom, the other through fear, and lastly, one through lies and empty promises. I'm sure you can put

# BUTTERFLY

faces to each of them."

"You're saying that it's the President who persuades his audience through lies and empty promises?"

"I never said it, Atwater Bey. Their actions throughout recorded history says it. I'm just a scholar, as you yourself. But yes, it would mean that it's the President who fits the bill. But he has two faces, because his executive orders are carried out through the threat of violence: he wears the faces of the haloed-politician and the terrorist."

"That's real."

"I know it's degradable when we have these high-power conversations and then we descend to talking about pimping. But there's no better way to understand the relationship between rulers and the ruled. Everything is a pimp/ho/trick relationship, and within those three divisions two pimps become brothers, two hos become sisters, and two tricks, brothers. You and I are brothers, but the rest of these fools in here and their weak minds, puts them in another division of hoes or tricks. They become hos by their weak minds and their inability to hold abstract thoughts and concepts. That's why the white man holds so dear to mathematics, physics, and all other pure sciences. Because that's where abstract concepts and theorems thrive; and their advancement with technology and civilization continues in an upward swing. These cats in here become tricks by being undisciplined and unorganized.

"But even if you organize a trick, he's still a trick operating under the guise of something bigger than himself. These COs are still tricks, and even if the rules and laws that they abide by are geared to rid them of trick characteristics, they're still tricks. And it's our jobs as pimps to find out what wets their beaks—and we own them. The President, the judges, all of them can have trick tendencies. But it's for a true pimp to find out what they are, and exploit them. That's where the power lies."

Old School brought their stroll to a stop as something became clear to him. What he'd say next, he hoped would help Atwater throughout his life. "When you get out, make sure you do what all great people do: build yourself an intelligence-base. Get you a think-tank that keeps you informed about everything."

Atwater chuckled. Old School had just given him an idea that made his mind spin. If people in powerful places were tricks, then they could be exploited and used.

It was the beginning of all the scattered plans in Atwater's head coming together. And what he envisioned would make peoples' teeth shiver from the chill as if they were in the harsh cold of Antarctica. But his plans couldn't be as twisted as he was considering now. Because that would mean . . . that would mean . . . he couldn't even bring himself to say it. But he played with the thought for the remainder of the day.

# BUTTERFLY

## Chapter Eleven |
### I cried my heart out.

Butterfly arranged everything she bought at commissary, and it proved to be a test to load everything in the semi-full space. And she didn't know what she would do with all the food she ordered, because she didn't know how to cook, and she wasn't really a big-eater. But she bought the things that Britney picked out.

Britney lay sprawled across the bottom bunk and wouldn't stop talking about how he wished he could have had a crack at Craze-zo for five seconds.

"I should have kicked his ass in there!"

"For what?" Butterfly asked. This was their tenth time going over it.

"So that he'd have to live with getting his ass whipped by somebody gay," Britney said.

Butterfly sighed.

"You're going to have to put some of that stuff in my locker."

Britney helped Butterfly put some of the things up, and he had come across Butterfly's receipt.

"Damn! You robbed a bank?"

Butterfly snatched the receipt away.

"Everybody in here ain't a flea-rotten prostitute."

"That's true. It's only us gorgeous 'hos. But you had money out there?" Britney asked, kind of shocked.

"I still do. I'm a model. I've ripped the runway, did the venue of all the Black magazines. I've done commercials and videos. I've done it all."

"How did you manage to get locked up then?"

# MICHAEL A. ROBINSON

"It's a long story."

Britney looked at her as if they didn't have anything but tons of time to waste.

"Identity theft and somebody talked me into cashing some checks for them, and I didn't know it was a set up. If truth be told, I've been using other girls' identities since I was young, but I had stopped busting checks."

"I believe you, and I know you're not lying. You're a pretty bitch, and it would be impossible to tell you apart from any other girl. But you were never scared that when you were modeling they would find out that you were a man?"

"Not really. I mean, besides, with this tiny appendage attached to my body, it's impossible to tell."

"I don't know—your hair is looking a little messed up." Britney laughed.

"That ain't fair. I don't know what to do with my nappy hair without a stylist in sight."

"Why don't you use mayonnaise?"

"Why would I do something stupid like that?"

"I don't know; I thought that was an Aunt Jemima's recipe. Plus, a lot of guys in jail do it to get waves."

"I'm not *that* desperate."

"I'm just making fun of you. You're gorgeous no matter how you wear your hair."

"Thank you, I really needed that. All of this prison stuff can really kill a person's spirits. I don't hate much, but I hate this place."

"Have you been feeling down?"

Butterfly shook her head.

"Here, have a seat and tell me all about it."

Butterfly left the remainder of the commissary to

80

one side of the bed as she recounted the story of how her life had turned into a nightmare.

"My ex's name is Clayton. I met him through his cousin Peyton, who I met while modeling. Peyton knew I was dating Clayton, but she didn't know I was a pre-op transgender. And I don't know how she found out about me, but it was like she found it out, and now I'm not so sure that she didn't know about me from the start.

"But she told their whole family," Butterfly said as she cried.

"Take your time." Britney consoled her as best as he could.

"After his family found out, they demanded that he leave me alone. When he realized that his family was against us, we packed up and moved to Richmond, Virginia. I was so happy." The thought of it choked her up all the more, and Britney pat her on her back.

At the time she didn't ever think that Clayton's family would take it out on Peyton. Butterfly couldn't have known, because Peyton never changed toward her, even though they didn't speak much after Clayton and Butterfly moved to Richmond.

"I was so happy living with him that I felt I had opened a new chapter in my life. But it hadn't been a month after we had left when one of his friends called and told him that his mother had died." More tears cascaded from Butterfly's eyes, and she couldn't hold back the flood. After she had gathered herself, she continued.

"Can you believe that his family didn't even tell him about his mother being in the hospital or dying or anything about the funeral? After he found out, everything went downhill from there. He blamed me for everything!"

"Don't cry about that. It's all behind you now. Don't cry, Butterfly."

"Life is so hard! Why is life so hard? Please tell me why life's so hard?"

"I can't tell you. I just know that you have to be strong, and every time you fall, you have to get back up, brush yourself off, and keep going like nothing happened."

"But I can't," Butterfly said. She wasn't even finished telling her story. "When Clayton found out about his mother, he beat me up so bad that I had to stay in the hospital for two months. He just kept hitting me and calling me sissies and fags and queers and gay and all types of horrible things! I just wished he would have killed me, because I still miss him so much, and I'm not mad at him for all the pain he caused me. I forgive him, because if this world is half as crazy for him as it is for me; I understand his pain and hurt."

"Don't say that. Nobody deserves to get punched on for whatever reasons. Don't say that, ever. You'll find somebody else."

Butterfly mended her heart as she cried on Britney's shoulder. The night outside had zapped the energy from her, and all she wanted to do was crawl in the bed and sleep a long, soundless sleep, and she didn't know if she'd want to wake again.

She thought about her childhood and all the negativity and hate for no other reason than people didn't understand who she was and that she had a beautiful heart that was generous, sensitive, and gentle. She wouldn't hurt anybody—it wasn't her nature. But for all the good she had, she attracted that much more evil,

# BUTTERFLY

and she couldn't help but wonder why people reacted like Clayton and nearly beat her to death. Or vengeful like Peyton to go through all that time faking a friendship to eventually set Butterfly up. Or people like her father, so hateful that he spurned the love of his own son. Or people like her uncle, who were so twisted in perversion that they would contaminate a kid's innocence. Could God be so cruel? And was there some other foreseeable plan for her future that would turn everything that had gone wrong in her life into something that could atone and amend for all the pain and suffering she had endured? And, as with life and all other complex questions, they seemed to go unanswered.

# Chapter Twelve |
### *She Could Never Shake The Demons Of Her Past.*

The following day, a dark, turquoise sky was outside, and the day seemed as if it would be cold and inhospitable.

Butterfly just needed another hour of sleep, and she'd feel completely rested. She'd get up, make her bed, and make something to eat because if she could help it, she'd never step foot inside of the chow hall again. Dog food looked and smelled better than the scraps they fed the inmates in the chow hall.

"Butterfly, you have to get up. You're on the call-out for an appointment."

Butterfly awoke to the sound of Britney brushing his teeth and splashing water on his face. She only heard him say that she had an appointment, but she didn't know what a call-out was.

"Appointment?"

"They have you for a psych evaluation at 9:00 a.m. They're going to have you running all over the place today and tomorrow, but they'll tell you. I have to go to work, and I'll see you later."

"Okay."

Butterfly had risen from the bed and freshened up. She guessed that it wouldn't be that hard to do her time here, because Britney and Buffy seemed like a good enough support team that she'd ever need.

She opened her locker and rummaged through it because she didn't know what she wanted to eat. But after a minute, she opted for oatmeal.

After she ate, she put on her shower flip-flops, a

shower cap, and grabbed her shower bag. She was about to head for the shower stalls, which everybody in the unit shared, when Sosa popped up in the door. There were three things Butterfly liked about him: he was cute, persistent, and he didn't care about the political stuff—which frightened Butterfly, but she found it thrilling and exciting all the more.

"Morena deliciosa, you're going somewhere without me?"

Butterfly thought he was cute on the bus, but now he had on a creased sweat suit with a gold necklace with a cross, and a gold Rolex watch that he had smuggled in the jail.

Britney's alarm clock read 7:45 a.m. Butterfly had an hour and fifteen minutes to kill before she had to be anywhere.

"You're gonna get me in trouble, Sosa," Butterfly said as she placed her shower stuff on the locker and sat back down on the bed.

"I got something for you, Morena deliciosa. Can I put up the towel on the door?" Sosa asked.

Butterfly had seen several people putting a towel on the door window so nobody could look in while they used the bathroom. The COs respected the inmate's privacy, and while some would knock to make sure the inmate was alive in the cell, other CO's would respect the inmate's privacy and not bother them.

Butterfly's breath was tense with lust. She wanted Sosa to spread her ass cheeks and spend his load deep inside her body.

"I don't mind."

He put the towel up on the door and came back and stood in front of the bed.

"So what do you have for me?" Butterfly asked. She could tell they were down to their wit's end.

He threw a cellphone on the bed, and Butterfly jumped as if it were a snake.

"How did you get this? I know you're not supposed to have this or that watch. How did you get this stuff?" Butterfly was extremely excited.

"I tried to tell you, Morena, that I got some good connections. Here, call somebody." He gave Butterfly the phone, and she didn't know who to call. She thought about calling Peyton to apologize for any and everything, but the mood wasn't right. So she called her mother, and when her mother picked up on the third ring, Butterfly hung up the phone because she didn't want anybody to know where she was.

"That was quick, Morena," Sosa said as he stood there. By now his dick had grown erect, and it was poking out in his sweats.

Butterfly scooted to the end of the bed, and by now she was horny for some dick after spending six months and a day in the County.

She caressed his dick and said, "I'm hoping that's not the only reason you're here."

Sosa was stuck on stupid looking down at Butterfly pull his five-inch dick from his sweats and take it slowly in her mouth. "Mi Dios, Morena!" he gasped as he fell back onto the locker for balance as Butterfly tickled his dick with her swirling tongue. She had been wanting to taste his Mexican dick ever since they met on the bus, and she slurped his dick without taking a breath.

"Morena, I want to fuck you."

Butterfly didn't stop. She took his balls in her mouth as she ran her tongue along the bottom of his ass while she jacked his dick with her right hand. When she looked up and saw the expression on his face, she put his dick inside her mouth and jacked his dick with her mouth until he shot a wad down her throat and collapsed on the ground. Butterfly kept his dick in her mouth the whole time as she swirled her tongue over the agonizing pleasure zone that had him trembling and pleading for Butterfly to stop. But she wouldn't relent, and after the strong pleasure waves passed throughout his body, his dick stiffened harder than it had ever been.

"I gonna fuck you now, Morena deliciosa."

"You gonna fuck me?" Butterfly asked as she laid her stomach flat on the bed after taking off all her clothes.

"Mi Dios, Morena. Tu cuerpo es mejor que jamás imagine."

"Yes, speak Spanish to me while you fuck me!"

"Deja me mirar a ese culo maravilloso."

Butterfly didn't understand a word he said, but she wiggled her hips side to side. Sosa bit and nibbled on Butterfly's ass and sucked on her cheeks. The ass was like his favorite star's ass, Jennifer Lopez. He plunged his middle finger in her ass when Butterfly told him to grab some Vaseline from the medicine cabinet. He wasn't gone a second, and he massaged it into her ass and on his dick and jammed his dick in so fast and hard that Butterfly had to bite down on her cellie's pillow not to cry out.

Right when they were about to get into it, there was knocking on the door. Butterfly's heart beat out her chest as she tried to get up, but Sosa held her still.

"Hey CO, I taking a fuckin' shit!" Sosa hollered, and he wasn't coming out of Butterfly to save his life.

"Who's in there?" the CO asked. "It's count time."

# MICHAEL A. ROBINSON

"What's your last name, Morena?" Sosa whispered.

"Moore."

"Moore's in here. Now can I take my shit in peace?"

The CO left the room because it was a dumb count anyway. It wasn't an official count, but sometimes they did it after 8:00 a.m.

"Hold on, Sosa," Butterfly said, because now she thought somebody would come in, and she remembered what Attenberger said about sending her to ADX.

Sosa stopped, but just to explain that the officer wouldn't come back. Then he started to hammer that ass until the speed and forcefulness made Butterfly have an orgasm at the same time that Sosa spent his load.

Sosa was barely able to drag himself from the cell because he felt so euphoric. But Butterfly saw that it was 8:45 a.m., and she had to hurry and shower and get dressed to go to her 9 a.m. appointment.

After she got out the shower, she put on the funny looking uniform that was mandatory for all inmates to wear, and she headed outside to see if she could find the Psychology building. Somebody was kind enough to point it out to her, or she would have never found it because everything seemed like the same building. She went inside the building and told the secretary at the desk her name. Butterfly was told to sit and wait for her name to be called.

They called her moments later, and she went inside the psychiatrist's office. The standoffish, cold, and calculating lady gave off every indication that she was as much a CO as she was a psych, if not more.

"Well, Ms. Moore, your record is very exciting," the lady said negatively. "My name's Mrs. Salinas, and by what I've read, it seems you've tried to commit suicide

# BUTTERFLY

more than enough times to be locked up somewhere in a straitjacket. But since that's not something I can recommend, is there something you'd like to talk about?"

"No," Butterfly said bluntly, because if Mrs. Salinas or whoever she said her name was, was going to be an asshole, so would she. And this was another reason why Butterfly hated to do the pre-sentence investigation report. It made her an open book to complete strangers.

"I'm going to keep you on hormones, as is your right, and I'll prescribe some medicine for your bipolar disorder, something you've had since you were ten years old. Are you still having problems sleeping?"

Butterfly didn't want anything from Mrs. Salinas, but she shook her head affirmatively to the question.

"Very well. I'll prescribe something for that also. That should be it, and if you ever feel the need to speak about something, feel free to come and see me."

Everything about Mrs. Salinas was tart, scripted, and phony and she had an aura of a genuine bitch about her. And Butterfly began to think that the majority of COs she had so far encountered had all been the same way: self-serving, nasty, egotistical, arrogant assholes, who all metaphorically had high horses they rode to work on. It was the most humiliating thing to be in prison.

Butterfly stepped back into the hall, and when the secretary smiled at her she was too far in her stink to return it. She was also mad at the fact that she couldn't immediately return to her unit, because of what Buffy explained to her about Controlled Movements, which meant, that there was no traffic on the compound except during prescribed hours. That prescribed hour happened to be an hour from now—on the hour and

89

every hour after that till 8:30 p.m. And the Moves would start again at 6:30 a.m. the following morning.

Two orderlies were cleaning the lounge, and when Butterfly looked up, she noticed that she was alone with them. One of them came and sat at her side. "You from DC, right?" His name was Tyrone, and everybody at the joint knew Butterfly was from DC by now.

"Yes."

"And you're coming here to get a fix? All you'd have to do is come to the homies, and they would have sent you to me. What's up? You wanna party?"

Butterfly was skeptical about everything, and she didn't trust anybody. After what had just happened in her cell with Sosa rocking an amazing orgasm out of her ass, she could use something that would wind her down. And she couldn't say she didn't want to get high to take an edge off the stress she felt. But she played as if she was a dimwit and asked, "What you mean party?"

"Hold up one second." Tyrone went over to Love, who was in the utility closet, putting the mop bucket away. It was funny that they could have passed for brothers, yet they had no relation at all. They were both slim, dark-skinned, and stood the same height. They both had a ridiculous youthfulness about their faces, even though they were in their late twenties.

"You still have those ecstasy-pills from yesterday?"

"Yeah, nigga, but why? You thinking what I'm thinking?" Love asked Tyrone as they both wore ridiculous smiles of agreement.

Tyrone shook his head. "Dr. Alonzo's office?"

# BUTTERFLY

"Let's go."

Love went to the unoccupied office as if he would clean it, and he took out the pills that he had keestered. He didn't wash his hands afterward, but he took out a couple of small bundles that had the content of crushed ecstasy-pills in paper.

The whole time Love was in Dr. Alonzo's office, Tyrone went back to get Butterfly. He wanted to fuck her so bad that he had a headache. She was fine and looked better than any female CO on the compound, or better yet, than most girls he had ever seen.

"Butterfly, right? My name is Tyrone, and my dude going in that room is Love. He's really good people. Look, I have some ecstasy-pills. I'll give you some if you wanna party."

Butterfly looked into his adventurous eyes, and she made the decision that whatever he meant by partying, she'd be down. She was still sexually charged from Sosa. She wanted to party, so she could forget about the fear she still had of the prison going into complete chaos because of something she had caused. Butterfly just wanted to feel secure, even if it didn't last for that long.

"Where are they?" she asked.

"We got them. You down?"

"Yes."

"Come on."

Tyrone led her back to Dr. Alonzo's office, and when they went in, they locked the door behind them.

"Ooh-child, you fine as fuck. Is those tits real?" Love helped himself to her busty breasts.

"Yeah they're real," Butterfly said coyly, loving the attention they gave her. They couldn't keep their

91

hands off her and they groped her ass and Love went as far as to kiss her on her neck.

"Damn, Butterfly. You're so fine, I'd suck on your daddy's dick!" Love said, completely taken.

"You won't have to, nigga. You can suck on my dick," Tyrone said as they laughed. "Where the shit at?"

"Right here-right here." Love made a kingly display of the lines of ex that he had under a paper on the desk.

"Snort it, baby," Tyrone said.

When Butterfly went down to take the straw and snort the fine powder, she felt Tyrone's dick grinding on her ass.

"God damn, baby, you're a real muthafuckin' girl. I thank the US Marshals for sending you here."

Butterfly snorted more than three lines of ecstasy and left very little for them. But they were too busy fighting over the privilege of grinding on that woman's ass of hers that put most women to shame. Even through the khaki, that ass was plump, phat, and she most definitely had a coke bottle shape that a nigga would kill for. Had they known better, they would've been running for their lives, because a taste of that sweet ass would awake love, jealously, and strife in them that they wouldn't be able to control.

When Butterfly had had her fill, she had an instant rush. She gasped pleasurably, and feeling the two dicks against her body felt lovely, and she wanted to be ravished on the spot.

Love was already feeling the line he had done moments earlier, and he started to kiss all over her. It was too much for Tyrone, just knowing the fact that Butterfly was a man, no matter how much she looked otherwise. He had to break up the party between them, as he whipped out his dick and grabbed Butterfly's head down to give him some head.

Goddamn, it was the best head he'd ever had; no matter that Love's dumb ass went to biting and gnawing on Butterfly's ass. Tyrone would have laughed if the head wasn't so powerful and thought-provoking as he looked at Love rubbing his face and licking his tongue in the crack of Butterfly's ass.

It felt so good to Butterfly that her ass was getting ate out through her khaki pants, and the more he ruffled her ass with his tongue and his face, the more she wanted to get fucked rough, hard, and final. She gobbled Tyrone's dick in the exchange and gave his dick her special and sucked it like she truly loved dick and he nutted uncontrollably. While humming a lullaby, she drank it down and took his dick all the way down her throat without gagging.

"Love." Tyrone trembled. He almost passed the fuck out! And Love jumped up and saw how Tyrone looked as if he'd died a heavenly death, and Love knew he had missed something grand.

Butterfly pushed Tyrone out the way and massaged Love's dick through his pants.

"Take it out, baby," Butterfly begged as she gently bit on the bottom of his hard dick. He collapsed against the table, and he didn't know if he would cry.

"I'm falling in love." He looked as Butterfly took his dick out his pants and sucked it as if he had juice inside of him. She slurped and twirled her juicy red lips around the helmet of his dick, and then dropped her mouth all the way down to swallow him whole.

Butterfly was so pretty that he would have sworn

she was the prettiest girl who had ever sucked his dick. She sucked his dick while Tyrone had gathered himself, and he was so cum-drained that he didn't have enough vigor to fuck Butterfly, who was by now, wagging her sexy ass like a bitch in heat!

"You don't wanna fuck me?" Butterfly asked Love with her golden and sex-hungry sparkling eyes as she wiggled her tongue over the base of his dick. He was too far gone, and when she felt his helmet flare, she slurped his nutt down her throat, and she loved the taste of it.

But she swallowed too much of his dick and she almost vomited as Tyrone handed her the trashcan. Nothing came up, but she was still coughing.

"Home girl, you all right?" Tyrone asked.

She waved him off. Love felt celebratory.

"I think she bit off more than she could chew," he said as he put his dick back in his pants.

"Shut up, fool, and get her some water," Tyrone responded.

Love disappeared to get her some water. When he came back, she drank the water and felt much better.

"Tyrone, I ain't never had head like that! She is pretty enough to tongue kiss. I'm in love."

"Hold down, Love. Fall back," Tyrone said.

"Butterfly, I know we ain't finished partying yet?"

Butterfly sat up. She felt much better, and she was still hot and horny as hell.

"What else you got in mind?" she said as she grabbed Love's dick again. He groped her ass and wailed like a brand new baby getting slapped on the ass.

"Shit, we got smoke, drink, and plenty more dick in

# BUTTERFLY

my unit. You down?" Tyrone asked. On the sly, Tyrone rubbed his fingers together. *Make money, fool.*

"I'm down for whatever, as long as your friend fucks me." At this point Butterfly felt so good and high that she didn't care about all the gangs, territories, and turfs. She just wanted to continue to have a good time.

Love couldn't take it anymore. He bit on his knuckles to restrain himself.

As promised, Tyrone snuck Butterfly in Unit-4B disguised with a low cap on her head and a big jacket. Tyrone brought out lots of hooch, weed, and he arranged for a few paying patrons to get a piece of her fine ass.

Love was first, and it took everything Tyrone had to pull him out of the cell after he had finished. Others had gone in and Butterfly serviced them all, something she had never done before, but she felt good for it. But the more she drank, the more she smoked. She lost proportion and felt herself falling into another nightmarish spell. Butterfly tried to fight against the impending gloom, but even though her body was in locomotion, she had drifted into the fogginess.

*She was a teenager again, lost in the mirror staring back at her. Yes, that's when she had found herself. It was the lady dressed ever so beautifully and whose face was made up and could have easily passed for her mother when she was younger. But Butterfly was much prettier than her mother. She was lithe, slender, supple, devilishly exotic, and she had a sex appeal that would cause men to lose their restraints—and this she knew! She smiled at the mirror, and to her surprise, the mirror smiled back. It . . . it—it was her in the mirror, and she was gorgeous! But the mirror cracked and split down the middle of her face. And she was on the ground and her father was pummeling her with his fists and screaming hysterically.*

*"Get out my house! If I ever see you again I'll kill you! I swear to God I'll kill you . . . Get out!*

*Butterfly's torn garments swayed in the wind as she ran, bloody and dizzy. She didn't know where to run, but she ran through the night, and the only thing on her mind was the image of seeing her mother crying like crazy trying to pull her father off her. But her brother just stood there and looked upon her with disgust.*

She tossed and kicked in her sleep till Britney woke her for the 4 p.m. count. Britney had just returned from work and had seen how Butterfly was strung across his bed with vomit everywhere. He just laughed till Butterfly started to scream from her hellish nightmares, which was around the same time the COs were counting. Britney cleaned the mess while Butterfly tried to get on her bunk at the top; but it proved too much a difficulty and she collapsed on the chair.

"You gutter mouth slut. You need to get your smelly ass in your bed. You smell, and I know your ass is soiled with nut."

"Leave me alone," Butterfly said pitifully. Her head was pounding, her ass was sore, and it took all she had not to vomit again from the sour taste she had in her mouth.

"Not ever. You have the whole compound talking about you, and you were probably too wasted to remember. What a waste!"

After Britney changed his bedsheets, cover, and sprayed disinfectant around, he lay Butterfly back in his bed. He then grabbed a bagel from her locker and spread

# BUTTERFLY

cream cheese and honey over it, and gave her aspirin.

"Eat this so it can absorb the alcohol in your stomach," Britney said as he coddled Butterfly and fed her. "You'll be all right, don't worry. A couple of more crashes like that, and you'll be fine. I'm here for you."

# Chapter Thirteen |
## *Dreamy Eyes And Passion*

B utterfly had been sneaking around the unit with Sosa, getting fucked every available moment. They fucked in the showers, in Sosa's room, and during the daytime when Britney was at work. Sosa's Mexican paisas would always keep watch while Sosa was with his girlfriend, Morena.

But little did he know that Black had caught wind of what was going on between them.

So a couple of days later during the evening, Butterfly had walked to the chapel. It was a good night to get out, and her first time outside since the orgy in Unit 4B and her days in the unit with Sosa. She didn't want to be seen for a couple of days because of the sheer embarrassment of what happened in 4B. Just the thought that she probably wouldn't recognize any of the guys she had slept with, even if they were standing in her face, made her feel like crap. But Black had sent word through Fraze for her to meet him in the chapel so he could speak with her.

It was good that he had brought her out the unit because she couldn't have stayed in the unit any longer. Although everything was good, she was scared Sosa might find out what she did in 4B, or that they would get caught fucking and a race riot would be because of her. And although Sosa was good to fuck, she didn't like him like that.

But once out and about, the air was crisp and cold and it sent a chilling shiver through her. She pulled her jacket tight and picked up her pace and she was

# BUTTERFLY

surprised when guys were saying what's up to her and greeting her as never before. *They must of heard about 4B,* she thought and picked up her pace again.

She saw Love and Tyrone walking to the gym. Love had puppy-eyes for her that were real and genuine and she thought it was cute. When she went inside the chapel, it was nothing like she had imagined. A hallway led to a main chapel and along the hallway were other rooms for different religious groups to congregate and hold services.

Black was the Grand Sheik for the Moorish Science Temple of America, and he had more rank than Atwater, who was the Assistant Sheik. They were both a part of the same faith, but they had never formed a tight friendship.

Inside the Main Chapel, the Moors were arrayed in their attire with red fezzes on their heads, Moorish pendulums, and shiny shoes. They had paintings of Noble Drew Ali on a chair and Marcus Garvey on another one. An American flag was at a corner of the chapel and a Moroccan flag at the other side.

Atwater stood at the podium and it immediately drew Butterfly to the door that was guarded by two doormen, and when they went to open it, Butterfly waved them off.

She couldn't hear anything that Atwater was saying, but she could hear the applause. She stayed there for a minute, watching him until somebody pat her on the shoulder.

"Excuse me. Can I be of some assistance?" Lazy Eyes (as was his name) asked. And as his name suggested, he had dreamy bedroom eyes that would make one feel intoxicated by gazing into them.

Butterfly had to snap out of it, because Lazy Eyes was most definitely good looking to say the least, and it completely caught her off guard.

"I . . ." Butterfly was lost for words, and Lazy Eyes, who was from Baltimore, wore a knowing smile.

"My name is Lazy Eyes," he said, drawing more attention to his dreamy eyes. "I'm the chapel's librarian. I know you're new in the system, but if you want I'll give you a quick rundown of the chapel's services." He was the perfect gentleman, nothing like Love and Tyrone who were just good fucks.

"I'm not really religious. I don't believe in God," Butterfly said, and she wasn't completely lying, but she didn't want to run him off either. Nevertheless, she was there to meet Black.

"That's all right. Tell me if you're Wicca, Santamaria, because you look like you have some Latin in you."

Butterfly ignored the fact that he was playing in an effort to converse with her. She was just there to speak with Black and leave. She was sure that he had heard about her escapade in 4B, and she could hardly think of anything else.

"I haven't even heard of any of that stuff."

"Okay, do you like music?"

"Yeah."

"Right this way, ladies first." He pointed her straight ahead. At first she was reluctant, but then she followed.

"I'm going to hip you to some good music." Lazy Eyes took her to a corner where a CD player was. He went into a closet and got out a couple of CDs and brought them back. He put on Dancehall and then Reggae because it was the only music the Religious Services had, besides Gospel.

Butterfly shook her head to the Reggae music. Lazy Eyes kept smiling and licking his lips at her and he was irresistible! He mumbled something, but she couldn't hear him because she had on the headphones.

When she removed them, he said, "You like that?"

"Yeah, but I liked the Dancehall better."

"So you can move those wide hips?" Lazy Eyes laughed. "I'll order some more for you. Can I let you in on a little secret?"

Butterfly shook her head.

"I think you are most definitely fine, and I ain't never swung like that, but since you came on the compound I've been wanting to get my hands on you."

Butterfly didn't wait for him to say anything else. She slid her hands between his legs and was satisfied at what she felt. She smiled seductively and said, "We can do something."

"When? Right now?" It was too much for Lazy Eyes to believe, and his dreamy eyes twinkled like shooting stars.

"Whenever."

"Go to the restroom, and I'll be in there when the coast is clear."

"Where's the restroom?" She knew she was pressing her luck, because she was there to see Black. But Lazy Eyes was too irresistible to pass on, and she could already taste him in her mouth.

"Over there in the corner."

She took her jacket off and left it in the chair, and as she headed toward the restroom and passed guys who were in other rooms, everybody turned to look at her phat ass. She had on her tight sweats pulled in the crack of her ass that looked like an ice-cream sundae.

Minutes after she had gone into the restroom, Lazy Eyes had arrived and shut the door. He took a minute to take her in. She looked like the devil from his wet dreams. Butterfly giggled lightly, loving how hungry he looked. He grabbed her tits and fondled them.

"Damn, baby, these are real?" was the question she'd always get.

Butterfly took one of his hands off her tit and put it on her ass. "This is real too," she said, kissing him on the lips. He tasted like peppermint candy. She slurped his tongue as if it was his dick and took his dick out his pants.

"God damn . . . shit!" he muttered, along with a bunch of gibberish that got lost at her mind-boggling skills. Once again she was overly concerned with giving him a ground shaking orgasm. She felt the rumbling, and his semen sluiced forth. Once she gurgled the tender head of his dick in the pit of her throat, he thought he might die because the pleasure was so great!

And she disappeared before he could realize that he wasn't sleep walking . . .

BUTTERFLY

# Chapter Fourteen |
*Black Out*

W
hen she emerged from the restroom, she
wiped the saline taste from her mouth and
went to get her jacket. She headed for a
bench that was on the outside of the main chapel and
moments later, the Moors had ended their service.

They mauled out and then Atwater emerged, trailed
by other Moors. When he looked over and saw
Butterfly, they locked eyes. He couldn't hide the hunger
rising in his throat, and he felt the urge so strong that
his heart pounded violently in his chest. Atwater felt
uncomfortable with the feeling.

Black came out seconds later and took the empty
seat on the bench where she sat.

"What up, home girl? How are you doing?"

"I'm fine," Butterfly said truthfully. It would have
been a lie if she hadn't encountered Lazy Eyes and
Atwater before he arrived.

"I told Fraze to tell you to meet me because I heard
about what you did in 4B."

Butterfly didn't know where this would lead, and
she looked off to the side where she saw Lazy Eyes
making pleading fuck-faces at her. She had to swallow
a welcoming smile and keep her eyes on Black so that
she wouldn't give him away.

"You trying to play me, muthafucka?" The easy
going Black had melted under a disguising mask of an
easily-triggered temper.

Butterfly was reeling from the fact that Black had
seen what had happened in the bathroom. "I don't

103

# MICHAEL A. ROBINSON

know what you're talking about."

"You know what the fuck I'm talking about!" Black's whisper could as well have been a scream, because it was just as hauntingly threatening.

Butterfly held her hands in submission, expecting a blow. "What did I do wrong?" She saw E and Berry standing nearby, and this all seemed like what she feared most about jail: being killed.

"You know you my bitch, right?"

"W-w-what?"

Black looked around to make sure nobody in the vicinity was looking. Then he grabbed Butterfly by her scruffy afro-tail. Tears welled in Butterfly's eyes from the searing pain.

"Yes, Black!" It felt like her hair was being ripped from its roots, and she felt his other hand wrapped tightly around her throat.

"This my ass-pussy, right! We 'bout to find out. You gonna give me some of that ass-pussy tonight! Bitch, I got all this time and you giving my ass-pussy away in your unit and 4B. I'll fuck around and kill all those niggas. I'm taking care of that right now as we speak. Now get your ass in the bathroom!"

# Chapter Fifteen |
## *War On The Down*

Sosa didn't know why, but he had a bad feeling something bad was about to happen. He was in the unit sitting at the table with Michoacán and a couple other paisas. Then he went to the cell and took his metal knife that he'd made in the plumbing shop at CMS, and he put it in his sweats and came back.

"Sosa, why you look paranoid? Pinche Morena leaves five minutes, and you can't keep your ass still in the seat."

"No me mames ," Sosa said, knowing why he felt alert.

"I wouldn't bullshit you," Michoacán said.

*Where the fuck is that pinche myate Fraze?* Sosa thought. He didn't trust Fraze at all.

Two minutes didn't go by when a team of six officers stormed into the unit and ran straight to Sosa's cell. Sosa was so mad because he had just left his cell, and he didn't put his cellphone and Rolex watch in the stash spot that he could have hit himself in the eye. He had paid $200 so somebody from CMS could put a hole in the wall where he could hide stuff. His phone and watch were sitting right under the pillow. Fuck!

Five minutes later, a CO came out of the cell holding his cell phone and watch in the air. "Sosa!" the CO hollered.

Sosa stepped up to the CO with Michoacán at his side.

"I'ma Sosa, but that not mine," he said as Michoacán came forward. He already knew to claim

# MICHAEL A. ROBINSON

ownership if Sosa were to ever get caught.

"That me cell phone and watch," Michoacán added.

"Nice try," the CO, whom they'd never seen before said. "That's not what our confidential informant said."

The other COs gathered around Sosa and put him in handcuffs. Sosa knew he'd never see his Morena deliciosa again, and he was so furious that they didn't even have the courage to give him a fight.

As the COs escorted him out of the unit, he looked back and yelled to Michoacán, "Mata el pinche Moreno Fraze y el Negro!"

Sosa knew nobody other than Black and Fraze would want to tell to get him out of the picture. He had paid COs, who had smuggled him in the watch and cell phone to give him a heads up if they were on to him. So somebody had to drop a kite. But he knew the pinche morenos would pay dearly. Because within two weeks after the majority of the Paisas had obtained knives from CMS, where they were made, there was gonna be a blood bath.

## Chapter Sixteen |
### *Knight With Shining Knives*

Black gave E and Berry the nod. Mysteriously enough, nobody in the chapel noticed what was happening.

Butterfly looked for Lazy Eyes, but he was nowhere to be found. She was pushed into the bathroom and Black shoved her face-first into the wall once the door was closed. Butterfly trembled with fear as her pants were pulled down and Black was about to fuck her in the ass until he heard the commotion outside.

Black pulled his pants back up and opened the door to see what was going on as Butterfly collapsed into the corner of the bathroom.

"What the fuck you want, pretty boy?" Black belched out at Lazy Eyes, who had his knife drawn on E and Berry. He wasn't alone. His closest homie, Raheem, held a knife in each hand. He wasn't as big as Black, but he had enough size to take E and Berry all by himself. But it would be an ambush because Black, E, and Berry didn't have knives.

"You trying to rape a man and you the Grand Sheik?" Lazy Eyes said. When he saw Butterfly in the corner, he wanted to stab Black in the throat.

"Don't worry about this!" Black said, knowing he was outmatched by the look on Berry and E's face.

"Nigga, I oughta kill you!" Lazy Eyes put his knife to Black's neck, and the overhead speaker announced the ten minute movement. "Get the fuck out of here before I change my mind!"

Black and his crew got out of there as fast as they

could, but everybody in there knew it wasn't over.

When Black and his crew left, Lazy Eyes made sure that the only CO in the chapel at the time was the Chaplain himself, and he didn't notice any of the commotion. It was clear the Chaplain hadn't seen anything as he sat in his office busy with something on his desk.

Lazy Eyes looked at Raheem and told him to give him a couple of minutes with Butterfly. They would be stuck in the chapel until 8:30 p.m., which was the official time when all the inmates had to report back to their units.

When Lazy Eyes went into the bathroom and shut the door, Butterfly jumped up and ran to him. If she thought she was afraid before, she was a hundred times more afraid now. She didn't know that Sosa had gone to the SHU, but she was thinking there would be a riot if he found out, because he kept promising her that he would protect her. But to make matters worse now, Lazy Eyes was in her mess. She didn't know what to do.

"Stop crying, baby," Lazy Eyes said, feeling Butterfly to the fullest.

"No, it's all my fault," Butterfly said with her head on his shoulder.

"It ain't your fault." Lazy Eyes grabbed Butterfly's chin so he could look her in the eyes. "I saw what that fool did, and I grabbed my knife and got my boy Raheem to watch my back." He always kept spare knives hidden in the chapel for times like this. It was just sheer luck that Raheem happened to drop by. "Don't ever say a nigga tryna rape you is your fault."

Lazy Eyes' words were comforting, and out of

everybody she had screwed since she got there she could see herself falling head over heels for him. To Butterfly, he and Atwater were the sexiest men alive.

"But he's gonna come back and get me!" The realization of Butterfly's own words scared her more than anything.

"Yo, fuck that nigga. I got you, baby. That's my word. I'd kill that nigga or get rid of him before I let him touch you. Now let me taste that sweet tongue of yours." They kissed passionately, like teenagers in love, until Lazy Eyes led her back into the chapel's lobby area so he'd have time to straighten the chapel and close up everything. But he made sure Raheem sat with Butterfly until the yard was closed and they returned to their units, on high alert.

# MICHAEL A. ROBINSON

## Chapter Seventeen |
### *Revenge, Revenge, Revenge!*

Black was steaming! He was with his cellmate E after 9:45 p.m. during unit lockdown where all the inmates were locked in their cells until the following morning. Black was doing pushups to knock out some of the aggression he felt. "I wanna kill that pretty boy nigga!" Black slammed his mighty big fist in the palm of his other hand after he finished a clip of pushups. His well-defined chest muscles were teeming together in a tight knot that stretched the outer skin. He went down and knocked out another set of 120 straight pushups without stopping.

"Yo, that bama ass nigga made us look real bad, Black. I want to personally get my knife in that nigga's throat," E said, who was sitting up in his bed. He was mad at Berry for not always being strapped and letting Raheem and Lazy Eyes get the jump on them.

Black hopped up and his bare chest was sweating as he paced back and forth. *Shit!* he thought. He'd just spoken to the institution's secret police and told them the information about Sosa that he got from Fraze. It was so easy to set that punk bitch beaner up by leading the police to his phone and thousand dollar watch. Black would have punished all the bitch ass Mexicans on the compound, but he was making too much money on the down low. Being that he was Grand Sheik, whenever an outside speaker of their faith came in to speak, Black made sure he was loaded down with nine ounces of heroin.

Once the heroin was smuggled inside the jail, he

110

could make upward of twenty grand a month. And because of the proximity of Schuylkill to DC and the ease and arrangement to get the shit in, Black would be a fool to get sent somewhere else by causing a riot.

"Fuck!" Black exploded as he thought about finally having Butterfly's sweet and fine ass to himself. He was so demented with having her as his wife that even if he would have had to 'publicly' step down as Grand Sheik, he would have done it willingly. His plan was to eventually keep Butterfly high off heroin and fuck her good every day until the bitch's heart was his. And then and only then would he marry that bitch for all time to come. Of course, it only meant for as long as the both of them were incarcerated, but he knew that once a person was incarcerated they would always return.

Black went down again to bust out another set of 120 pushups. He'd just gotten Sosa out the way and now Lazy Eyes popped up. *God damn, how many other contenders were going to pop up on the radar?* he thought. It would have been easy to have sent Berry and E over there to stab Sosa up, but Black was gonna need them for what he was doing with the heroin thing. The barbershop was where they stashed and sold everything, and after a week of officially being in business, the shit was already highly lucrative.

He knew he had to take his time with Lazy Eyes. The nigga was a nut all right. Black couldn't do anything rash that would fuck off what he had going on, and he couldn't keep going to the institution's internal police, because he didn't need rumors traveling about him being a snitch. He'd have to wait until Lazy Eyes slipped up and then punish his ass. Then Butterfly would be left all to him.

# Chapter Eighteen |
### *Prison Dreams*

H ey! You wanna get drunk?" Love had been standing outside of Butterfly's window during the ten minute move.

Butterfly nodded yes and looked over at Brittany. The weekends usually consisted of leisure time for the inmates and newly released videos would be shown on all the flat screens in each unit.

Minutes later, Love came in with a gallon of hooch that he had brought from his unit, and the three of them sat around eating and drinking.

Since Britney didn't have to work, he made a delectable fruit salad, barbecue chicken, rice pilaf, and refried beans. All the items had been smuggled into the unit from the kitchen and would be cooked in the unit's microwave.

"Bad Breath Britney, time for you to bounce," Love finally said, wanting an hour or two with Butterfly. But before Love had come in the unit, Butterfly had already told Britney to stay in the cell with her, because she wasn't doing anything with anybody. At least until she knew what she wanted to do about Black and Lazy Eyes.

"This is my cell—hello!"

"But I'm trying to get some of mommy right here."

"Not today, baby," Butterfly said and she meant it. With what was running through her mind because of Black, she couldn't think of much else as of late. Black scared the living god out of her, and no matter about the protection of Lazy Eyes, she was going to

113

stay put in the unit.

Her Latin lover, Sosa had been taken away. That Sunday morning she found out that he had put six thousand dollars on her inmate account. When Britney saw that, he just shook his head as they both laughed.

When Love realized that she wasn't talking about anything, it was time for him to bounce.

Once he left, Britney wanted to get out of the unit. He was drunk and he wanted to go to the gym.

"Come on, girl. Let's get out of this unit."

"Ain't nothing to do out there. And you know Black wants to kill me." Butterfly had told Britney everything during the night.

"So what. You can't hide from him. Get your drunk ass up and let's go."

They headed to the gym, and it was Butterfly's first time going. She didn't know the jail housed this many people. She thought she had seen a lot of people during chow, but there were tons of people she had yet to see.

When she walked in the gym, every eye turned on her. The sexual charge was so powerful and thick, she could cut it with a dull knife. The guys who were playing basketball couldn't even concentrate on the game, because they were distracted looking at Butterfly in her shorts that were pulled tight into the crevice of her ass, and the T-shirt she wore went above her belly button and was knotted at one side of her waist. It was no way to explain to these sex-depraved men that Butterfly wasn't Rihanna coming to pay them a special visit. There was even hooting and hollering.

"If that's a man—I'm gay, my nigga 'cause I'd fuck the shit out of that bitch!" somebody yelled.

"What, nigga! We already ran a train on that

# BUTTERFLY

muthafucka, and the pussy and the head was the bomb!" another person from 4B responded.

"You punk muthafucka. Why didn't you get me?"

"Nigga, you was too busy working for Mr. Charlie."

Butterfly couldn't help but feel shy and sheepish and when she heard them calling the ten minute move, she begged Britney to take her back to the unit. All she could think of was Black lurking in some dark corner ready to jump out at any time. But when she turned, Lazy Eyes bumped into her and quickly whispered in her ear for her to go to the library's bathroom immediately.

Butterfly acted perfectly normal and held her poise as if he hadn't said anything to her. She grabbed Britney's hand and told him to take her to the library, which he did.

Once she went to the library, she headed straight to the bathroom where she waited while Britney sat at a table and kept watch.

Moments later, Lazy Eyes came in primped and preened as only on a rare occasion, and his cologne could be sensed from afar.

When he walked in, he took a minute to look at the tasty treat who was smiling from ear to ear. Lazy Eyes was most definitely her type, and she was instantly a girl of giggles and loose chatter in his presence.

"Why you haven't been coming out? I've been trying to get at you for a minute?" Lazy Eyes asked. He was most definitely sweating her.

Butterfly loved it a little too much! "I've been thinking about you too, baby," she said as she ran into his arms and ran her tongue over his lips. Lazy Eyes acted as if he was still terribly mad that he hadn't seen her for what seemed like a year of endless longing.

"I had a fool clean this bathroom, scrub the fuck out of this shit, and the chapel bathroom, waiting for you to come back and see me. So when we finally were together, we'd be in a clean ass place."

"I'm here," Butterfly said, grabbing his dick and massaging it. And if he was mad before, he was hot and horny now.

She kept kissing him, knowing that would make him truly happy. "I want you to fuck me, baby," she whispered and kissed his ear and his neck while massaging his dick.

Lazy Eyes hadn't thought of anything for days on end that he'd spent without her and he hated it all the more. No girl had ever had him fucked up in the head as Butterfly had him, and he didn't know if it was just because he was in jail or not. But he dreamed of her, woke up thinking about her, and he could smell her scent everywhere he walked. He wanted to fuck her so bad his head was throbbing.

"I don't want to fuck you," he said, but it was a lie, and his face had betrayed him. Shit, he had already put his life on the line for her.

Butterfly turned and brushed her ass against his stiff penis. She rocked back and forth while asking, "You sure you don't want to be inside this ass? Baby, it's cold outside, and I got thrice shelter, passion, and hearth."

Lazy Eyes had to laugh, but he really wanted to cry! He knew if he fucked whatever Butterfly was, woman/man, he'd be head over heels. And when he looked down, his dick was already head over toes.

He grabbed her perfect 36Cs from the back and

# BUTTERFLY

pulled her to him. "You want me to fuck you?" He grinded his dick into her ass and she moaned pleasurably and smiled seductively.

"I want you to fuck me until you nut inside my tender ass. Butter my guts, baby." Butterfly pulled her sweats down so Lazy Eyes could see what he was about to sink his teeth in, and her ass was perfect! Heart-shaped, full, and she didn't even have a pimple or a blemish. Her ass, completely hairless and a bowl of joy! It had a pronounced arch that tapered into the fall of her back, and her teeny-tiny waist, and the composition of her body would make Melissa Ford envious. Lazy Eyes had to bite his bottom lip from sheer disbelief!

"You don't like what you see, baby?" Butterfly sounded like a sex-nympho, and she knew what she was working with. It was conceit in her question and thirst in her eyes.

"Hell muthafuckin' yeah!"

"Drive that dick in me. You have a CDL to drive on these wet streets?"

"Fuck no. I got an eighteen wheeler with no brakes."

"Oh god!" she said as she lightly giggled, loving to sex-talk while getting fucked.

Lazy Eyes was prepared. He squirted Vaseline in his hands from a tube he brought with him, massaged it onto his dick and some into her ass. She wiggled into his fingers and one or two of his fingers slipped into her ass and she moaned. He was done waiting, he slammed his dick inside her, and she reached around and assisted him.

"Go deep, baby. I can take all ten inches." Butterfly opened her legs more and guided him deeper by

117

pressing against him.

He groped her tits, and he was scatter-brained as she crashed into his mid-section with her soft and virgin-feeling ass, and when she knew he was about to cum, she turned her head to the side and passionately kissed him as he drained his contents inside her and fell limp.

With all the shit in the air with Black and Lazy Eyes, there was no way to tell when Butterfly was with Lazy Eyes. He made her feel completely secure, and his fuck game was bananas! She had most definitely made up her mind that it was going to be Lazy Eyes.

## Chapter Nineteen |
### *Rendezvous Gone Wild*

Butterfly and Lazy Eyes had kept up their secret rendezvous every day for three weeks straight. He met her every night at the same spot, and sometimes they would meet earlier in the day at the chapel and then they'd go back to the library at night to finish off their incessant deeds.

On one of these nights, after they had left the bathroom, he sat down and explained why he had to keep everything with her on the down-low. It was hard for Lazy Eyes to say what he had come to say next. It was something he had been thinking to say for as long as he had been messing around with Butterfly.

"Look, we ain't got a lot of time, but let me put everything out there so you'll know where my heart is."

Butterfly was still sucking on Lazy Eyes' neck.

"Damn, you listening or what? And stop fucking with my dick."

"I can't. I love that big fat dick."

"Hold up. I'm tryna come clean." Lazy Eyes gripped Butterfly's ass and sat her on the bathroom counter. "I ain't like none of these 'ho ass niggas. Whatever I do, I put my heart in it, and I don't like this coward down-low shit."

"You coming out, baby?" Butterfly chuckled.

Lazy Eyes smirked. "That does mean I'm a homo-thug. But it don't matter, cuz' whatever I do I stamp it with my thug insignia. But look, my shit is complicated. My wife's father is here."

# MICHAEL A. ROBINSON

"What!"

"I know. But when she be coming to visit me, all I can do is think about hugging, fucking, and kissing your fluffy ass lips." By now, Lazy Eyes was smooching all over Butterfly's face while she giggled and welcomed the wet nothings.

What he told her was the truth. He was married, and his father-in-law was on the same compound with them. He hated the fact that he had to keep it on the down-low, because he wanted everybody to know that Butterfly was his bitch, and at this stage in the game, he didn't give a fuck who knew! But out of respect for his father-in-law, family, and wife, he tried to keep it on the down-low as much as possible.

Butterfly, at the same time, had avoided Black, and whenever he sent Fraze to get her, she'd act as if she was sick with the flu or indisposed. There was always a reason, and she was lucky enough not to have had to go to commissary the past three weeks, or he would have impressed upon her the fact that he was still going to make her his wife.

By now Butterfly was in love, and her love was mutually shared with Lazy Eyes, and unlike many, he was a real nigga and didn't give a fuck if she was born a man. She had the best pussy and head game he'd ever had, and she looked as good as his finest 'hos. *Fuck what a nigga thought,* he'd reason.

But secrets are seldom held, and on one velvet night, Lazy Eyes had eaten Butterfly's ass out. She had bought some X-lines from Tyrone, and she and Lazy Eyes did more than enough X-lines to take their already heightened sexual experience far higher, and make their sex intensely sensitive and devastatingly more gratifying.

He slivered his tongue in and out of her sweet smelling ass and nibbled all around it. Then he grouped four of his fingers together and ass-screwed her.

She loved it, but she preferred his big dick over tongue and vice. She turned around on the sink and sat her ass on the very edge of the counter, and he fucked her from the front and stuck his jellied tongue in her mouth as he fucked her brains out. His pounding was so mesmerizing that she had an orgasm inside the folds of her sweats and had another one minutes later as Lazy Eyes jammed faster inside of her.

Gladly enough, Butterfly had a rare condition of being born with a micro-dick, which meant that her penis was a little over two-inches hard. In addition to the hormones she was given, she didn't have much at all, and when Lazy Eyes had first seen it, he laughed and said, "You wouldn't have been much of a man anyways. Women have bigger clits than that." So there was no way he could tell that she was having an orgasm while he fucked her.

Lazy Eyes was hitting her buttermilk ass hard and meaningful, and when they thought Britney to be vigilant and watchful, he was busy flirting with somebody at the copy machine, and somebody had slipped by them.

The person who had slipped by Britney was a brother from the Nation of Islam. He opened the bathroom door and switched on the lights, and Butterfly's bare ass was in the air with ten inches pumping in and out of it.

"What the fuck, nigga!" the brother from the Nation asked.

"Shut the fucking door, muthafucka!" Lazy Eyes

said, but he didn't dare pull out of that sweet ass.

The brother from the Nation of Islam looked at the filth before him, and he slammed the door behind him!

And over Butterfly's protest, Lazy Eyes wouldn't stop until he had finished.

# BUTTERFLY

## Chapter Twenty |
### *Visitation, Meaning Family Feud, And Love!*

The next day, Atwater went to work out with Craze-zo, and while they were working out, they heard the only talk on the compound, which was how Lazy Eyes got caught fucking the punk in the library bathroom. The brother from the Nation of Islam spread his discovery and demanded that the Baltimore Cart, which was a gang that Lazy Eyes ran with, check him into the SHU. But Lazy Eyes troubles weren't so easy to resolve. He had a peculiar situation because his father-in-law was on the compound with him, and he was surely going to find out.

When Atwater and Craze-zo heard the details of the 'Romance of Dicks,' as Craze-zo styled it, Craze-zo felt that he was right for wanting to beat up Britney that night at the barbershop because he felt that, that would be the only way to prevent homosexuality: by checking in any 'faggot' that came out of the SHU. Of course Atwater agreed, because he didn't feel comfortable with the sexual urge that came over him when he was in Butterfly's presence.

While Atwater was working out with Craze-zo, he heard his name called over the loud speaker, and when he went to the CO, he was told that he had a visit.

He had to run back to the unit, shower, and put on his visiting clothes. He knew Shonda was on some surprise shit; but he didn't care.

When he went out to the visiting area, there she was: fine, fresh, and fabulous. She wore a zesty orange Stella McCartney ankle-length dress and off-white YSL

# MICHAEL A. ROBINSON

platform pumps that set out her 36-22-38 bust, bends, and curves. Her naturally black long and curly hair was in a flat twist-out much like Corinne Bailey Rae's coif.

When Atwater saw her, he laughed, knowing she had scored a low-blow on him for her to surprise him with the visit and looking zesty, tasty, and relishing. But in her eyes was a valid apology for her having said that she had raised the kids all by herself. And this impromptu visit was more than warranted. They talked about everything, and she loved Atwater all the more. She shared with him how she had made a dinner for the kids and they didn't show. They were young adults who didn't have time for their mother.

\* \* \* \* \*

When Shonda saw Butterfly enter the visiting room and sit across from them, she couldn't believe her eyes! It couldn't be possible for them to have women at this jail, and if that was a man . . . The nerve of it all was maddening, and she was instantly jealous and preoccupied with a thousand and one things. And she watched Atwater's eyes, because the eyes told it all. She thought her 36-22-38 measurements were mouthwatering, but as she took recognition of Butterfly's measurements, it looked as if she was outmatched by the remarkable composition of 36-22-40 busty breasts, nonexistent waist, and ass for days, which meant for any man: heartaches, sexual longing, and urge.

It all seemed unjust to Shonda!

"What is that!" Shonda asked, livid and beside herself, as she nodded over to Butterfly.

Atwater wished she hadn't seen her. "What?"

"You know what I'm talking about!"

124

# BUTTERFLY

"Shonda, don't start that bullshit. How can I stop who they bring in here?"

"Is *it* a girl?"

"*It* can't be a girl and be in here," Atwater said. He didn't like comparing Butterfly to a senseless object by saying "it" as if a person was a thing.

\* \* \* \* \* \*

Butterfly had a rare visit from her mother, and she hadn't seen her mother in years, or ever since her father ran her from the house. Her mother entered, and she was beautiful as ever. When her mother saw her son sitting there as a woman, she couldn't help but cry.

"Momma, I don't need you to be here if you're going to be crying."

"Bobby, I'm sorry." She hugged her son, and it was too hard for her. "I miss you, baby. No matter what, you're still my baby boy."

Butterfly was hurt. She couldn't sit here and allow her loving and doting mother to continue to make her feel bad for who she was. Especially considering the fact that Butterfly had been kicked out of her father's house when she was a teenager, which forced her to have to hustle to make it, which eventually landed her in federal prison where she had almost been raped! And as always and with everything bad that accompanied her life, her parents had something to do with it, one, indirectly for being weak and the other, directly, for being hateful.

"I'm not your baby boy. I'm a grown woman, and you're either going to accept it or you can leave." Butterfly pointed to the door. It was as hard for her as it must have been for her mother. But she wouldn't apologize any longer! She was who she was and that

125

much was final! But in her heart-of-hearts, she was praying that her mother would never leave her side.

Her mother took a second to weigh what she was being offered. She missed her baby boy. She missed the . . . daughter that she never had, and if that's what she'd have to do to have her baby back, she'd do it for the sake of a mother's love.

"Those look really, really, real," Sandra said, laughing with tears in her eyes.

"They feel real too." Butterfly took her mother's hand and placed it on her breast.

"They do!" Sandra said as she laughed, and a CO came over to them.

"No touching," he warned.

"This is my mother!" Butterfly snapped as the CO walked off.

"I missed you, Bobby. I know it's been hard on you because of your father and brother, but I never knew what to do."

"You should have left him, Momma." And even though it sounded crazy, Butterfly truly felt that way. She knew her mother had always contemplated it, but her love for her husband was stronger than any words could describe.

"You don't understand," her mother said. "I didn't know what to do."

Seeing her mother like that hurt her to the core.

"I'll never talk to them again," Butterfly said, referring to her father and brother. "They tried to make me hate myself, and they almost succeeded." And now Butterfly was the one crying in her mother's arms. She didn't know that she had all that hurt and pain inside of her, and the fact that she still longed to be loved and

126

accepted by her mother.

"I love you, Bobby, and I'll always be here for you even though I never knew how to handle the situation."

"I love you too, Momma, and if you really love me then call me Summer."

Sandra knew what it would take to have her child back in her life and that was all that mattered. "I love you, Summer."

They had an emotional hug, but only time would tell before her mother would tuck tail and desert Butterfly again.

# Chapter Twenty-One |
### *Trouble In The Camp*

The compound, in the meantime, was singing another sad tune. B-Rod, who was Lazy Eyes' father-in-law, was in his mid-fifties, and he was the official shot-caller for Baltimore.

B-Rod was big, and the strength he looked to possess belied his advanced age. He didn't have a lot of patience for bullshit, and as soon as the issue with Butterfly and Lazy Eyes was brought to his attention, he was all over it.

He was coming from outside where he had been looking for Lazy Eyes, and when he was passing the kitchen, he saw Lazy Eyes heading the other way.

"Lonny!" he called Lazy Eyes by his first name. "Come over here!"

When Lazy Eyes saw who it was, he knew it was going to be some bullshit. But he walked     over to B-Rod, nonetheless.

B-Rod didn't say what's up or anything. He got straight to the matter at hand. "Tell me about this rumor going around that you got caught fucking a boy in the library restroom."

Lazy Eyes dropped his head, because he wasn't going to lie to any man! A man only lied to a person he was intimidated by or scared of, and he wasn't scared of anybody!

"Lonny, this is not the type of shit you do being married to my daughter!" B-Rod could have smacked his son-in-law. "Have you forgotten about your kids with Brandy?" B-Rod had to take a minute to calm

# BUTTERFLY

down, because he loved his grandchildren, and he didn't want to let one mistake define an individual, an individual whom he had respected for the longest. When it dawned on him what that meant, he calmed down. "I won't mention it to Brandy, but I bet not hear about you being with that boy no more, all right?"

Lazy Eyes shook his head, because he wasn't lying to anyone, least amongst them—himself.

"You don't understand. I'm in love with her."

"Her—who the hell is 'her'? Brandy?"

"No, I'm talking about Butterfly."

B-Rod snatched up Lazy Eyes by the collar. "This is my daughter we're talking about! You leave that boy alone, or I'm going to check you in."

Lazy Eyes looked at his father-in-laws hands, and it was obvious that B-Rod didn't understand that he didn't run shit!

"Yo, take your hands off my shirt!" Lazy eyes said as he pushed B-Rods' hands off of him.

B-Rod looked around and seeing that he was about to get them sent to the SHU, he walked off.

Lazy Eyes was going to meet Raheem by the Commissary, but they had already ended the move, and it wasn't that many people on the compound.

When he headed toward the Commissary, he didn't know there was an ambush waiting for him.

As he came around the corner, Berry grabbed him and E punched him in the throat. They backed him into a corner and were about to poke holes in him with ice picks.

"Hold up! Lieutenant Muncy coming! But hold that bitch-nigga's mouth and keep him still!" Black said as he kept lookout.

129

While they were watching for Lt. Muncy, Lazy Eyes broke their grips off his shirt and walked calmly by Lt. Muncy who passed him. He was shaken up a little, but the lieutenant didn't even notice anything out of the norm. "What are you doing outside and there's no move?" Lt. Muncy asked Lazy Eyes.

"I'm coming from outside. I forgot my ID and I was trying to go back to the unit to take a shower."

"Go straight to your unit. And the next time I see you out of bounds, I'm going to write you an Incident Report."

"Yes sir." Lazy Eyes said and he couldn't have thanked Lt. Muncy More. Lt. Muncy didn't know he had just saved his life, and Lazy Eyes scurried off to his unit, almost skipping.

Black, E, and Berry went into the barbershop, which was accidentally left unlocked by the compound officer who was in charge of securing the compound's buildings. They didn't know that Atwater was in the cleaning room wringing out the mop when he overheard them come in.

"Black, we have to alert the homies and let them know this shit is about to go down, because I know that nigga is going to get all those niggas from B-more," E said, mad that he didn't get to kill that nigga Lazy Eyes.

"Damn! The fucking lieutenant picked the perfect time to be walking around!" Black said.

"And that bitch-ass nigga squirmed away," Berry added.

"I swear—by the end of tonight, that's a dead nigga," Black said. Even with what he was making off the heroin, he couldn't continue to let the threat that Lazy

# BUTTERFLY

Eyes presented go unchecked. The botched ambush was going to cause a war between the 200 strong DC Cart and the 185 strong Baltimore Cart.

\* \* \* \* \* \*

On the unit front, Lazy Eyes went straight to his cell, crawled under his bed, and busted a hole in the wall and brought out three long knives from his stash spot. He placed them on his bed, and for a minute he looked long and hard at them.

The more he thought about it, if he was to go to war with DC niggas, they'd just put him in the SHU and ship him off to another joint. In short, he'd be fucked because he'd be without Butterfly, and now that he had that heaven-ass, he couldn't live without it. It'd be unbearable. He returned the knives back to his hiding place, grabbed a sheet of paper out of his drawer, and scribbled something on the paper. *It was always good to have something on somebody,* he thought. He went downstairs, and when nobody was looking, he kicked the small paper underneath the CO's door, and he walked off to wait and see how his plot would hatch.

*And he really thought that would be the end of all his troubles . . .*

\* \* \* \* \* \*

Atwater had just returned from his lovely visit with his wife. Shonda was most definitely a keeper, with the qualifications and criteria to be a boss player's *numero uno* wife. She was a dime piece, educated, and had fly shit to offer. *At times she did get a little carried away and jealous, but there was no real passion without jealousy,* he thought.

He washed his face while his cellmate Thompson Bey was about to read the book on his chest.

131

Atwater heard the front door to the unit open, COs marched in, and he didn't know what to think.

"Damn, about ten COs just came into the unit."

"They must have found some wine."

"No, I think they're getting somebody."

"Who?" Thompson Bey asked, crouching over on his top bunk to see over Atwater's head.

"They're taking Black, E, and Berry out," Atwater said, and it all made sense to him of what they had been talking about in the barbershop.

After he had come from his visit, he went to the barbershop to make sure all the cutting stations were clean, and that's when they were in there plotting on Lazy Eyes. But Atwater couldn't figure out how they could have done anything from the time they had left the barbershop till now because everybody was waiting in the unit to be counted.

So after they were taken out of the unit, Atwater broke the scenario down to his cellie of what he had heard in the barbershop.

# Chapter Twenty-Two |
### "Why does everybody die of HIV in this book!"

Butterfly was reading a book that Britney had given her called *Convict's Candy* by Amin Meadows, which was an *Essence* best-seller.

The CO had just cleared count and popped the door when Fraze came charging into their cell.

"They just took Black, Berry, and E to the SHU."

"What?" Britney and Butterfly said at the same time. It was the best relief either of them had expected.

"Yes, and word is that Lazy Eyes did some hot shit and dropped a kite on them. Tonight we're going to have a meeting. So be careful around here because the shit can go up any minute from now."

When Fraze left, Britney couldn't stop laughing. "Butterfly, you have this place going up in smoke because of that good pussy of yours."

"Shut up!" Butterfly snapped as she climbed on her bunk to try to lean over and see if she could see Unit 4B from her bed. She couldn't see anything, and she didn't know if they had made the ten minute move yet, or if Lazy Eyes would go to the gym during the chow move.

"Give me a mirror." Britney handed her a mirror, but she still couldn't see shit from her angle.

"I'm going to the gym on the move," Butterfly said.

"Stay out of it, Butterfly," Britney advised.

"I can't," Butterfly said.

Since Butterfly wouldn't listen, Britney resolved to say, "Be careful. He just told you something was about to happen."

"I know, but I'm gonna go out on the rec and come back when they open for mainline."

"Just be careful."

\* \* \* \* \* \* \*

Lazy Eyes was already in the gym plotting with Raheem. Nobody had come out yet, because they still hadn't called all the units for evening chow.

Raheem was Lazy Eyes' best friend in jail. Even though Raheem never agreed with Lazy Eyes messing around with Butterfly, he'd still die at his homeboy's side.

Lazy Eyes had his sweats turned inside out, and his pockets hung like rabbit's ears at his side. He had brought his knives because even though he got rid of Black, E, and Berry, he wanted to make sure anybody from DC walked a tight rope around him.

"Are the homies coming or what?" Lazy Eyes asked briskly.

"Yeah, nigga. Calm down. They're going to be here after dinner. Yo, shit is fucked up. They're saying you dropped a kite on Black and them."

Lazy Eyes didn't lie to anybody for nothing. Fuck that! "So what! Yo, between me and you, I did that shit. I let them know where them niggas' heroin stash spot at. Them DC niggas are bitches without them three. What? You think they'll send scary-ass Tyrone or Fraze? Them niggas is through."

"Yo, word up, dog," Raheem said as they slapped hands and laughed.

"Word up, I wouldn't even worry about them no more. They'll send some kites out da SHU suggesting I did it, and I'll just deny it. It ain't like they can prove I done it. Them niggas are through!"

"What about B-Rod? He's trying to get the homies to check you in."

"Fuck that. I'm uncheckable. But B-Rod could be trouble. But he's family, and I don't think he wants to see me fucked up. He's just mad."

Right then, Butterfly walked in looking a bit wan and pale, as if she was frightened. It was truly feminine, and Lazy Eyes' heart poured out to his beauty.

Butterfly went to the bathroom and that was his cue.

"There she goes. Watch out for me," Lazy Eyes told Raheem.

"A'ight," Raheem said as Lazy Eyes disappeared into the bathroom.

Butterfly was in the last stall, which was the biggest. It was a handicap stall and the bathroom was filthy, but it offered them the privacy they needed. Outside, people would be coming to the gym after evening chow had ended, and whatever they had to say, they would have to make it quick.

"You all right?" Butterfly asked, looking as if she'd been crying. She had on a big T-shirt and her tight sweats, which looked like she'd just hopped out of bed and came out to meet him.

"Told you that I'd get rid of that nigga for you. Now it's just me and you. I love you to death." They kissed, and he could taste the salt of her tears and the love of her heart. She tasted bittersweet with her velvet lips, high and soft cheeks, and creamy body! Fuck—he wanted to be with her come hell or high water.

"I don't want you to get hurt, baby," Butterfly said. She could feel Lazy Eyes fondling her tits because there was always a strong sense of lust, urge, passion, and hunger that went before the perils of danger hovering overhead. "Everybody from DC is supposed to meet up tonight. What's going to happen, baby?"

"Nothing ain't gonna happen. Them niggas are bitches without Black and them. Don't worry about nothing. I got everything under control. I'ma wife you, baby. We can be the first to get really officially married. Obama back this shit now. You gonna be my Mrs.?"

"Forever, baby." And Butterfly meant it as she grabbed Lazy Eyes' dick. "Let me suck it, baby."

"Not right now."

"Fuck that. Let me suck it," Butterfly Insisted.

Lazy Eyes' dick was harder than Damascus steel, and Butterfly went to relieve him of that aching madness. With Butterfly at her oral industry, it was moments in the making before Lazy Eyes shot a load off, and Butterfly had her supper.

"Yo, Lazy. B-Rod is coming with the homies!"

"What?"

"Come 'ere."

Lazy Eyes fixed his pants, still lust dumb, but he had to get his head out of his pants. He pulled away from Butterfly, who started to cry again, but she followed him as he came out of the bathroom.

B-Rod had a squad of eight homies from Baltimore with him, but Fraze was with them too.

"What y'all got that DC nigga with y'all for? Them niggas tried to kill me today!" As Lazy Eyes spoke, Raheem stood at his side, ready for whatever.

"Lonny, you gotta check in."

"No, nigga, y'all gotta check me in. I'm uncheckable." Lazy Eyes pulled out his knife and handed one to Raheem. Lazy Eyes looked over at

# BUTTERFLY

Butterfly and said, "Watch out, baby."

"No, I'm going with you!" Butterfly cried out.

"Get your homeboy, Fraze," B-Rod said. But to Fraze, it didn't matter if they fucked Butterfly up too.

"Butterfly, get out the way," Fraze said, but he didn't move to go over and get her.

"No!" she said, still really scared.

After B-Rod and the other Baltimore guys took out knives that were just as big, she saw that it was going to be worse than she had imagined.

"Butterfly, get out the way!" Fraze screamed.

"I said no!" Butterfly had the nerve to reach for the other knife Lazy Eyes had in his pants.

"Just grab him!" B-Rod ordered.

"I'll stab a muthafucka if you touch my girl!"

"Get his ass!" B-Rod commanded.

They converged on Lazy Eyes and Raheem, and Lazy Eyes shot out like a soldier and stabbed one of those fools in the throat. One went to stick him in the side, but Raheem stuck the guy first, and they swarmed on Raheem, who was jabbing his knife as he took two hits for every one he swung.

Lazy Eyes took out his other knife and had one knife in each hand. He went to get them off Raheem, and they scattered when he came from behind them sticking them like a madman. "'Ho-ass niggas! Uhn uhn uhm! Take that, nigga!" he screamed and stuck. When B-Rod came from his blindside and hit him in the chin, Lazy Eyes was dizzy.

Butterfly tried to run to his aid, but Fraze jumped on her and held her down while she watched them butcher Raheem and Lazy Eyes until the COs came in and broke up the melee.

# Chapter Twenty-Three |
*Surprise, Surprise*

Fraze rushed Butterfly out of the gym, so they both wouldn't be sent to the SHU with the rest of them. She could barely walk the whole way back to the unit as her mind kept replaying seeing Lazy Eyes getting butchered like that. It was too much to have seen!

Once Fraze managed to get Butterfly back to the unit, she was hysterical. Fraze wanted some get back on Butterfly for getting Black, E, and Berry sent to the SHU. He just always had the feeling that somehow Butterfly was tied to the three being sent to the SHU.

The COs were all responding to the commotion that was going down in the gym. As soon as Fraze took Butterfly to her cell, he turned to see Michoacán and Ramirez coming up to him.

"My friend, what happened out there?" Michoacán asked with a smiling face. Everybody knew something had happened because they saw all the COs running to the gym.

"It ain't nothing, amigo. Just some shit between them Baltimore niggas." Fraze was too busy talking to see Michoacán slip a knife out his pants. He jammed the sharp pointed end into Fraze's neck as Ramirez started to jug holes in his side.

"HELP!" Fraze screamed as he tried to get away. He could go nowhere because Ramirez delivered a solid blow to Fraze's chin that leveled him to the ground. Once he hit the ground they continued to butcher him.

Butterfly could only hear the commotion going on

# BUTTERFLY

outside her cell as she was about to tell Britney what had happened. But when they heard the cries for help and heard the Blacks screaming, they ran to the door to look.

"Stop! You're gonna kill him!" Britney screamed as Butterfly fainted.

Michoacán and Ramirez kept on, knowing full well there were no COs to respond to their vicious attack, because all the COs had run to the gym.

The Paisas had the attack so planned out that at the same moment while this was going on, the Blacks were being attacked in all the other units. Tyrone got butchered while he was talking on the phone, being that they couldn't kill Black for snitching Sosa out, they killed another one of Black's homies from D.C.

It took the Blacks in all the units to realize that they were being surprised-attacked. But once they did, every single Black man took down three Mexicans. They would take the knife from the Mexicans and stab them up.

When the COs saw that they had a riot on their hands, it was too out-of-control for them to do anything about it. They went to a secure place and called back-up from local police and nearby jails. They put on riot gear and returned with a superior fighting force. They shot rubber bullets that stung like hell, shot tear gas all over the compound until they gained control of the prison.

When the smoke cleared, three Blacks were dead, twenty were injured to four Paisa's being killed and thirty injured.

The administration locked down the joint because at least a hundred inmates who were instrumentally involved in causing the riot would be prosecuted federally and shipped across the country. The lockdown would last for three weeks until the administration felt the inmates no longer posed a threat to themselves.

Raheem and Lazy Eyes had almost died during their scuffle with B-Rod and his men. But they were rushed to the hospital in a helicopter and lucky enough they both survived. However, their days were numbered at Schuylkill as well as Black, E, and Berry. All of them would be shipped to another prison. Sosa, Ramirez, and Michoacán would also leave the prison. The riot would go down in prison history of when the Paisas ambushed the Blacks.

# Chapter Twenty-Four |
*Wings Of Wind*

Once the administration deemed that the inmates no longer presented a threat to one another, they let everybody off lockdown. But being that the SHU was now full, they had to let out some people, and Buffy's time had come. He thought he would have been gotten out, but he was wrong.

And it wasn't even lunch before they let Buffy out, who looked scruffy and SHU-ridden.

As always, he came out talking boss shit, and everybody was mad they had put him in their unit, Unit 2A where his girls were. He dropped his property in front of the CO's office as Butterfly ran up to him and gave him a hug.

"I thought you wasn't ever gonna get out," Butterfly said.

"You've been here a little over two months, and I hear the compound went up in smoke because of you." He smacked his lips. "Bitch, ya poison ivy. I gotta talk to you."

"Adams, get in here!" the CO said from his office. "You're in cell #216. Try to stay under the radar this time."

"Okay, cutie-pie."

Butterfly helped him take his bags up to his cell. And when they got there and dropped everything on the floor, Buffy unpacked his things.

"Has Funky Breath Britney been messing with my man?"

"No, not that I know of," Butterfly said

unconvincingly.

"Bitch, ya lying. But anyways, Black was mad about you trying to defend Lazy Eyes fine ass. His feelings were more hurt than anything, but he told the homies not to touch you. Gurl, you must got some good pussy." They laughed.

"And Lazy Eyes . . . out of all people. I didn't even know he was going. He got a wife and kids, and he was willing to leave them for you, let me tell you. They're gonna start calling you Sunshine like the chick in the movie *Harlem Nights*. Remember that Italian guy left his wife and kids?" Buffy smacked her lips again.

Butterfly was glad to know that Buffy had no indication that the Paisas' ambush of the Blacks was because she was fucking Sosa. Even though she had fainted when the riot began, somehow she knew it was because of her. The thought of people being dead all because of her made her sick to her stomach. But the three weeks on lockdown was good for her to get needed sleep and emotional support from Britney.

"What are they saying about Lazy Eyes?" Butterfly asked. Now she was sad again. And she was prettiest when lost in her sadness, and it made Buffy love her all the more.

"Don't worry about him. They're back there selling death-threats, door-banging to the fullest." She smacked again. "Let me tell you." They laughed, because they knew door-banging was threatening another inmate while you were locked in a cell, meaning you really didn't pose a threat.

"When is he gonna get out the SHU?"

"Bitch, are you crazy! He's getting transferred, somewhere across the planet, let me tell you. Black, E,

# BUTTERFLY

and Berry too, and all those idiots that were in that race riot. I'm just glad I wasn't here because somebody would have tried to kill me. Forget about them. Tonight I'm going to get my hair cut, and we're going to party! We're going unit to unit: dick-a-treat, let me tell you." They laughed.

"You just keep that good pussy of yours away from mine, and we won't have no qualms. A man get a taste of that sweet ass of yours, and he think he can do supernatural things, like fly, or stab eight people to death, let me tell you. Bitch, I gotta go and wash my sexy ass. See you in a minute."

Butterfly most definitely felt sick that Lazy Eyes was no longer there. But even with him gone she felt a great weight lift off her chest, knowing that she wasn't going to have to worry about Black, E, Berry, Fraze, or Tyrone.

The night settled on the wind and the trees and darkness roundabout the prison were warm and settling. Three weeks after the racial riot there was a peace that settled over the jail. Everybody that was left behind had pretty much done some dirt and got away with it. Neither race could hold bad blood against the other, because they had to live with one another in close quarters, so they had to make the best of an impossible situation. Fresh off lockdown brought genuine respect and a calm that seemed beguiling.

# Chapter Twenty-Five |
*Blossoming Calm*

About eight people were in the barbershop waiting to get their hair cut, and they were talking about all the stuff that was going on.

"What high-power forces ail you to patronize this humble establishment?" Atwater asked Old School, who on a rare barbershop visit picked the choicest chair by the door to seat himself. He knew Old School would have some deep thoughts about the race riot, even if he didn't voice them now.

"I saw a light on a hill and I ascended." Everybody laughed.

"Riddle me that," Atwater responded.

"There's no riddle to my old fables. I just came to see how you were getting along in this place of constant madness."

"You see what I'm doing. I'm in here perfecting my craft. Besides that, I'm putting my plans together. Planning far and beyond."

"Don't try and sell me nothing. I ain't buying."

"It's more than one way to skin a cat." As Atwater said that, Britney, Butterfly, and Buffy walked in, laughing and giggling. They all wore tight clothes and looked primped and preen.

Old School tipped his hat. "Good evening, ladies." Always the perfect gentleman, no matter how he felt.

"Hey, Old School," Buffy said dismissively, knowing he was being sarcastic.

"Tone or Atwater, can one of y'all cut my hair?"

"Sorry, mami. I got a couple of heads to cut that been here at the move. Come back manana." Tone was Puerto

Rican, and his accent said it best. Being that he was Puerto Rican, he wasn't involved in the race riot because Puerto Ricans didn't run with the Paisas or Blacks.

"Sike! Atwater, ya gotta help me out." Buffy wouldn't take no for an answer.

"I got you—let me finish this head."

After that, Buffy was fussing with Britney for whatever trivial qualms he had against him. And even though Butterfly was in mourning over her lost love, Lazy Eyes, she still couldn't keep her eyes to herself. When she came in the barbershop or wherever else she chanced to see Atwater, her eyes belonged to him.

"I know you were fucking Ray Ray," Buffy fussed, trying to keep his tone to a minimum, but that was like pulling teeth.

"No, I wouldn't do that. Not to you, girl." Britney was lying through his teeth.

"Bitch, please!"

Their conversation was a bit tart for Old School's delicate ears, so he asked Atwater, "Where's your shadow at?"

"Craze-zo went to commissary. He's supposed to be bringing me an ice cream in a couple of minutes. Why, you wanted to holla at him?"

"No, I was just asking. I always see y'all together."

"He's like my brother."

"Brother from another mother?"

Atwater had finished cutting the guy's head who sat in his chair. While the dude was checking out his haircut, Atwater brushed off his chair and made eye contact with Butterfly on the low. She smiled at him because she couldn't possibly contain it. She was melting.

# MICHAEL A. ROBINSON

"All right, young blood. I'll see you later," Old School said, and Atwater thought he'd been caught.

"Love, Old School."

Buffy went to get in his barber chair. "Two with the grain. Caesar all the way around."

"What? No taper fade?" Atwater asked, which was Buffy's usual.

She gave him her signature smack." "I ain't got time for all that. I just got out the SHU, and I have to make my rounds."

"Excuse me." Atwater laughed playfully.

"How's your wife?" Buffy asked. He had seen Atwater's wife several times during the visit.

"She's chilling. She was just up here last weekend."

"The same one I seen when we were on the visit together?"

"The one and only."

"You've been down for a while, haven't you?"

"This will be eighteen years."

"And your wife's been with you the whole time?" Buffy sounded shocked. Atwater zipped the clippers over her ragamuffin naps that snapped back into a smooth even surface.

"Yes."

"I don't know how she's doing it. I couldn't imagine going on dick celibacy for eighteen days." Everybody in the barbershop laughed.

"Eighteen minutes," Britney added.

Atwater held the clippers and thought about how to handle that. "Y'all wrong for that."

Tone laughed with them. "Mami, y'all foul."

"Just keeping it real, sugar, let me tell you. So what's your secret?" Buffy asked Atwater, who was focused on

146

# BUTTERFLY

Buffy's haircut. But Butterfly was focused on him!

"It ain't really a secret." He looked up into Butterfly's dazzling eyes that were fountains of immeasurable love and the promise of creamy dreams.

"Sometimes people don't know what to do with themselves, and when you give them purpose, they'll run after you."

"That's whas' up. Didn't she move from St. Louis to be closer to you?"

"How you know all the details?"

"Everybody knows the details of romance in paradise. You're a good guy."

As Atwater finished, he brushed his chair off. Butterfly was too shy and abashed to do anything but look at him. And when he looked at her, she couldn't hide the smile or the incredible speed of her racing heart.

But Buffy had other plans for them, and they headed to Unit 1B where Ray Ray lived. And now Buffy could fuss at Britney, but only if Butterfly would shut up of her crush!

"Damn, he's fine. I have to have him!" Butterfly said.

"Who?" Britney asked.

"The barber," Butterfly said.

"Tone?"

"No, Atwater. Didn't you see how he looked at me?"

"Bitch, worry about Lazy Eyes. He's a married man"—She smacked her lips—"but I guess that never stopped you before."

"Oh, that was clever," Britney said. "But I did see him staring at her."

"He must've heard that all he'd have to do was say hello to her, and she'd give him a mind-boggling orgasm with her fast, good-pussy-having ass."

# MICHAEL A. ROBINSON

"You're hating, 'ho," Butterfly said, and they all laughed.

"Ain't that the truth," Britney added.

"Bitch, you got your nerve. We about to go in here and confront Ray Ray. It's Buffy the Body or Toilet Face Britney."

"I got your toilet face, stank bitch."

"You impotent, dick-sucking harlot," Buffy shot back.

"Ya momma's a strumpet on Planet of the Apes."

"With your herpes in the mouth and gonorrhea in your ass." The three of them couldn't help but laugh at the back and forth between them. And as they neared unit 1B, Franco and Slim stood outside in the front of the unit where they lived.

"Look at Franco," Buffy said.

By now everybody had heard about how Franco and Slim put in work during the riot, and it was sheer luck they weren't being shipped to another prison.

"He ain't never got on drawls," Britney said.

"Dick just a swinging back and forth. And I know he has a foot of dick—his big strong ass. It'd a be like fucking a gorilla on Viagra, let me tell you," Buffy said.

And as they approached, Franco said, "What the fuck y'all bitches laughing at?"

"Shut up and shave your hairy chest, you gorilla looking muthafucka," Buffy snapped and smacked her lips.

"Fuck them punks," Slim said, who was always super fly, sly, and cool. This time Britney didn't pay him any mind because he was on his way to get higher than a kite.

They snuck in the unit and went straight to Ray Ray's

148

cell on the second floor. He was a tall, light-skinned guy with ruffled braids, and a shaggy and sparse beard. He had just gotten out the shower and was drying his toes with a towel when Buffy and his gang barged in his cell.

"What up, Ray Ray? What's this I hear about you and Britney?"

"Damn, you could at least see how I'm doing."

"I told her nothing happened between us," Britney said defensively, trying to lead him.

"I ain't trying to hear that shit right now," Ray Ray said.

"Oh, ya not? Don't make me set it off in this bitch."

L, who was Ray Ray's friend, came to the door and knocked. He was making his rounds in the units, selling his wares, and he happened to see them in Ray Ray's cell.

"What up, L?" Ray Ray said.

"Nothing. I just came to say what's up to the home girls," L said. He had taken over supplying the joint with drugs from where Tyrone left off.

"Hey, L," they said together, having met him on another occasion.

"I got some Bang Bang. Y'all trying to hit that joint or what?" L asked, because he wanted to party after coming off lockdown.

"Probably, but we not trying to get stuck on the move," Britney said, knowing it was getting late and they had to leave on the 7:30 p.m. move, or they'd be shit out of luck.

"Y'all can leave at pill line at 8:00 p.m. The CO working is cool as a fan," L said, taking his wares from his pocket.

"What's that?" Buffy asked.

"Sex'stacy."

# MICHAEL A. ROBINSON

"Enough fa' all of us?" Buffy asked.

"Chill out. I got you."

L spread lines on the table and they blasted off.

Butterfly floated back to the unit as in a creamy dream. Her feet moved, but she didn't feel like she was really walking. When she got to her bed, she passed out. And it was as if the last dream she had not too long ago was still in progress.

*She was running, from who or from what, she couldn't say. She just knew that her father had just kicked her ass, and her clothes were ripped, and her face felt shattered in two.*

*But as she ran she saw the headlights of a car ahead, and she felt blinded by the dazzling lights. She tried to cover her eyes, but when she did, she uncovered her eyes and she was on a runway modeling clothes.*

*She strutted down the runway as cameras whipped and flashed away, and she felt as if she was on top of the world. But, but . . . she almost tripped and fell and when she reached out to grab for balance, she suddenly was shaking the extended hand of her business manager.*

*"We're going to make a lot of money off you," the manager said with a cunning smile that read dollar signs.*

*More lights flashed, and she covered her eyes from the brilliance of the light snaps, but she saw her face spread across magazine covers like Straight Stuntin, Show, Curve, Essence, and Don Diva.*

*But the blinding light that she covered her eyes from was her father pummeling her to the ground with hateful fists, disgraceful fists, fists, fists, fists and nonetheless.*

*"You'll never amount to anything, you faggot! Get out!" her father screamed with phlegm and gall pouring from his mouth.*

*Butterfly was fleeing her father as much as she was her*

# BUTTERFLY

*dreams, nightmares, her fears. She was dressed in drag, and she knew the woman's clothes that dressed her body were supposed to be there. And when she looked down at the gash on her wrist, she was in the back of a car and her hand was holding a small straw and there were lines of cocaine before her, and she snorted them and felt the sudden charge. When she leaned back on the seat, she felt the sunrays resting on her skin, and when she opened her eyes, she lay in her special orchard with butterflies drifting poetically on the wings of wind.*

# MICHAEL A. ROBINSON

## Chapter Twenty-Six |
### *I Have To Have Him*

Two days had passed, and Buffy had gotten settled back in, and the compound had returned to normal. Almost. It was the weekend, a Saturday evening, and it was cold outside.

They headed to the gym where a basketball game was in progress, and it looked like a riot. The guys threw elbows and tripped one another. Bystanders and homeboys kept their hands on the hilt of their sharpened knives, waiting for something to pop off. Murder-ball was in full swing.

L and Ray Ray were playing on the same team and Buffy and Britney cheered away. It was so loud in the gym that it did them no justice to scream and act a fool.

Atwater was in a group of Moors, and his cellmate Thompson Bey sat at his side. Butterfly, who if she moved to go anywhere, would have all eyes in the gym following that phat pretty ass of hers.

"Stop staring at him so hard. You might offend him," Buffy warned Butterfly, but the bitch was in an unrestraint heat, and she was on her scent.

"I can't keep my eyes off him." Butterfly had puppy-eyes and it looked sick and cute at the same time.

"You can't stop talking about him neither. I feel bad for Lazy Eyes."

"Out of sight out of mind. Cupid done shot that bitch with a new dick," Britney said.

"Straight in the ass," Buffy added as they laughed.

Butterfly gave them the finger.

Atwater got up and raced to the restroom, so he

wouldn't miss that much of the game.

"There he goes, horny 'ho," Buffy said. "You better skedaddle if ya want to catch him."

"Right now?" Butterfly asked as if she was a dimwit.

"No, bitch, when a full moon comes out and turns Britney into a werewolf," Buffy responded.

"I'd probably still could give better head than you, vampire."

Butterfly summoned her courage and went to the bathroom. When she went in, she saw Atwater at the urinal, and it made her a little mad that all eyes were on her as she walked to the bathroom. But when she went in, she went straight to the handicap urinal in the back and acted as if she had to piss. She waited a second, and when she came out there was a short line for the guys waiting to wash their hands at the sink which had a mirror over it. But Butterfly was lucky enough to stand right behind Atwater.

When the guy at the sink left, Atwater offered Butterfly to go before him. She washed her hands, but she was looking at him on the sly through the mirror. They held eye-contact, which seemed like forever and silently communicated volumes.

She walked back into the gym, now certain that Atwater felt the same way she felt about him. And she just didn't know how to make the first move.

They watched the end of the game and the ten-minute move was called at 7:30 p.m. Butterfly went to the library because Buffy thought Ray Ray wanted to meet him there, but when they got there, Ray Ray didn't even show up. So they were stuck on the move, and when Butterfly looked up, she saw that Atwater was there with his cellmate Thompson Bey, and they were in a room watching videos.

She couldn't contain herself, and she let Buffy and Britney know. "Atwater's in the library now. What should I do? Should I just go in there?" Butterfly said fidgeting with her shirt.

They just said, "Calm down, you horny bitch."

Atwater emerged from the classroom where they watched videos, and he headed for the bathroom.

*It's now or never*, Butterfly thought. Buffy was going to be the watch, because Britney already proved to be useless.

When Butterfly went into the bathroom, Atwater wasn't pissing. He just stood there and said, "I've been waiting on you." A sure smile framed his mouth.

It was music to Butterfly's ears. "I can't keep my eyes off you."

"You're going to get me in trouble." Atwater knew it! But he was too far gone to give a fuck.

"How so?" Butterfly asked, narrowing their distance until she stood right in front of him.

Atwater felt his dick lurch in his pants. He didn't think Butterfly had seen it, but her hand dashed out to grab it, and he couldn't stop her from massaging his dick.

"I know you want me. I see how you look at me." It was the moment of truth, and as Atwater stared into Butterfly's eyes, he felt like he was looking into the face of Rihanna.

"I want to fuck you so bad, I don't know what to do." The words trailed off Atwater's tongue before he could guard them.

"You wanna fuck me?" Butterfly asked senselessly,

# BUTTERFLY

because she already knew the answer. She took Atwater's dick from his pants and sucked it on the spot. Atwater flung his arms back to close the bathroom door, but Butterfly stopped him.

"Leave it open."

Atwater looked confused, but Butterfly peeped down the hallway to make sure Buffy was watching out for them.

"I had to make sure my girl was watching."

"Damn, I wanna fuck you bad!" Atwater said as if he was lust-drunk.

Butterfly pulled down her shorts and bid him on. "Fuck me then," she said as she leaned over the sink. Their encounter reminded her of her creamy dreams that she made with Lazy Eyes when he used to pound ten inches of thunder through-and-through her body. And she felt fever in the night.

"I ain't got no protection," Atwater said, and he was serious. He wasn't the one. Fuck no! Not after doing eighteen years and to come home with HIV or worse! He had heard all the stories, and he wasn't the one, not today or ever. Atwater would have never thought about having sex with a man, until he saw Butterfly, who didn't resemble one at all.

Butterfly pulled her pants back up, because the mood was hampered. But she knew they were going to meet back up again.

"What sign are you?" she asked.

Atwater thought it was funny that she had asked. "I'm an Aries."

She remembered it. "When are we going to meet back up?"

Atwater arranged his pants. "Meet me at the gym

155

tomorrow night." The pm shift, which started after 2:00 p.m. for the COs, was the best time because there were less COs on the compound then.

The rendezvous point, tomorrow night, was music to Butterfly's ear. She was going to have him in every way possible.

# Chapter Twenty-Seven |
### *Can't Get You Out Of My Mind*

Atwater needed the walk down the walkway to clear his head because he didn't know what the hell just happened back there. He went back to his unit from the library, knowing he was overly-attracted to Butterfly, and he even thought about the things he'd do to her, if nobody knew. But he never thought he'd actually act on it.

*Damn me!* He knew the urge was beyond him when he took the image of Butterfly back to the unit with him: her soft neck, her high and soft cheeks, and those fluffy lips. She had measurements that he yearned: a mouth-watering display of a supple 36-22-40. Yes, her waist was teeny-tiny and the arch in her back, the bow in her legs, her thick thighs, and her busty breasts. He was damned—he knew! He couldn't wait to get his big dick in her sugar-buns and wax-wane until he spazzed out. He'd hold her hips and shatter her spine with his diesel load.

*Fuck!* He had to get control of his thoughts. The whole time he was thinking about nutting so hard in Butterfly, his cellmate had been talking about miscellaneous things. He could have been talking about hidden treasure, but it still would have been miscellaneous. *Shit!* Atwater felt fever in the cold and unnerving air.

He went straight to the shower, took a cold shower, and thought about his fine wife and beautiful children. The cold-draining shower was good to clear his throbbing mind. He just couldn't do it. He couldn't drive head first, speeding into a head-on collision that would end with a plummet off a mountain peak. But that was exactly what it was if he made love to Butterfly. *Oh my god! Did I say make love?*

Atwater soaped his dick up and started to jerk it as fast as he could. He knew if he shot off a wad, he'd gain some semblance of control. But as he stroked his dick, he felt every callous on his palm, and he was just tired of jacking his dick. It had been eighteen years of fucking his hand, and plus, he was taking a cold shower, so his hands felt like fucking an empty soda can.

He dried off and went to his cell. It was lockdown anyway. Atwater slammed the door behind him, and Thompson Bey looked up at him as if he was crazy.

"What's up?"

"Nothing, just got something on my mind," he said. After he brushed his teeth, he grabbed Robert Green's *33 Strategies of War.* He read it, but still had the same thought of Butterfly's light skin and her fluffy, rosy red lips sliding up and down his shaft until he nutted down her throat. Frustrated, he slammed his book closed.

And it was as if his cell mate knew the content of his mind.

"Mace, these brothers are a trip. The homies are talking about checking Love in. They said that, that fool was in a homo-orgy a few weeks ago."

"He from St. Louis?" Atwater asked, feeling like Thompson Bey had to know what he was going through.

"That's the only Love the homies would be concerned with. But Moor, I find it impossible that a man could come in here and get turned out." A shadow of guilt shaded over Atwater's face. "And it's always them DC

# BUTTERFLY

niggas that got all those fags."

"Must be something in the water out there," Atwater said, and he could have punched himself.

"I don't really agree with checking Love in though, because I know T got personal issues with him, and he's just trying to use this as an excuse. You know Love be into everything, and I know it's some ulterior motives. Really, who's checking brothers in for fucking punks?"

Atwater sighed. "Hardly ever."

"I think the only reason the B-More Cart checked Lazy Eyes in was because he was married to B-Rod's daughter."

"You're bullshittin'!" It was the first time Atwater had heard that.

"The truth is far from bullshit. I feel B-Rod too. That boy Lazy Eyes was fucking probably got the package; he's always at pill line. I saw him headed for pill line tonight when we were leaving the law library. You know them DC niggas be having that shit. HIV in DC is as high and as worse as places in Africa.

"But what trips me out even worse is the whole time Lazy Eyes was fucking that boy, he'd be out there on the visit tongue kissing his wife. I always say if you pitch, you'll eventually catch." They laughed.

"That's foul." Atwater brushed the light perspiration from his brow.

"I heard they ran a train on Lazy Eyes' boy, who they call Butterfly in 4B when he first got here. I can't even front; I ain't never seen men react to nobody like that. When that punk came into the gym tonight, it got so quiet I could hear hearts beating." Thompson Bey laughed to himself. "Real talk, in my pimp days, I would have had to put that punk to work."

159

# MICHAEL A. ROBINSON

"Islam Moor," Atwater said, which was supposed to instill value in the conversation they were having. It was improper to talk about things that were debasing to men, and Atwater knew he was fronting to the max.

"Islam Moor." Thompson Bey started laughing. "I'm just keeping it real."

"No, I understand. I think it's just the novelty of having somebody on the pound that looks like a girl."

"Yeah, Moor, and not just any girl—that fool looks like Rihanna." Thompson Bey laughed harder. "But you're missing what I'm saying. I guarantee that even on the streets that boy got dudes going. I think women would even be curious. It's a live wire in the human psyche to marvel at anything exotic. And he fits the bill. Pure psychology."

Atwater was lightly relieved that Butterfly had even affected his cell mate. "You may need to stay away from that boy talking like that."

"Islam Moor. I'm going to bed. I've got to go to the plantation tomorrow."

Thomson Bey turned the lights off, and Atwater was left to his thoughts. His mind went on to the conversation he had with Old School when they walked the track. There were only three divisions of people: Pimps/'Hos/Tricks. He had to keep his mind above the water and seize the opportunity of the prospects Butterfly had. It was chancy, risky, even dangerous, but he still had the semblance of a plan forming in his mind of how he could take pimping to another level. If what he thought could work, hell, he could even get Old School out of jail. He laughed and was too excited to go to sleep. He tossed and turned, thought about his plans, his future, and the egging

160

# BUTTERFLY

thought that he couldn't get out of his mind: the touch of Butterfly's soft ass, which he thought about thrice as much!

# MICHAEL A. ROBINSON

## Chapter Twenty-Eight |
### *The Fantasy*

Unlike all the other images and nightmares that passed through Butterfly's mind while she slept, for the first time she had a lovely dream.

She was laid out in an orchard of soft red roses and Atwater had her legs straight up, ramming his dick inside her. He moaned, and she felt as if she had a g-spot that he was hitting. The head of his helmet flared, and she knew he was buttering her buttermilk biscuits as she took his sugar tongue into her mouth while he released his mother-lode.

His eyes were doting as he peered into her eyes, and she loved the feeling of having that power over him. His massive member was wedged between her cheeks, still hard, and he fucked her with the foremost passion ever. She had completely surrendered, abandoned to his strong arms locked on her hips and his manly prowess selfishly seeking its climax as she welcomed his toll. His dick felt like pure fire, and it was the most warming, satisfying and soothing feeling she had ever had.

Butterfly awoke as her evanescent dreams fled. And for once, she had woken with a smile on her face.

Britney had already left for work. So Butterfly got up and refreshed herself by washing her face and brushing her teeth. She threw the towel up over the door window so she could have some privacy. Butterfly then stripped naked and did a once-over in the mirror.

It was so rewarding for her to look at her shapely body in the mirror. It was all perfect! Everything was

# BUTTERFLY

sleek, smooth, and firm. She clasped her tits to her chest and the cleavage looked sexy and appealing. She twirled on her heels and looked at the emphasized arch in her back and her phat butt and she celebrated! Oh but for her hair and lack of makeup and clothes!

She shaved her legs, armpits, and pubic hairs and at once she felt her comfort zone return. Then she made something to eat, because tonight she knew she was going to need all her energy for her amazing tryst. That dreary turquoise evening, Atwater and Craze-zo went to work out in the weight room. It was always crowded with people. The good thing was there were two weight lifting areas: one outdoor and one indoor. They went to the indoors, and since it was cold outside, everybody was in there.

They were on the incline bench and Atwater was lifting as Craze-zo spotted him.

"One more. Push!"

When Atwater finished, a Mexican came over to ask if he could have the bench next, which was always the case. You had to call the weights and wait in a long line for the group of however many were finished, and then you could have your turn.

"We have two more sets," Atwater responded to the Mexican as Craze-zo went to do his set.

While Craze-zo was getting ready to do his set, Butterfly and Buffy came to the door to peek into the weight room. Butterfly shot Atwater a quick knowing-eye, and Atwater felt his heart leap. But Craze-zo gave Butterfly and Buffy the evil eye and they took off.

Atwater laughed. "You're a funny dude."

"No, man, those faggots is vicious. They got this whole compound off balance. What kind of shit is

163

this? Niggas are going. And from what I hear, the Rihanna punk got trained in 4B, was fucking Black, Lazy Eyes, and that Mexican, Sosa. Word is before the orgy in 4B went down, Love and Tyrone—rest in piss, were fucking that faggot. On my hood, had you let me stab that one punk that night in the barbershop, them faggots wouldn't be so bogus right now."

"You can't stab somebody up because they're gay," Atwater said, but he hadn't known that Butterfly had been tossed around like that. He was just happy he didn't slip up and fuck the punk. The head was cool because it wasn't like you could get HIV or AIDS from a blow job.

"Why not?" Craze-zo asked, his face completely blank of understanding Atwater's statement. "Me and my homies from my hood used to fuck punks up in Hollywood all the time. Shit, every jail I've ever been to them faggots have some shit in a twist. Look at these clowns around here. All them fools went to the SHU, and I know that race riot had something to do with the punk because all the key characters were fucking him. To add to that, one of them niggas was ready to leave his wife for that punk! Mark-ass niggas! Cuz, they got to get me out of this region before I put a plug in one of these busters!"

Atwater laughed because he had his doubts. If the power of temptation was so strong, how could he resist it? "Your set, Moor."

While Atwater and Craze-zo were lifting weights, Butterfly and Buffy stood in the entranceway of the gym, which was right next to the restroom. Butterfly was having a fit because Atwater hadn't already come out to meet her. She had been thinking about him all day, and it was just too bad he had his evil and hateful friend with him, whom she hated! But she kept it courteous, and spoke to some of the guys who passed them by on their way to the weight room.

"Damn, what is taking him so long?" Butterfly had, had it!

"Calm down, bitch. You probably about to get the best dick on the compound, let me tell you," Buffy said playfully.

"I've been thinking about him all day. Every time he's with his friend he never even makes eye contact with me," Butterfly fussed.

"He's probably fucking him."

"Shut up, bitch. He ain't gay!"

Franco and Slim came into the gym like they owned the place. Franco's chest and chin was to the sky, and even when Slim worked out he was still fly with his new baseball gloves on, sweats turned inside out, and his long sleeve T-shirt white and crisp. He wore a doo-rag under his cap.

"Look at Franco," Buffy said, but she was looking at his slog poking out of his shorts. "Hello, Franco."

"You better stop talking to me, faggot, before I beat you up," Franco threatened.

Butterfly and Buffy laughed.

And after Franco and Slim went into the weight room, Butterfly started to stress again.

"Where is he?"

"Calm your hot ass panties down, bitch!" She smacked.

"There he goes," Butterfly said, finally relieved!

As by design, Atwater headed straight toward the bathroom and went to the handicap stall.

# MICHAEL A. ROBINSON

When Butterfly entered the restroom, somebody was in there, so she acted like she was using the urinal until he disappeared, and then she stole a chance to go to Atwater! She went into the handicap stall and closed the distance between them in milliseconds. Atwater was so hungry and lust-dumb, he welcomed the grand gesture as if he just hadn't had the conversation with Craze-zo. And she melted under his kiss and fell listless in his hands.

For a moment he kissed her until she was dizzy, but she wanted to feel her dreams of this morning resurge!

Butterfly dropped to her knees and yanked his massive dick from his pants and gave him mega head! She took his sex lever into her mouth, and when his dick was deep in her throat, she gurgled. He thought Butterfly must have known sorcery! Never in a million years—Lord forbid! She whirled her mouth around his dick and slurped the pre-cum dribble and jacked her head back and forth, and he knew she was a genius. When he nutted in her mouth, he grabbed her arms so hard she thought he would snatch them from their sockets. She gurgled deeply in the back of her throat, the whole time his orgasm was in a twist!

Atwater shivered like a man pulled out of an iceberg. Butterfly loved it, but she wouldn't give him leave! She nibbled on his pulsating helmet and slurped at it. In a rare occasion, his dick responded to the sapping slurps, and he was hard again and she continued to ply her trade. Atwater began sweating. Her head was so supernatural he could have easily mistaken her for a snake charmer par excellence. He shot another wad down her gurgling throat, and he almost collapsed to his knees. If she continued, he knew he'd need a

166

gurney to carry him back to the unit.

She licked her lips like a demon-nymph that had just feasted on a prey. She asked, "You all right?"

Atwater was still absent-minded and paralyzed with pleasure. He still couldn't feel his legs. "I think so."

Butterfly laughed, and she didn't need anybody to tell her the full merit of her skills. She had left many bewildered, better yet, everybody.

They heard somebody enter the restroom and the spell was broken. Butterfly helped Atwater up, and his color returned to his face.

"When am I going to see you again?" she whispered in his ear with her soft lips, and with her super-soft hands grabbing his pulsating dick gently.

"Whenever," Atwater said, and he meant it. She had him as one of the worst divisions of people: the trick!

They heard the guy leave, and it was Butterfly's chance to steal her exit. "I'll see you later." She pecked him on his cheek as she left abruptly.

Moments later, he was about to leave, but when he looked down, he saw her ID on the ground. Atwater picked it up and placed it in his front pocket.

*That was the best head ever!*

# Chapter Twenty-Nine |
### *Rendezvous Point*

Shonda came right back to visit Atwater again. But this time, she brought Mason and Macy, their children.

Mason didn't look anything like his sire, but Macy was a blend of her mother's good looks and Atwater.

"What up, Pops!" Mason said as he hugged his dad, standing an inch taller.

"Daddy!" Macy said, who wore skinny jeans, a designer top, and heels. She hugged her father, and she didn't want to let him go because she missed him like crazy.

And as always, Shonda looked completely mouth-watering with her pendants, jewels, and snug-fitting dress and superbly whipped hairstyle. She kissed him like it would be their last.

When they all sat down, Shonda was first to speak. "We have some good news to tell you, and that's why we came up here because they wanted to tell you in person."

Atwater smiled. "What good news?"

"You sure you don't want to eat first?" Shonda asked. They would have to eat out of a vending machine for lunch, which consisted of 85% junk food, and the remaining 15% were sandwiches and sodas.

"We can wait. I want the news first."

They all looked to Mason, who was smiling from ear-to-ear.

"You know how you've always been talking about getting into positions of power, networking, and strategizing success? Guess what? I've been accepted into West Point."

Atwater was breathless. He couldn't believe it! He knew such a position meant power, connections, and above all else, influence.

"That's what I'm talking about! Give me a hug. Damn—you make me proud!" Atwater yelled.

"Hold it down, Atwater," the CO said, who sat across from them.

"My apologies. My son just hit me with some good news."

"I understand," the CO said and went back to monitoring the visitors.

Atwater had to know everything. "How did you get in? Doesn't a Senator have to refer you?"

"That's why I have you to thank. You were so instrumental in getting me accepted, you just don't know. To keep it real, when you told mom to put me in military boarding school, I hated you. But now I understand why you did it. That's where I met Timothy Hathaway, and his father's a Senator out of Maine. His father wanted to refer a minority to West Point, and he immediately thought of me."

"My son's going to be a Five Star General."

"And an engineer," Mason added.

"Damn—you make me proud!" And Atwater couldn't have been happier. Everything that Old School had been drilling into his head was coming to fruition. Everything was owed to Old School's thoughts and ideas, and Atwater felt as if he owed the old man a prince's boon.

Shonda was in tears. "All of this machismo's making me cry." But it wasn't the machismo. It was seeing her husband with their son and seeing the love everybody had for Atwater that made her happy.

And seeing her mother crying tears of joy, Macy was also choked up.

"Macy, tell him your good news," Shonda said.

"There's more?" Atwater was shocked.

"Daddy, I'm going overseas to get an education. I'm going to Oxford, and I have a full scholarship because I'm a Rhodes' Scholar. I'm going to the same college that so many powerful people went to—like Bill Clinton."

Atwater was choked up. "I need a minute to get my head together. This is too much," he said as he dropped his head to cherish the moment. Macy hugged him.

"You were right about strategizing success," Shonda added.

"I love y'all," Atwater said. They had a family hug, and the CO didn't say anything.

"You just make sure you come home soon. Stay safe," Shonda said. They ate lunch and talked about everything until the visit ended. What stood out above all else during the visit, was the fact that Atwater's mind couldn't stop thinking about Butterfly. And he didn't know what it meant.

### *Jealous Passion...*

The next evening, Butterfly raced out of the unit to meet Atwater. It was 8:05 p.m. and pill line had just been called.

Atwater was already up the walkway when Butterfly left the unit. He took a detour toward the automated machine by the commissary and barbershop, feigning as if he was checking his account, but he was waiting for Butterfly to catch up with him. She came up behind him, wearing a cap on her head. Her face looked luscious with those rosy red lips, and her ass looked full and wide. And with those thoughts, Atwater could forget everything.

"Where have you been? I thought you were going to meet me last night?" Butterfly sounded hurt. It made Atwater laugh because this was really a woman! He hadn't felt the feeling of being possessed by a woman in a long time. It was different with Shonda. She'd always been there.

But before Atwater could respond, Butterfly said, "You were with your girlfriend?"

Atwater didn't know who she was talking about. She couldn't have been talking about Shonda. How could she have known about their visit?

"Who are you talking about?"

"Your friend."

"Craze-zo?" Atwater could have guffawed. "That's like my little brother."

Butterfly gentled at the softness of his eyes feasting on her busty breasts and wide hips. She knew if she had been a piece of candy, she would've dissolved!

"I've been checking up on you. I know you're from Virginia, you and the guy you're in the cell with."

Atwater laughed.

"Somebody's been feeding you bad information. I ain't from Virginia."

Atwater was talking to her, but at the same time he was still trying to be discreet. But he could tell Butterfly didn't give a fuck who saw or listened. She could have tongue kissed him in front of everybody with a middle finger to them!

"If this is going to be too much for you, you need to let me know right now. I'm falling in love with you. I just can't stop thinking about you." Butterfly had been thinking about getting that off her chest all day, and she had finally said it.

"Calm down. You're all right." Atwater's sheltering voice and soft words were assuring.

He then tapped the automated machine and the screen went back to its entry page, and they started to walk off side-by-side. And Butterfly, who was anxious to be with him the past couple of days, was now settled and calm.

"When I'ma see you again?" she asked with hidden promise in her eyes.

"Tomorrow night," Atwater promised. He knew he needed her again. Her mouth was a honeycomb. By now he had ruled out the possibility of ever fucking Butterfly because there was no way he'd ever get a condom.

"Why don't you come out during the day time? That would be good too."

"I'll keep that in mind," Atwater said with his sly smile. It was powerful and magnetic, and Butterfly couldn't keep from smiling herself.

"I'll see you then."

## Chapter Thirty |
*True Love Never Dies*

Bobby Moore!"
The following afternoon during mail-call, Butterfly had heard her name called. She shot down the steps and grabbed her letters. Some were from her mother, who was probably the only person that knew she was in jail. But the other was from somebody with a return address that she didn't recognize.

When she opened the letter, she knew exactly who the letter was from. It was from Lazy Eyes, and he had sent the letter to somebody on the streets and they had sent it back in, addressed to Butterfly. When she opened it, she smelled his scent strongly, and had forgotten how much she had really missed him.

Buffy had come over to her and asked her who it was from. Then they ran to her room so that she could read him the contents.

*Butterfly,*
*I'm fucked up back here. They're talking about sending me to USP Florence in Colorado. I can't stop thinking about you. I broke my fist against the wall because I can't be out there with you with that good pussy of yours. The best ever! Hands down . . .*
*My wife wants a divorce because her dad told her about us. But fuck that bitch. I'm in love with you! I swear I'm going to wife you when I get out in 3 years. I've been thinking a lot about that, and if you steal a woman's identity, we can get married! Real talk, you look better than my bitch anyways. Shit, you look better*

*than all my baby mommas put together. Lol*

*Yo, check your account: I had my homie put $10k there. And you better get a job before they stick your ass in the kitchen. Go and talk to the secretary at the chapel where I used to work. She'll look out for you, because I told her about us. I got you, baby: Forever my lady. Love you. Oh yeah, when you get out of jail, I'll have you a spot, clothes, and everything you need.*

*Love you.*

After Butterfly read the letter, she and Buffy fell out on the bed laughing.

"Bitch, you got some good pussy!"

### Where Is He?...

The next day, Atwater had come out to chill with Craze-zo. They were walking the yard and talking about what Atwater was going to do when he got out in a couple of months. Atwater had so many ideas now that he met Butterfly that it seemed crazy. He couldn't tell Craze-zo, but he kept his youngster in suspense by telling him of how he'd be living, traveling, and doing it real big.

Butterfly and Buffy were also walking on the track too, and Butterfly just needed Atwater to steal a minute away with her. She knew he was on the down-low, but damn, how down-low did he have to be? It was frustrating, and she had too many options to be tripping off him. But she knew better.

Buffy was even tripping. "He should have been gone to the bathroom." He smacked his lips like always.

"He knows I'm here waiting for him. Every time he

# BUTTERFLY

gets around that idiot, he acts like he don't know me,"
Butterfly fussed. It was so unlike her to be so uptight all
the time.

"I told you they're probably fucking, let me tell
you."

"I told you he ain't gay," Butterfly said, knowing
that if she didn't look as much like a girl as she did, he
wouldn't be fooling around with her either.

"Shut up, gurl. He ain't all that." He smacked once
more. "Lazy Eyes looks better than him."

"Shut up."

Butterfly was furious when she was unsuccessful to
meet with Atwater, and she had to take a walk of
shame back to the unit. She fumed and fussed the
whole way back to the unit, while driving Buffy crazy.

She couldn't wait till they called pill line, and when
Britney came back from work, she fussed and fumed
some more.

Pill line was finally called and Atwater was at the
automated machine. Butterfly walked as fast as she
could to give him a piece of her mind.

When she walked up to him, she had a whiff of his
cologne and she wasn't as mad as she'd been a second
earlier.

"I'm so tired of you and your shadow. Y'all must
have something going on I don't know about. You
didn't even try to go to the bathroom earlier."

"Chill out," Atwater said. He liked that shit, but
everything was difficult for him too. "At least say
what's up first."

"You know how I feel about you. I'm falling in
love with you. You need to let me know how you
feel."

175

Atwater backed up from the machine, and Butterfly went up to the machine as if she was checking her account.

"I like you. What are you tripping about? Everything is going to smoothen out."

"I ain't trippin'. I just can't take having these feelings for you and being completely ignored. It would be easy for me to fall deeply in love with you. You have stirred me up." Butterfly kept tabbing the machine. But she couldn't stop thinking about the last time she had brought Atwater to his knees, in the velvet clutches of her gurgling throat. She smiled and faced him. "You tasted so good the last time."

Atwater laughed. Damn—he was so fond of her. They started to walk off again toward the walkway.

"You mind if I write you a kite," Butterfly asked.

"No, I'd like that."

"I have to ask you something. When are you going to stop being scared and fuck me?"

Atwater couldn't believe that question. "Real soon," he lied. "That's my word. I'm going to take my time with that ass." Atwater eyed her ass mischievously.

"I'ma see you tomorrow," Butterfly said. She could've skipped to pill line as good as she felt.

### If Truth Be Told...

Atwater was in the band room listening to live musicians who played so good he thought he was at a concert. The guitarist plucked and strummed the guitar so skillfully that Atwater felt his neck hairs ruffled.

Outside the music room, it was nighttime, and the

sky was filled with smoky clouds, and the trees from far off whipped freely in the wind.

Atwater could see Butterfly coming down the walkway, and he thought this would be a good chance to give her back her ID. Over the past few days he didn't know where the budding relationship would lead, but he felt that they would be life friends. She was tied to a lot of his plans for the future, and that's why he wasn't just fucking her. He wanted to develop her mind better, and he thought it was no better way than by seeming to be preoccupied with other things. For her to understand him, she had to understand that he handled business first, and pleasure was a product of success and not vice-versa.

He headed straight to the restroom, and Butterfly saw him as she entered the yard. He was waiting for her in the handicap stall when she entered. She melted in his arms, and for a minute, she didn't say anything.

"Missed me?" Atwater smiled.

She looked up and kissed him. "Yes, I've missed you. And I've missed this." She brushed his dick. "I'm going to make this mine and mine only."

"You wouldn't know what to do with all that," Atwater teased.

"I'm sure I could put it to use." They laughed, and Butterfly slipped her note in his pocket.

"I'm going to read it before I go to bed. And here's your ID."

"You had my ID? I was looking all over the place for it."

"You dropped it."

She kissed him again. "I'll see you later."

"All right."

# MICHAEL A. ROBINSON

Atwater left the bathroom first this time, and Butterfly followed closely behind him.

Butterfly went to the entranceway where Buffy and Britney were waiting for her.

Atwater was about to leave, but he held Butterfly's gaze for seconds, until he heard his name called. He turned and Old School was sitting in the basketball bleachers, unbeknownst to him, checking out the exchange between him and Butterfly.

"Atwater, one second. Hit a couple of laps with me on the basketball court," Old School said. The gym was empty and they'd be alone. "I'm not interrupting you, am I?"

And that's when Atwater knew that Old School's suspecting-self would have seen anything going on between him and Butterfly.

"No, I was about to get my stuff. I was over in the band room listening to Jeffrey Bey and his group."

They started to make their laps, and Old School set out on a brisk pace. He was never one to beat around the bush.

"The Greeks used to say: women are for childbearing, and boys are for fun."

Atwater was aghast! Old School just couldn't have known about him and Butterfly. This was a perfect time to tell Old School how he appreciated the guidance he had given him and how his family was reaping the benefits.

"Come again?" Atwater said wanly.

"The deaf and foolish shout and scream because they don't understand that signs and symbols are for the conscience mind. Riddle me that. A wise man could decipher dark sayings, break down enigmas, put the

# BUTTERFLY

pieces of puzzles together.

"Have you heard about King David and Prince Jonathan from the Bible?"

Atwater didn't dare answer that question. Even if he had known the answer, he wouldn't have said anything. Old School was on a spiel. "King David wrote the dead Prince a eulogy. He said: *The love I had for him surpassed the love of any woman.*"

"Islam Moor. What are you trying to imply?" Atwater was a bit offended, and he didn't like the fact that Old School could read him so easy, bare him so shamefully.

But Old School kept digging. "You ever read the book of Psalms about King David getting persecuted? They say it's a prophesy for Jesus Christ. But I say King David got persecuted because of his affair with Prince Jonathan."

"Old School, I don't know where you're going with this."

"You haven't read about Alexander and Hephaestion, or Set and Heru, or the Sacred Band, or Sulla of Rome, or at least 80% of Hollywood's major actors?" Atwater shook his head and was about to drop his head to the ground, but Old School brought Atwater's attention to Butterfly, who was still standing in the entranceway, laughing with Britney and Buffy. "Look at him. He has the silhouette of a woman. His whole body, spirit, and manner is that of a woman. He's far prettier than any lady CO on this compound, or any I've ever been to.

"You think I'm judging you?" Old School leveled the question at him, and it was then that Atwater looked up at him. But that was it! He felt that Old School, who had been his counselor, his mentor, in short, a father to him had judged him, and it was more than he could take. But

# MICHAEL A. ROBINSON

the more he looked at Old School, the more Old School's eyes had shone with understanding, sympathy, and empathy even.

"No, I don't think you're judging me." Atwater was certain of it now, and he had to come clean. "I fell into my low. I've been down eighteen years without the merest touch of a woman. I've missed the banter of a woman's laughter, her frailty, the lyric of her walk, and the taste between her sweet thighs. And when I saw Butterfly, she gave me some of that and some. I knew I was too far gone when I used to take her image back to the unit with me, and I didn't have anybody to talk to about it. I let Butterfly get into my head, and I started feeling like one of those tricks you were talking about the other day.

"She has the softest lips, and her ass feels soft, and she gives the best head I've ever had. But I ain't trying to be another Lazy Eyes, and I most definitely ain't trying to take nothing home to wifey."

Old School was the perfect listener, and it was as if he understood what Atwater was going through. "Did you kiss him?" Old School asked.

Atwater had just told him she had the softest lips in the world. He just shook his head.

"You got it bad. What's your ulterior motive with him? You ain't tender-dick, are you?"

"Hell no!" Atwater said emphatically. Of course he had ulterior motives that would help him and Old School. "I'm most definitely going to get some money."

"What's your angle?"

"I'm putting that pretty thing on the Internet. Get a couple of tricks to contribute to his legal aid. When I was at Terre Haute, a cat from Atlanta was getting

180

# BUTTERFLY

plenty of money like that." But Atwater couldn't tell Old School his real plan. It was to be kept a surprise.

"What's plenty of money?"

"How much a high profile attorney cost? What $60k to $90k, and they were getting a lot of different Johns," Atwater answered.

"Strategizing success," Old School added.

When Old School said that, Atwater told him about his son and his daughter and the good tidings they had brought him. Old School truly felt a part of Atwater's family.

At that minute, the ten minute move was called over the loud speaker. To that, Old School said, "Young Blood, I'm going to always trust and roll with your judgment-call. But remember, amongst all the emotions you'll have with him/her, keep the presence of your mind."

Atwater looked at Old School as if he knew that already. "Come on now, this is me you're talking to. That's why I like this chase, because I have to struggle with temptation. I like living on the edge a little bit."

Old School laughed. "What happens when he gets possessive and starts demanding more and more of your time? Young Blood, don't get emotionally attached. Don't be like Lazy Eyes. You have too much to lose."

"Never that," Atwater said as they headed toward the exit. "You're like a father to me. I'm hearing you on everything you're saying, but I have to take this ride and see where it leads."

"You better. How else would a man test his mettle and wits? Iron sharpens iron and man sharpens man—no homo." They laughed.

Atwater went straight to the unit. He brushed his

teeth, washed his face, and got his clothes out for tomorrow.

His cell mate jumped on his bunk, and once he saw that his cell mate was occupied reading a book, he hopped on his bunk and read Butterfly's letter.

*Aries,*

*I'm trying my hardest to be patient. I know you're on the down-low, but how down-low do you have to be? You have me waiting outside, walking the yard trying to get your attention, and sometimes you don't even go to meet me. I just be giving you a hard time when I talk about you and your shadow, because I know y'all don't have nothing going on. But I hate the way he looks at me. My brother and my father used to look at me the same way. It's a long story.*

*If this is too much for you, please let me know because I wouldn't play you like this. What's worse is you keep kissing me and holding me tight as if this is something that you want. I'm confused! Let me know what's on your mind.*

*Distant whisper . . .*

Atwater just smiled. She was too much.

# Chapter Thirty-One |
### *I'm Tired Of Prison*

M rs. Mires was the wicked bitch of the prison. If she could be nasty, she'd spite herself to be even nastier. She had no sense of being cordial. Being decent could never have crossed her mind. And it made her little stump legs and fat body seem grotesque. She wore her blue CO uniform, and it became her personality, as if her blue uniform and badge could compensate for her foul mouth, nasty manners, and her ugly and shapeless body. With her short hairstyle, she looked like a short-stop who should be spitting Chew with a shit-dribbling horse stuck between her legs and a straw in her mouth.

That morning, Mrs. Mires called Butterfly to her office that was in a hallway between two units. Butterfly did as told. There was nobody back there with Mrs. Mires except the secretary and an orderly, who was emptying the trashcans.

"Princess, go to the chapel when you hear the call for the ten-minute move," Mrs. Mires told Butterfly.

"For what?" Butterfly asked. She didn't like the sneer in Mrs. Mire's eyes.

"Because I said so. And also, put on your boots and take off those tight pants. And if I see that you've altered another shirt, I'm going to write you an incident report."

"What's that?"

"You'll find out when I write one. Now get out of my office and go and put your uniform and boots on."

Butterfly padded out of her office and went to change her clothes as she was told. When she put on the two-piece uniform and the gangly boots, she felt like the horse-bitch Mrs. Mires truly was.

They called the ten-minute move, and Butterfly marshaled out with the other inmates. She went to the chapel and it was quiet and empty inside, nothing like how she had remembered the last time she was there.

When she went in to the Chaplain's office, there was nobody there except a sharply dressed white lady in her early forties, clad in D&G transitional frames, with a body of rigorous and hard-fought for curves, shape, and a unique type of definition. And Butterfly knew that this must be the lady that inmates would line up outside of her office to ask her a meaningless question just to get a sneak-preview of her jazzy attire worn over her flawless body.

"Hello," Mrs. Hoover said, a stark difference from Mrs. Mires. She seemed urbane and cordial.

"My counselor Mrs. Mires told me to come down here," Butterfly said, using her kitten voice, because she liked the lady at first sight.

"Hello again, Butterfly." She smiled and winked an eye. "You'll be taking over Lonny's old job as a library clerk. He sent me a kite and told me to give you his old job and to look out for you." She squeezed Butterfly's hand over the counter that was between them.

"He told me a lot about you too." She shook her head. "And you are every bit as pretty as he said. "Wow!"

The phone rang. She told Butterfly to give her a second, and she would show her around. So Butterfly stepped out of her office and started to prowl around the chapel. She walked by the bathroom and remembered that was the first time she had made out with Lazy Eyes and then she thought of the other times. Yes, the library had a wealth of memories with him, and if she sniffed the air, she could still smell his musk, his cologne scent, and feel his thrust in her lubricated bend. It was a pleasing thought that she was suddenly pulled from when the lady emerged from the office, whose name was Mrs. Hoover.

"Sorry about that." She giggled.

"You're going to basically do everything Lonny was doing. Your job is very simple, and I'm sure we're going to get along just fine. You'll hand out books, CDs, DVDs, and any other religious apparel needed.

"Those lockers are where we keep everything, and I'll unlock it as need be.

"You have the Sunnis locker there, the FOI there, and the Rastafarians over there too. On the other side are the Hebrew Israelites who share the same locker with the Jews, Wicca, and Santamaria. The Jehovah Witness and Protestant's lockers are there. And of course, the last locker in the corner is for the Catholics."

Butterfly laughed because it was a lot to remember. "I'll try to get it remembered."

"You will. I'll show you the library where you'll spend most of your time undisturbed."

They walked to the room that Lazy Eyes came out of the night when Butterfly had met him. It was diagonal to the main chapel.

When they walked in, it was just as Mrs. Hoover had said, spacious, relaxing, and it did offer privacy because there was a door that could be shut and locked!

"We have books on every religion, no matter what it is. Here's a religious catalogue." Mrs. Hoover held up a *Yellow Pages* sized book. "The CDs and DVDs are in that drawer. They have to fill out this sheet and give you their ID to rent them.

# MICHAEL A. ROBINSON

"Now that, that is all done, I want you to tell me about you and Lonny. He's already told me so much about you."

Butterfly smiled sheepishly, but she still hadn't warmed to Mrs. Hoover yet.

"I understand. I want you to call me Kathy, okay? You don't have to call me Mrs. Hoover and be all official." She laughed. "I'm not all gung ho. I'm only a secretary. I collect my check and that's it. I'm here to be your friend, you understand? And I was friends with Lonny. That boy is crazy!" She laughed. "He talked so much about you. I feel like I know you already."

And that loosened Butterfly's tongue, and as first sight impressions went, Butterfly knew she'd like her.

"What did he used to say?" Butterfly asked. And that's how their friendship began.

## *Love's Like A Rollercoaster...*

Atwater and Craze-zo listened intently to the music Jeffrey Bey and his band played in the band room, but Atwater's mind was on Butterfly. He needed to see her tonight just to ease his mind. He had been uptight lately about getting out. It wasn't easy for a person to have done eighteen years and then get released, and responsibility hit him all at once. He had been holding everything down from jail and that was simply his comfort zone, and he knew it would be different. Everything would be different. *Don't fret,* he told himself.

He saw Butterfly sauntering those juicy thighs up the walkway and her disheveled hair. It was obvious she didn't know what to do with her hair, and he thought she probably was the type that figured beauty and body overcompensated for anything as trivial as a hot comb and some hair-gel. He just laughed.

She saw him and headed to their honeycomb hideout, and he appeared instantly into her arms.

"What kind of letter was that?" he asked as she kissed him.

"A 'truth be told' letter."

Butterfly wanted to suck his fruit dry of its succulent juice, but he pulled away and handed her a letter. "Read this. I'll meet you tonight at pill line. I have to get back to the music room."

"Is that it?" Butterfly said. She wanted much more. "You ain't gonna let me get any nourishment."

"If you keep drinking this bull's milk, you're going to lose that pretty figure of yours." They laughed.

"Do you like me, Aries?"

He laughed. Up till that point, she had never called him by his name.

"Hell yeah! Let me feel that ass. Damn!" he said as she brushed her ass against his dick and pushed it against his mid-section.

"What?" she asked skeptically. "Let me guess—feels like a woman's ass is what you're thinking?" she asked sarcastically, shameful that she had to go through this with him. But how was he to know?

He just shook his head affirmatively.

"When will you accept the fact that I'm a 100 percent Black woman?"

"I'm a 100 percent convinced now. That's on the prophet!" Atwater added, exasperated.

"I'll see you at the pill line. I'm gonna read the letter

right now."

### *Testing The Water…*

The moon cast a pale silvery glow over the night, and Atwater had to put his jacket on against the chill in the wind as he made his way to the pill line. He saw Butterfly walking up the walkway at a fast pace, and he had to damn near trot to catch up with her.

She slowed down when she saw him coming, and when he saw her face, she seemed as if she had been crying.

"What's up with you?" he asked.

"I've never been more insulted in all my life! I don't need a pimp. Everything you put in that letter just says that you want to use me like my manager did. I'm already on the Internet. Here's my Facebook picture." She gave him her profile picture that was on the Internet, and damn was she even prettier! "That's how I look when I have a stylist and a make-up artist."

"Why are you surprised? I hope you didn't think I walked around the streets with my hair like this. I'm a model."

"Calm down," Atwater bid her. At least till they were able to walk to the automated machine, where everything wouldn't be put on front-street. But he couldn't keep his eyes off the picture she had handed him. She was ever more gorgeous!

"I have plenty of money," she continued to fuss in her hushed manner. "I don't need a pimp. Here's my commissary receipt. I always keep three zeroes on my account. If I love somebody, Aries, I'll give them whatever they want. But those were hurtful things you said in that letter. Asking me why I go to pill line. I'm bipolar! But you don't listen to me." Butterfly disappeared into the night.

Atwater smiled. He had done what he had wanted to—shaken up her foundation. And now she had given him the key he needed to get her to do what he needed her to do. What did she say: 'If I love somebody, Aries, I'll give them whatever they want.' *How relishing.* The key to unlock her had come to him so easy.

# MICHAEL A. ROBINSON

## Chapter Thirty-Two |
*Make Up To ... Busted*

As had been different from the past few weeks that Butterfly had been seeing Atwater, she had woke up from the bed sluggish and feeling heavy with slumber.

Butterfly dragged herself from the bed and Britney had already left. He left a note on her bed saying that he was going to whip them up a meal that night and for her not to eat anything until he returned from work.

She had to put on her gawky uniform and gangly boots and trudged to work feeling uncomfortable in the men's clothes.

When she went into Mrs. Hoover's office, aka Kathy, after the chaplain had left to attend a meeting up front, Kathy had made Butterfly a refreshing cup of coffee that snapped her back instantly, and she was as giddy and graceful as ever.

When the chaplain returned, Butterfly headed for what would now be her office. She went inside and cleaned and arranged everything to her liking. She had to give the place a woman's touch and knew that if she could appreciate it, so would Kathy.

But while she was cleaning up, Atwater stumbled in, without as much as knocking.

"You got some trash in here that needs to be emptied?"

When Atwater looked up, he couldn't believe it was Butterfly sitting behind the desk watching TV. She just rolled her eyes at him.

Atwater went to empty the trashcans. But an

# BUTTERFLY

awkward moment passed, and when it had, he didn't feel like letting Butterfly off the hook that easy.

"So you still following me around I see."

"I didn't know you worked here," Butterfly said with an attitude without looking back.

"I find that hard to believe. I thought you had your informers who told you that me and my cellie were from Virginia and blah blah blah. I distinctly remember you saying that." Atwater had a smile that read victory.

"You know what? Fuck you!" Butterfly added. She didn't want to look at him, because she wanted to stay mad at him.

"Was that Bobby or Butterfly talking? I did hear you last night when you said you were bipolar. I read your real name on your ID."

"Keep on," Butterfly said. Finally she looked up at him, and she was mad that she had.

Atwater set the bag he held in his hand on the ground. He was enjoying himself too much to just leave.

"Check this out, I didn't completely accept in my mind that you were a real woman till last night, as crazy as that sounds. This is all new to me. When I wrote you, I thought I was being helpful. I didn't mean to hurt you. And plus, I didn't know you were laid like that out there. But I respect that."

"What led you to believe otherwise?" she asked curtly as Atwater pulled the door closed.

"Don't even go there."

"Don't go where?"

"You don't think I know about what you did in 4B with Tyrone and Love? I know the details of how you let them get you high and drunk. I know

191

about Sosa, Lazy Eyes, and Black."

"You sound jealous." Butterfly leveled.

"Fuck you."

"You wanna meet Bobby, talking to me like that."

Atwater loved this shit. He got two inches from her face as she sat in the chair. "Yeah, show me Bobby."

Butterfly grabbed his arms. He wiggled away, and she jumped up to grab him again, but he bear-hugged her and trapped her and planted kisses on her gorgeous face as she bit for his. That was until Kathy came in.

"Bobby . . ." She was shocked seeing them hugged up together, and she just smiled as Atwater jumped back. "I didn't see anything." Kathy smiled mischievously. "Excuse me, Bobby, we need you to put the new items in the lockers when you're finished in here. I'm sorry, that's all I wanted."

Kathy pulled the door tight this time, and when she left, Atwater picked his bag up and he was about to leave.

"Thought you were busted, huh? With your 'keep it on the down-low ass.'" Butterfly couldn't stop laughing.

"Islam Moor." Atwater exited.

Once Atwater left, Kathy ran back into the room when she saw that he had gone to the bathroom.

"You got you a cute one!" Kathy said, all smiles. "But be a little more discreet. Next time, put up this TV sign here. See this side: 'Do Not Disturb'. And keep the door locked."

Butterfly smiled. She had her a friend. "And hide these." Kathy had handed her a fistful of condoms, and Butterfly couldn't believe it. "I have plenty whenever you need them. Just let me know. But don't tell anybody I gave them to you. Nobody."

# BUTTERFLY

Butterfly placed her left hand over her heart and swore. It was the only hand she had free. "I can't say thank you enough."

"A singular thanks would be plenty. Now I have to get back to work, and you have to think about what you're going to do with those."

*Make-up Tips...*

After work, Butterfly floated back to her unit, as if she had butterfly's wings. She now had a job where she could have privacy, and her boss was the coolest in the world. When she returned to the unit, she grabbed her mail from the officer, and she saw that she had a letter from her mother, Sandra. She read it and didn't understand why, but it seemed as if her mother was trying to be real cool about their relationship.

When Britney came back from work, Butterfly told him and Buffy everything about her day, and they couldn't stop laughing.

"Bitch, you got to be the most luckiest ugly duckling in the pond," Britney said.

"Let me tell you," Buffy added.

"Whatever. Tomorrow we're going to make love."

"Go on and give him that worn out pussy," Buffy said.

"Ain't that the truth." Britney slapped hands with Buffy. "She lost all her grippers in 4B." They laughed.

"You guys have to help me get ready for tomorrow. I can't go in there with my hair all over the place." Butterfly wanted to look irresistible.

"It never stopped you before," Britney said.

"Shut up, funky breath." She smacked her lips as always. "I got you, gurl."

# MICHAEL A. ROBINSON

Up until that point, Butterfly didn't know that Buffy had possessed any skills. However, Buffy shampooed her hair in the sink, braided it really tight in corn-rows, and put on a doo-rag and a tied a shirt tight around her head. He waited forty minutes until they opened the cells after 4:00 p.m. count and unwrapped her head. He took it out of the corn-rows and wet her hair again and took Murray's wave grease and put her hair in a silky, wavy bun at the back of her head. Buffy then made lipstick with Kool-Aid and used a pencil as eyeliner, and hooked Butterfly's face up.

That was the look she wanted! But she wouldn't see Atwater until the next morning, so this process would have to be repeated the following day in the morning.

The next day when Butterfly woke up, Buffy was the first to the door when the CO unlocked the cells.

"Get up, bitches," he said, but Britney had already stirred.

"I have to get ready for work," Britney said as he got up and arranged his bed.

"'Ho-please, we about to give the finishing touches." Buffy went over to Butterfly to shake her. "Get up, bitch. You have to get ready for work call."

"Just give me five more seconds."

"Get up, bitch," Britney said.

Buffy laughed as Butterfly stirred. "Please Britney, I got her from here. Just brush your goddamn breath." She smacked.

"It's teeth bitch, not breath," Britney said, making sure he blew as much of his breath on Buffy as possible.

"I don't even think I should ever breathe again," Buffy said as Butterfly laughed.

"'Ho, it is too early."

Britney went to freshen up while Buffy had given

# BUTTERFLY

Butterfly the altered pants of her old uniform back to her. "I hooked your uniform up. Wait till you put it on."

"Na-hum, you're going to get that bitch sent back to the SHU altering her clothes," Britney said with toothpaste suds all over his mouth.

Buffy just gave him the stop sign with his hands.

"Damn, bitch. What did you do to them?" Butterfly asked as she held them out in front of her. They looked to be skintight and they were tapered at the bottom.

"I hooked them up. Now get your ass up. We have to douche you, let me tell you."

"I'm not doing that with y'all in the cell."

"I don't know why not." Smack. "It ain't like you know what you're doing anyways. It ain't like the streets, bitch. You have to use this shampoo bottle."

Buffy held up a shampoo bottle in his hands. "Come on, bitch, and Britney get the fuck out the way."

"'Ho, I'm almost finished anyways."

"Good, because after I douche her ass, I'm going to douche your mouth, let me tell you." They laughed.

Butterfly took off her shorts that she slept in and went over to sit on the toilet and that was the first time the two of them had seen her penis. They both laughed.

"What?"

"Bitch, you know what. What the hell is that? You sure you're supposed to be in a men's prison?" Britney asked.

"That's not even possible to be that small," Buffy said, slapping hands with Britney.

"Charming. Can we get on with this?"

Buffy gave Butterfly the shampoo bottle and Butterfly douched right in front of them while Britney was getting dressed for work. When Butterfly flushed the toilet the smell was horrible!

# MICHAEL A. ROBINSON

"Damn girl, you smell like a dinosaur decomposed inside of you eons ago," Britney said.

"'Ho, it's no worse than your breath," Buffy said.

"I got bad breath from sucking your daddy's dick."

"You sure it wasn't from sucking the puss from his ingrown toenails?"

"I wish the both of y'all would shut up. I'm trying to concentrate," Butterfly said.

"Please, like you need to concentrate to flush your ass," Buffy said.

"Some people do. All ass and no brains."

Butterfly gave them the finger. When they finished, Butterfly looked better than she did the day before. Her hair was whipped back in a nifty and wavy bun. The button down shirt was altered by Buffy, as were her pants, and she tied a knot on the side and it showed her belly button. Her pants were skintight. She would have to put another uniform on top of her sexy clothes in order to go to work. She'd also have to hide her makeup by putting a cap on her head. But the good thing was that it was cold outside, and she could put her big jacket on and blend in with everybody else.

Butterfly went to work, and when she got there, she called Kathy into her office.

"What are you doing?" Kathy asked with a smile as Butterfly took off the uniform that she had on top of her sexy apparel.

"If I tell you, then you're going to have to write me an incident report." They laughed.

"That is too nice, especially considering what you have to work with. How did you put that together?" Kathy thought it all too cute, the way Butterfly's ass was hiked up in her skinny pants, and the shirt tied to the side and the belly button for all to see.

# BUTTERFLY

"Tricks of the trade."

"I'll tell you one thing. I'll make sure you're not disturbed," Kathy said as she walked over to grab the `Do Not Disturb' sign. "Just promise me that you'll tell me details when you're through."

"Cross my heart and hope to have some wild and savage sex."

Kathy laughed to that. "Just be sure to use the condoms, and nobody should be able to hear you." Kathy was about to walk out the door, and then she turned back around and said. "You have a hot ass and a hot body."

"Thank you." When Kathy closed the door, Butterfly twirled around in a celebratory circle.

Then she turned on the radio to soft jazz, lit candles, and turned off the lights. She didn't know what she could use on the floor, which would be their temporary bed. Butterfly couldn't find anything, so she neatly laid out her uniform on the ground and waited for what seemed like forever! *Where was he?*

# MICHAEL A. ROBINSON

## Chapter Thirty-Three |
*Creamy Dreams*

W hen Atwater had gone to work, the first thing he always did was make sure that all the trashcans were empty, and then he'd clean the bathroom. But as soon as he went into Kathy's office, she had been very direct and even rude, which was unlike her.

"Atwater, go and clean up the chapel's library."

"Okay, Mrs. Hoover. I'll go over there as soon as I'm done here."

"I said now!" she said, and she was stern about it.

He looked at her for a moment. She didn't give him any clue as to what she was up to.

When he left out of her office, he saw the `Do Not Disturb' sign on the door and returned to let Kathy know.

She told him that she had put the sign up because the place was so dirty and that she was disappointed at his work performance. He was momentarily stung, because nothing seemed right with her this morning. Atwater hunched his shoulders, completely confused about everything. Then he went inside the chapel's library, and when he went in, he couldn't believe his eyes!

Butterfly was lying on the ground, her lips red, her hair whipped up in waves and pulled into a neat bun, and her eyes were shaded and lined. Her cleavage was mouthwatering, her stomach flat, her ass fat to death! She had on footsy socks and her ass looked like it would bust out the seams of the skinny pants that Buffy

198

had made for her.

Atwater dropped the bag in his hands and wiped his brow. "Get the fuck out of here!" He was lost in her awesome beauty, and for a minute, when he thought that he might have been tripping to have wanted to fuck her, now he knew he was right on point! As of late, he had been second-guessing everything. He questioned his sexuality and everything. He didn't understand what was wrong with him. But now that he saw her sprawled out on the ground and her lust-ridden eyes, he knew that it was the fact that she was a woman!

There was nothing that could tell him otherwise, but he knew he could never fuck her, because there was no way in hell he was going to raw dog her. He could never live with himself if he carried something home to Shonda, and he was so close to going home.

"Damn, all this for me?" he asked, dubious, unsure of how much control he had over this situation.

"And much more." Butterfly displayed the condoms.

"Where did you—" he was about to ask, and then it all made sense to him. Kathy's strange behavior, the candles, the soft jazz music . . . it was all Mrs. Hoover, aka Kathy's doing!

"Don't ask," Butterfly responded.

He gave her a knowing smile. And the talking came to an end. Butterfly was undressing him with her eyes, and she couldn't wait to deep throat him and fuck him reverse cowgirl style.

He looked kind of indecisive and skittish. She had gotten up with graceful, seductive movements and brushed her ass against his bulge in his pants. Butterfly

# MICHAEL A. ROBINSON

danced and unbuttoned one of the buttons on her shirt and swung her ass, and then backed onto the desk. She made her ass clap, and he touched her soft ass to make sure it was real.

Then he grabbed her up, and he kissed her from behind. She stuck her butterscotch tongue in his mouth, and she moaned deeply because she wanted to feel his full measure.

He groped her breasts and dug his crotch into her full ass, and he could have lost his head!

Butterfly turned and unbuttoned his uniform one button at a time, as she looked him in his eyes and played her lips against his. She took his shirt off to see a well-developed chest and broad shoulders that she kissed every tattoo on them until she made her way down to his pants.

She unbuckled them and then she sucked on his dick. He thought he would bust wild, unchallenged in her throat amongst her gurgles of pleasure. But she stopped and sucked on his balls and kissed his thighs until his passion was raw and gripping and he couldn't take anymore! He went to take over the intermission, but she had stopped him with a single commanding finger to suggest that she was in control.

"You ain't gonna fuck me until I ride the pony."

His face was drawn up in anguish. The more he heard her soft gentle and sexy voice, the more he wanted to nut so hard inside of her.

"Ride the pony then."

"I want you to talk to me the whole time that fat dick is in my ass," she said, unpeeling her tempting shirt off. Her tits sprang forth, and he hadn't seen real tits in eighteen years. Atwater groped and sucked on

200

# BUTTERFLY

them.

Butterfly pulled down her pants, and when she did, she pushed Atwater into the chair. She kissed his thighs again, and then slurped the full scale of his dick and put a condom over the span and then she greased her butt.

She turned, and when Atwater tried to guide his dick into her ass, she slapped his hands away and did the guiding. She put the helmet of his dick in her ass and twirled her hips without dropping down.

"I got plenty of this for you," Atwater promised.

"Do you?" Butterfly moaned.

"Yeah, baby, dick and butterscotch."

"Oh, you wanna tease me?"

"You're teasing me. Go on and let that thing drop before I pull you down."

"No, you might hurt me with all that dick."

Butterfly slowly wiggled her hips and took each inch slowly. His dick was as long as Lazy Eyes' but much fatter, and she knew she was going to be in for one.

"I'm gonna let you ride this pony, but when it's my turn, I'm gonna fuck you so hard." He gnarled like a wolf.

"How that feel, baby?"

"Feel like you need to stop fucking around."

Butterfly slammed down on his dick and took him all the way in, smashing down hard on his midsection. FUCK! she wanted to scream, feeling his massive member in her stomach.

She balanced her weight on his knees and popped her ass into his dick. He couldn't take anymore. He pushed her on all fours and pounded in and out of her as hard as he could. She wanted to scream with pleasure, and he bit down on her shoulder when he nutted inside her.

"Ahhhh . . . " she gasped. What more did Atwater have in store for her? She'd have to find out.

## *Flight...*

They passed weeks after that inseparable of each other. Whenever they closed the chapel's library door, they were in a world of their own. There, they could share intimate conversations, have sex, and get away from being judged.

When Butterfly thought that she had been deeply in love with Clayton, lying on the floor with Atwater made her think that she had never known what true love was. It was true that she loved fucking Lazy Eyes' more, but something about Atwater had taken her breath away. She would go back to the unit and tell Buffy and Britney everything, and they thought she was the luckiest ugly duckling in the pond.

"There's nothing I wouldn't do to make you happy," Butterfly told Atwater with a mist of admiration and deep love in her eyes.

She had not changed at all since the first day of her make over. And she lay there naked and the candlelight danced a shadow on the surrounding walls. The air from the air conditioner was cool, and she had goose bumps all over her skin. She wrapped up in Atwater's big arms and pulled tight against him.

"Is that right?" Atwater said and he had to know. He knew the way to her heart, and he was fast on the trail. She had told him that she'd do anything once she was in love, and only time would tell.

# BUTTERFLY

"If you still want me to get on the Internet for you, I'll do it."

Atwater didn't even have to game for it. "When?"

"Whenever you want. I love you." Butterfly didn't look into his eyes when she said that. She just didn't want to see if his eyes would read other than how she felt. And if she was lying to herself, let her live the lie.

Atwater said nothing. His heart was split. Shonda most definitely came first, and he didn't know if he had taken this fling too far. It was supposed to be about money and nothing else. But he had gone tender-dick, and he knew that Old School better not find out.

"How did you get these scars?" Atwater asked, touching the scars on her wrist. He noticed them a long time ago but never wanted to ask because he didn't want to be prying in her personal business like that.

"I tried to kill myself." Butterfly was disappointed that he didn't say anything about her love for him. But if he wanted to be hushed about it, so would she.

"Why did you try to kill yourself?"

"It's a long story."

"And we have all day. You're gonna hold it back from me when you just told me you'd do anything for me."

Butterfly had to think. His lips were kissing her earlobe, but she wanted to look at him while she told him what he should know. So she turned around to face him.

"Men only love me when it's easy for them. When they have to go through what I've always had to go through, they leave me."

"What did you have to go through?"

Butterfly looked at him as if it was obvious. "You'd

never ever understand."

"Try me."

"Imagine being disowned by your family. When my mother came up here to see me, that was the first time I'd seen her in years. And she still doesn't want to accept the fact that I'm a woman. She still sees me as her little Bobby. She writes me, but I just don't trust her.

"Plus my father and brother have always looked at me as if they hated me or as if I disgusted them." Butterfly was choked up and tears formed in her eyes.

"That's okay, you don't have to tell me if it makes you mad."

"No, I'm going to tell you. My father and brother treated me as if I wasn't there. Whenever my family would go on fishing trips, vacations or outings, they wouldn't take me. And since I didn't have my father's love, my mother had always kept me at bay."

"That's fucked up, baby."

"I know it is. And I haven't always been honest about who I am or what I am. I've lied so much about it. Being that I can pass as a woman, I don't always tell people otherwise, like I was born . . ." She let the moment pass. "I guess Clayton was shocked at first, but he left it at that. But somehow his family found out and his cousin Peyton blamed me for everything because she hooked us up. And that's why I'm in jail: vengeful justice."

"What?"

"Peyton set me up. She had some guys act like she owed them some money, and they said they'd kill me if she didn't pay them. So I did the only thing I knew how to do to get that much money on such short notice: I started busting checks. And the whole time it

# BUTTERFLY

had been a set up."

"We gotta get that bitch back," Atwater said, and he meant it.

"No we don't. It's my fault. She's right. I should have said that everything about me is complicated. I should have said that I don't want people to know I was born a man, because I love them and I want them to love me as who I am not what I am. And if that sounds complicated there's no better way to explain it.

"And that's why I said that when somebody has to face what I've faced my whole life, they'll leave me. They'll end up blaming me for being who I am. But this is who I'll always be. I can't change."

"Have you ever felt like you should have never come out of the closet?"

"Of course I do. I regret that I am who I am every day of my life. But it's pretty obvious. It's not like I can hide this woman inside of me. It's who I am and the sooner people'll realize it, the better off the world'll be. People act like somebody gay would go through all this discrimination and hate for some excitement. But this is who we are.

"I think—" Butterfly just couldn't bring herself to say it because it would shatter her dreams.

"You think what?"

"I think you're gonna leave me, too, when you're faced with the reality of what you're doing . . . watch and see."

"I ain't going nowhere. Don't even think like that. I'll never abandon you. That's my word . . ."

*"That's my word . . . That's my word . . .* "The words waded through Butterfly's mind that night when she

205

# MICHAEL A. ROBINSON

went to sleep. His voice was so settling, and she almost got lost in the words. The words were so comforting that she felt herself drift off into her favorite place in the world.

*She was in an orchard, and the sun was warm and the skies clear. She was running, and she felt her adolescent youth in her spree. She was a kid again, seven to be exact, and she was flying fast across the orchards.*

*"I'm a butterfly! I can fly!"*

*She twirled in a spot as the sun shone on her face. She spun and did a dance with a butterfly that waddled by and whispered love to it.*

*She didn't know, but her uncle, Kevin, was standing by a tree watching her with a smile on his face. He thought his young nephew was so beautiful, and it took all in his power not to get excited every time he saw him.*

*"Bobby, come here."*

*When Butterfly heard her uncle's voice, her sunny day had instantly become gloomy, and dark clouds hovered overhead. The sky passed and was eerie and dreamy and she was transported back to her uncle's study in his big mansion.*

*She was crying, and her uncle was pulling down her pants as she stood stark still. She couldn't move, because her uncle forbid her to.*

*"I love you more than your own dad," her uncle said, and it was true, but it was a love that was tainted by perversion, and his eyes were crazed with lust.*

*"Please don't, Uncle Kevin! Not again!" Little Bobby's pleas were sincere, his cries piercing. But his uncle didn't yield to his pleas.*

*His uncle kissed him and Little Bobby hated it. His*

# BUTTERFLY

uncle made him get on his knees and he instructed Bobby on how to put his mouth on his penis and suck it. Bobby did as he was told, because . . . because . . . his uncle was the only one in this whole wide world who cared about him or ever showed him any affection. Bobby knew what they were doing was wrong, but who could he tell! His father already hated him, and his mother was scared of her husband, so there was nothing to do but comply.

Little Bobby's uncle turned him around and he felt his uncle thrusting inside of him and he felt the searing pain. Sweat poured out of Little Bobby's pores, and he felt drenched in water. He felt dunked in a tank that was filled with water.

He was drowning and a hand held his head fast in the water. He fought against the water and his hands splashed back and forth, and he tried to breathe, but he only sucked up more water. Then she felt his head yanked out of the water, and he was in his uncle's hands.

They were at his uncle's church and his uncle was baptizing him!

"He's reborn again, Lord Jesus. He's renewed in your Holy Spirit! He'll never be the same again, because he was born to you! He's yours! He's yours!"

But Bobby was Butterfly now and her uncle tried to dunk her in the water again, but it was as if time had stood still. She could feel his hand on the back of her head but when her face was about to hit the motionless water, she could see her face on the surface as if she was looking into a mirror.

Her face had changed from that of a youthful boy to that of a teenage girl. Her lips were full, she had on make-up and her hair was flat ironed. She was beautiful *and she had gotten lost in the image. Her beauty was dreamy, and she loved what stared back at her. This was her: she knew then that she had found herself. She had been lost up until this point. The only thing that was missing were breasts and wide hips. But everything else was all she could have ever wanted.*

*She was lost in her beauty and had lost track of time, and seconds later, she heard her father enter her room and everything went into chaos.*

*"GET OUT MY HOUSE! I DON'T EVER WANT TO SEE YOU AGAIN WHILE I'M ALIVE!"*

*Butterfly felt her father's hate unleashed, and his fists were his vengeance. He tried to kill her, and he would have had her mother not come to her aid. But her brother just watched. He just stood there to let his mother struggle to daunt their father's strength. He just stood there as if he had no love for her. He enjoyed it as much as her father hated it. And when she ran away from her home, she knew that, that home had never been home. And now, she knew that she didn't have any place to go. She didn't belong to anyone. She was in this world all alone!*

*Butterfly stumbled through the streets, and she couldn't help but think that her mother wouldn't come looking for her and the thought hurt her terribly, because she didn't know if her mother had ever loved her. She ran even faster and blood leaked from her face. Her hair was now disheveled and she was nothing like the beautiful girl who had just found herself. She didn't know where to go, but there was only one place in the world where she knew she'd always be welcomed.*

*"Don't worry. I'll take care of you. Come and sit on my lap while I nurse your wounds. You look really nice*

# BUTTERFLY

*dressed like this." Her uncle was sick—she knew! And at the same time that she hated her life, herself, and was confused about everything, she pitied her uncle and his love, and accepted it because he had the only love that she had ever known.*

*Uncle Kevin led her to the top of the house, where his wife couldn't find them. He led her to the third story, and when Butterfly walked to the top and stared down the steps, it was as if death was calling her. Death seemed so cozy, welcoming. She wondered if death's love would be as queer as her uncle's. But she felt tired, and death looked like a good bed to rest in. She felt the warmth of it, and it reminded her of her orchards filled with butterflies.*

*She saw the butterflies waffling around in the wind, and she knew that she could fly too, if only she stepped forward.*

*"I can fly . . . I'm a butterfly. I can really fly!" Her mouth uttered in a sort of distant jubilation; and she would have taken the step to meet death, had her uncle's beckoning arm not grasped her back. Bobby . . . Bobby . . . Bobby . . .*

# Chapter Thirty-Four |
## *Can I Forgive Him?*

**B**obby Moore! Wake up, you have a visit," the CO said, and Butterfly was pulled from her dreams.

She thought her mother had made another impromptu visit, and she dressed casually in the uniform that she must wear.

Butterfly went through the usual, being strip-searched before she could go out to the visit room, and then she walked out to the visiting room and the first person she laid eyes on was Atwater and his wife. Butterfly had to walk pass them to go to the CO's desk in the front of the visiting room.

"You have any picture tickets?" the CO asked.

"No," Butterfly answered, hating that the COs were always mean and rude.

"You may be seated."

Butterfly found herself an empty seat, but she sat in a place where she could keep her eyes on Atwater. She thought that Shonda was cute, but to be honest, the bitch was barking up the wrong tree. Atwater would be Butterfly's one day, she kept saying to herself. And she dreaded the truth behind it. And just when she was lost in endless thoughts, her uncle, whom she had been having nightmare after nightmare about, came out to pay her a visit.

He had the nerve to smile!

Uncle Kevin always looked good, dressed in a beige Brioni suit with a sky blue tie and handkerchief. He wore waves and he was tall. His demeanor was warm

# BUTTERFLY

and friendly, but this same demeanor had a way of making Butterfly's skin feel like bugs were crawling on it.

"Where have you been? I've been worried sick about you." Her uncle looked honestly worried. And for the most part of her past, her uncle would drape her in fine linen, buy or give her anything and everything she had ever wanted. He was totally against her modeling, because modeling meant that she would have her own money, and she wouldn't have to depend on him.

Butterfly didn't answer him, because she had ice in her eyes. And it had always been that way. She never showed love or kindness to him, and when he fucked her, she just stiffened up. She would lie still, and he would pour his seed in her while grunting over her. It was nasty to think about!

"I've been calling all over the place looking for you. I thought you were dead. But your mother happened to call me, and she slipped up and said that she had been writing you. And I pressed the issue, and she finally told me the truth. How could you do this to me?" His eyes were pathetic, and as always, he looked sick or ill, and when he looked that way, Butterfly felt sorry for him! Imagine that, the prey feeling sorry for the predator's hunger, knowing that it was at the destruction of its own life that the predator could feel happy and whole.

Butterfly was so mad and indisposed that she didn't recognize until after a second that Atwater had been watching her secretly for a while. Was that jealousy in his eyes? Because he wouldn't have known the relation between her and her uncle.

"What family? Have you forgotten that my father disowned me?" Tears welled in Butterfly's eyes, and

211

she hated that he had come to visit her.

"I've never disowned you. I don't care what your father did. I've always been here for you. I've always loved you unconditionally."

"Why are you here?" Butterfly couldn't take any more. "Do you want me to sit on your lap?" Butterfly said seductively, but she still had ice in her eyes.

He was embarrassed. "This is the wrong place to discuss or say something like that." He looked around to see if anybody was looking. And Atwater was looking right at him. "You know better than to put family business out in the public like that. Did you check your institutional trust fund account? I put money on your account."

"I have plenty of money, and I don't need yours." As usual her uncle would pour gifts and money on her to get her to accept the fact that he would always be her benefactor.

"Why are you so evil-spirited? I've only raised you to love the Lord and do God's will."

"Don't come back here anymore. If you do, I don't know what I might do to you." Butterfly gave him a look that could kill, and for the first time, her uncle realized that she wasn't a kid anymore.

Butterfly got up and ran to the back to terminate her visit. She was crying, and she didn't want anybody to see her cry. She just ran.

\* \* \* \* \* \* \*

"There that boy is again," Shonda said, who had been eating lunch with Atwater. For some reason, she felt her life was tied to Butterfly's, but she could never understand what the feeling meant.

Atwater was worried about Butterfly, but he didn't

# BUTTERFLY

give himself away. "What?"

"Turn around and look before *it* leaves."

Atwater turned to see who he knew was there. He played it off. "What? It's just a fag. What you tripping for?"

But Shonda knew something. "I didn't like the look he gave me."

# MICHAEL A. ROBINSON

## Chapter Thirty-Five |
### *It Starts Out Good*

Butterfly and Atwater signaled to each other when they left the visiting room that they would meet each other at the automatic machine at pill line. Since it was the weekend, they wouldn't be able to have privacy.

Atwater had got there before Butterfly had arrived. The night was chilly, but spring was setting in. Butterfly had on a jacket that made her look flimsy and little. She had gained back her color from when she had run out of the visit, and the thought of seeing her run out of the visit had been egging at Atwater all day.

This time Butterfly didn't stand behind Atwater in the line as she usually did, but she stood at his side.

"So that's your wife?" Butterfly knew the answer because this was the second time she had seen them together.

"What I tell you about not saying hello and seeing how I'm doing first before you start getting all crazy and shit? But yeah, that's my wife."

"You look happy with her. You sure you got time for me?"

"Yo, real talk, I'm trying to get back to the unit so that I can handle the business at hand. Did you get the pictures I told you to bring?"

Butterfly took out six pictures and handed them to him.

"That's my baby girl. These are perfect."

"Perfect for you. Ya already with somebody else."

# BUTTERFLY

Butterfly's admission was a slip, but on too many occasions she had let him know that she loved him and wanted to be with him.

Atwater studied her for a while. "Come on, I'm gonna walk with you to pill line. What's really on your mind? I'm a little amped up about all this, and I forgot to ask you about your visit. Who was that, that came to visit you today? And why did you run out?"

"That's my uncle and it's a long story." That neither one of them had time to talk about. "And don't change the subject. I said you're already with somebody."

"Don't start tripping on me now. This is a complicated and complex situation as it is, but Shonda got twenty-two years with me. But she ain't no threat to you when it comes to my heart. I got a big piece cut out just for you. But I'm not trying to crash twenty-two years of being with her over two months of being with you.

"I'm throwing this ad on the net to see how we handle challenges together. Shonda, on the other hand, is tried and tested. I just need you to trust me. Keep your head clear and stress free. You're with me?"

Butterfly waited before she answered his question. She nodded.

"You're gonna let me hit that tomorrow."

Butterfly smiled and they walked to the pill line.

After they had left the pill line, Atwater hurried back to call his home boy Tyler. He had to stand in line to wait for a phone to become available. The unit was as loud as ever, and he was just anxious to speak with his partner.

Tyler's phone rang twice before he answered it, and after the automated operator said the call was from jail,

# MICHAEL A. ROBINSON

Tyler pressed five to accept the phone call.

"What's up?" Tyler said.

"I'm chilling. What's going on with you?" Atwater asked.

"Apple snacks and money stacks. What's on your mind? I sent that money to Shonda."

"Good look. I got some pictures, and I want you to start a website. You could either do a Facebook, but I don't know none of that shit."

"Dog, you already got enough flicks of yourself to last you a lifetime on your Facebook."

"It ain't for me. It's for a boy. I'm trying to get paid. So when you put him on, make sure you put out an All-Points Bulletin for all tricks and johns."

It was making sense to Tyler what Atwater was talking about, but it took a minute to dawn on him.

"Mace, you coming out of the closet on me?"

He didn't know whether to laugh or cry. "Fuck no! But even if I were, after eighteen years, I'd deserve to indulge. But real talk, I got this boy in here who looks better than Rihanna. You'll see in a couple of days. Put the pictures on the net and in a couple of weeks I'll send you a list of johns who I want you to request as friends."

"Nigga, you done lost your mind in there." Tyler laughed. "How the boy look?"

"I just told you: as pretty as a little girl." They laughed. Atwater knew he could tell Tyler anything, and Tyler would never judge him.

"Don't be bringing nothing to the streets. They'll have your ass sucked up looking like ET on crack."

"Don't worry about that. I got a hefty supply of jimmies, provided by the BOP."

# BUTTERFLY

"Don't let me find out you're catching as well as pitching."

"Ah, that's some shit, nigga! Fuck you . . . I got to go. I'll send the flicks."

"Love." Tyler said as he ended the call.

Atwater was feeling himself, he knew he was about to get paid off Butterfly.

*The Plan Unleashed . . . Phaze One...*

The next morning, Atwater had gone to work and when he got there, Butterfly didn't want to do anything else but suck on his dick. She had been adamant, and once they shut the door, she pushed him on the ground and sucked his dick until he was cumming back and forth.

He had to talk to her, but he kept nutting so hard as she gurgled his tender dick in the back of her throat. His orgasm balled up and then it shot out in loads, and he pleaded for her to stop. She'd laugh because she knew nobody could compare to the head and satisfaction that she gave. And she knew she would make it impossible for his wife to ever be able to please him truly as she had. And that was the thought that kept his dick in her mouth for hours on end.

She then dressed his dick with a condom, and she shoved it up her ass. She rode his pony like a sex-crazed girl, and when he thought he could nut no more, she had him begging her to stop. But she couldn't because his dick was hard as steel and she loved the feel of it barreling down in her stomach, and it took her breath away and she had gotten so much pleasure by seeing him pleased.

"I can't take anymore." It didn't sound like something a man who had just did eighteen years would say, but Butterfly had a way of making a person feel like he was exhausted.

She laughed. "You don't want no more of this soft ass?"

He cried, because the sound of her voice made his dick stiffen again. She got on all fours and purred like a cat and wiggled her ass and giggled, and blinked her eyes at him.

"Fuck!" He had to hit that. He stood up and kneeled enough to slide his dick inside of her and went all the way to the hilt. He dug inside her and she pulled his arms tight around her and he held her breasts and fucked her good. She gave it back to him, and gnarled at him. "Fuck me harder, faster!"

"What that dick feel like?"

"Feels like thunder's rumbling in my stomach, and a jackhammer smashing into my ass."

But Butterfly would feel her orgasm building by the incessant pounding and she tried to give as much of her ass to him until she felt it building and building and then she released it on to the floor as she cried. He placed his hand on her mouth, because she was going to give them away. But she couldn't help it. His dick was so hard in her and her body melted under him. She cried and sucked on his fingers, and he pounded and pounded until his charge had discharged and he collapsed on her back.

"I could fuck you all day," Butterfly said when she came to herself.

He sighed. "I don't have any energy to get off the ground. Damn, I wish you were here my whole bit. It

# BUTTERFLY

wouldn't even have felt like I was in jail."

Butterfly laughed. "This is like cheating them out of the time they gave us. Sometimes when I'm in here with you, I don't even feel like I'm doing time. I feel like I'm just away on vacation. Take it out," Butterfly said as she wiggled her hips and he slipped out of her with a moan.

"How you know I was finished?"

"You are, because if you weren't, I'd finish you off with my mouth."

"I could take another hour."

"I bet you could." She laughed.

"Turn around so I can look at you." It was Atwater's first time saying that. Although she lay naked in front of him many times before, he had never asked her to take a look at her whole body.

"For what?" She was still apprehensive.

"Turn around."

She turned and it was the first time he had ever looked at her whole body. "What is that?" He laughed because it didn't look like much of a penis.

"It's a dick," Butterfly said with an attitude.

"A baby's dick, if that."

"Go ahead and lick it then." They laughed.

When they were finished clowning around, Atwater looked at Butterfly for who she was. It didn't make sense, but this was a human being with fears, and a love for life. A being who wanted to be loved and cherished and who, as with everybody else, hated to be judged.

And Atwater had been raised to hate gays. It was taught to him by his friends, family, and everywhere else he went. He had remembered when he was young, and he would tease certain boys because they acted like girls.

But now that he was here with Butterfly, he couldn't explain what he had felt for her. He had to question everything. Why would God create them? And if it was so bad to be gay or if it was a defect, the defect was none other than God's defect himself.

He kissed Butterfly passionately, and he thought if he could actually love her stronger than he did his wife. And when he thought of that, he laughed to himself. It was a trip, but he wanted to know more about her, something that went beyond their fuck-crazed days together.

"That day at the visit, why did you run out of there like that?"

By now, Butterfly was snuggled in his arms, and if jail was supposed to be meant as a punishment, she'd take this form of punishment over having liberty.

"I told you it was a long story."

Atwater looked her in her eyes. "I want to know everything about you."

When he said that, Butterfly couldn't think of anything else but when Clayton had said that to her also. That was the time when he had fallen head over heels for her and chose her over his family. And if it was up to her, she would have never made him choose between her and his family. Love shouldn't be based on a condition of entanglement and choosing between other people. Love should be free and for all. And it was a feeling that made her emotional, and as she looked into Atwater's eyes, she felt that this was going to end the same way that her relationship with Clayton ended. Because people would never let them be them. It would be different had Atwater been truly gay, but it

# BUTTERFLY

wasn't the case. The only reason she felt like he was with her was because she looked like a girl. He wasn't with her because she was a man, as was the case with her for why she was with him.

She loved the musk of a man, the hardness of their bodies, and she wasn't fooling anybody to believe that Atwater would ever accept in his mind that he was gay. It was far from the truth, and she couldn't blame him, because she'd never date a gay man. She had slept with Buffy and Britney. But not sexually because there was nothing that turned her on about them. They were bitches too. And that was it. She couldn't date a gay man any more than he could, and by the grace of her womanly fortune, she had Atwater's love.

"Why are you ignoring my question?"

"I don't know?" She brushed away a tear, and he wiped it away. "I just don't like talking about when I was a kid. I have a lot of nightmares about being young. I'm looking at myself for the first time dressed as a woman, and my father comes in and busts me and he beats me senseless. But the nightmare isn't a dream. It really happened to me."

Atwater didn't want to rush her. He wanted her to come clean in her own time.

"My uncle is a pastor of a famous church. When I was seven years old he molested me."

"That punk ass nigga!" Atwater said, angry. "Muthafuckas like that should be killed."

"I know. But the sad thing is that he was the only one who ever showed me genuine love. I took the abuse to win his affection, because I didn't feel like I was worth receiving love from anybody else."

"Damn, I'd never know it was that fucked up for

being you. I can't imagine, because the first time I saw you I thought you were a woman, and it took me a second to realize that this is a men's jail."

"That's my blessing and my curse at the same time. If people could just tell I was born a man, they'd know and they wouldn't get close enough to me if they didn't like the idea. But because I look so much like a woman, people get close and when they find out—"

"I know. But fuck that shit. Fuck your uncle—he was fucking a seven-year-old *boy*." Atwater sighed, and he wanted to murder him. It hurt him to his core.

"I hate my uncle and love him at the same time. It hurts when I hear you say fuck him. I don't know—it's just how I feel. He'd make me suck his dick, and then he'd fuck me in the ass. I guess he regretted it because he'd always spoil me with all kinds of presents.

"I know his wife Debra knew, but she acted like she didn't. They could never have kids, and I was the closest thing to their child."

"Like I said: fuck him and her. There's only one way for us to get back at the muthafuckas who raped us. We have to get power. We have to use wealth to increase our power, and we have to use our power to get back at all the people who did us wrong."

"Mace, what are you talking about? Who did you wrong?"

"I just did eighteen years, and you're going to ask me that question? The system did me wrong! This shit is bullshit! They found me in a house with drugs that wasn't mine and because they didn't have anybody to put it on, they put it on me. But instead of them saying that it was a possession charge, they put me on some big conspiracy and fucked me over.

"And you're gonna help me get them back."

Butterfly lightened to the idea. She'd help him any way he needed.

"What do I have to do?"

"First, we're going to get a decent savings of money. I'm going to request some tricks and johns to your web page, and when they come up here to visit you, you're going to run game on them."

"How? What am I going to tell them?"

"You see how you're excited now? I want you to act just like that when they come and see you. You have to be very flirtatious, touchy, and they have to be the only ones who exist in this world. I have a list of johns who are millionaires."

"Where did you get the list from?"

"Don't worry about that. I have my means. But when you go out there you have to be assertive, and you can't ever give them time to think and place details together. You have to control the conversation and always keep the topic on sex. And this is what you're going to tell them . . ."

# MICHAEL A. ROBINSON

## Chapter Thirty-Six |
### *Dear John*

Butterfly had been kind of nervous because she didn't know what to expect. But Atwater told her that the Johns had responded to her ad as he had expected they would. When Atwater had spoken to Tyler, Tyler couldn't believe that Butterfly was the *boy* that he was talking about on the phone.

Two weeks later was Butterfly's first visit. Butterfly wore her skintight pants, and her busts were full in her shirt, and her hair and makeup were nice.

She entered the visit room and waited in a chair in a corner by the vending machine. When the middle-aged black man came in, she didn't know if he was the trick until he looked directly at her and the lust in his eyes said it all.

Smartly dressed in expensive digs, the chubby man wore wire-framed glasses. He looked like the type that would fumble a ball if he had ever played football.

"You're prettier in person than in your picture. You're beautiful," he said and she could tell that he was nervous by the way he kept looking all over the place.

As Atwater had instructed, she was as flirtatious as ever. "I couldn't wait to see you. Your letters got me so hot and horny." She brushed against his dick as she hugged him and they sat down. "Here, let me see you without your glasses. My god! Now I can imagine you fucking me." Butterfly was doing her job all too well, and she had him stumbling for words. She led the conversation from the minute they sat down!

# BUTTERFLY

"When? When can I fuck you? I wanted you the minute I saw your picture. When are you going to get out? I keep asking you, and you keep avoiding my question."

Butterfly slid her hand between his legs and felt his snub dick that was hard in his britches. "I'm scared to tell you the truth. If I tell you, promise me that you won't leave me?" Butterfly's eyes sparkled, and she massaged his dick in his pants.

"I swear to God! Just tell me when!" He felt that he would nut in his pants as he pictured her mouth wrapped around his dick, and he felt sick.

"I have eight more years to do."

"What?" His shock was apparent.

"See, you lied! That's why I didn't want to tell you in the first place. Now you hate me." Butterfly took her hand off his pulsating dick. He felt like she had shattered his heart. He was minutes away from nutting right there on the spot, and Butterfly knew it!

"I don't hate you. I'm a bit shocked, that's all. I just want to know if I could do anything to get you out sooner? I mean, anything?" His passion was real, and he had desperation written in his eyes.

"There's an attorney that keeps promising me that he can get me out, but I'm a foster kid. It's not like I have family who'd pay him. Nobody loves me enough to help me." Butterfly then brushed her lips against his. Her seductive and blatant behavior should have compelled the COs to have ended their visit a long time ago. But the COs sat there and watched because they got a laugh from it.

"Are you sure he can do what he promises? How much time did he say he could get you?"

225

"I'm sure. He's the best, and he promised me that he could get me out in under six months."

"Give me his info, and I'll arrange everything."

It was just as Atwater had said he'd do, and Atwater already had all the information she'd need to give him to send the money and set everything up. This excited Butterfly all the more.

"You don't understand. He's a high profile attorney, and he's very expensive."

The John smirked. No money was too much for him. "What's expensive?"

"He told me to give him a $25k just to retain him. That doesn't include all the legal papers and process after that." By now Butterfly had her hand on his dick again, massaging it. His eyes fluttered. She couldn't tell if he had nutted in his pants or if he was about to.

"As I said." He composed himself. "Just give me his info. I want you home, and I'll do anything to that end."

"When I come home, daddy, are you going to pull my hair when you fuck me?"

He was choked up. He never wanted to fuck anybody in his life more! "I'd love to."

"I can't wait! You'll do all that for me?" She kissed him on his lips, and his mind was gone.

Later on that night, Butterfly had met Atwater at the money machine, and she couldn't wait to tell him how much of a success she had been. She told him everything that had happened, and he let her know that he had a different John coming the following day. It was all too fun to her, and she was happy she could help him out in whatever he was doing. The only apprehension she had was

# BUTTERFLY

any of the Johns finding out it was a scam and doing something to her.

## *Those Who Accomplish to Plan, Plan to Accomplish...*

Several weeks had passed and everything that Atwater had said was happening. He had arranged for somebody on the streets to act as an attorney, and the money poured in. Butterfly was juggling six multi-millionaires. It was funny because to give a $100k to her legal fund presented no problem to them. She had begged Atwater over the weeks that followed to tell her where he had gotten the list of the rich tricks, but Atwater wouldn't relent! It drove her crazy, because she felt like she had no power in the situation but to be a ploy in his game, but she loved him all the more for it.

Butterfly thought she had been doing well for herself while modeling, but the most she had ever made was $2k at any one gig, and usually she never made that much. But she wasn't really a big spender, and her uncle had always bought her big item wants, like cars. He paid her rent and had given her plenty of plastic. But now, the bank account that Atwater had set up for her on the streets had almost $200k, and she knew that he had stashed away another $300k for himself. It just seemed unreal that she didn't have to have sex with these guys or go out with them. She just had to go on a visit and give them the impression that she would rock their worlds once she was out. This was the easiest money ever. She didn't even have to read or respond to the letters they sent, because Atwater had paid a few people who wrote the guys back around the clock. The letters were always sex-ridden and charged with underlying adventure that kept the guys in a trance and on her trail.

She and Atwater had accomplished something, and their relationship became more than just fucking and sex. They would sit up all day and talk about how she should go to the next visit and what she should say, do, etc. It was all too amazing for her. She loved the way his mind worked. And he was never conquered, not by his situation or any circumstance. He just saw past everybody and focused on what he'd do. He was a very special person.

Atwater had over $300k that he stashed in a bank under an alias. He didn't want to get released on Supervised Release so his probation officer could track his movement by tracking his money. He wanted to do a lot with that money, and he had to be discreet. He had big plans, and what he was doing now was just the beginning!

Things were getting a little wild though. He couldn't really stay on the down-low with Butterfly because of the simple fact that he had to communicate with her more effectively, and to wait to have a five minute conversation with her at the money machine while she was going to pill line, limited his communication with her. And the money that they had rolling in, he thought: *fuck what anybody thought!*

It was time for him to splurge a bit, and he called his wife Shonda.

"Hey baby. You are truly too much!" She sounded excited and he knew why.

"Tyler must have gotten those things to you guys?"

"I'm wearing the diamond necklace and the bracelet right now. Mason and Macy didn't wait five minutes to leave after the BMWs you bought them showed up. This scares me."

He should have known. "Shonda, chill out and enjoy what I got for you. I promise it's all good."

"I hope it doesn't have anything to do with Tyler because I'll give it back!"

Atwater laughed. "All right, I'll call him right now and tell him to come back and get everything."

"Well, just let me keep the bracelet." They laughed. "Just tell me that when you come home you're never ever going to go back to jail?"

"I promise, baby. I'm going to tuck you in every single night. Damn, what's that I hear in the background? Sounds like water."

Shonda smiled. "I'm taking a hot bubble bath, and I'm drinking champagne."

"Ooo-weeee! I have three weeks and I can't wait."

"Just remember that you promised to tuck me in at night," Shonda said seductively.

"I want to tuck you in right now. Slide your hand between your thighs and tell me how hot and wet the tub is."

"I'll tell you how hot and wet it is, if you tell me what you're going to do to me when you get out."

"After or before the candlelit dinner?"

"After, baby," Shonda moaned as she massaged her pussy and imagined it was Atwater sucking on it. The phone call ended with the sound of her climaxing and Atwater's simmering plans once he was released in three weeks.

***Out Of The Closet And On To The Floor…***

# MICHAEL A. ROBINSON

"Atwater is a good man and a hustler, let me tell you," Buffy said as she took another gulp of the strong and savory jailhouse hooch that had him feeling good.

Britney, Buffy, and Butterfly were in their cell eating a lavish nacho bowl with refried beans, melted cheese, chopped vegetables, diced beef and turkey log over nacho chips. Butterfly had paid somebody to make her a sweet potato pie, and they sat around drinking hooch and were all feeling good.

"Ain't that the truth. Butterfly has been able to put money on my account, and I've spent my commissary limit three times in a row. If I keep this up, I'm going to tell Mrs. Bowers to go to hell with that Unicor job. I'll just sit here all day and eat, drink, and get fucked," Britney said as all three of them laughed.

"Yes, Mace is my hero," Butterfly added.

"He must be"—She smacked—"because he has you geeking on his dick. Bitch, you act like you too good to get high with us now."

"He don't want me to! He doesn't like when I do that stuff, but he don't mind if I drink a little."

Britney mimicked her. "He don't like when I do that stuff."

"Maybe he needs an X-pill and to fuck you with a choo-choo train of other niggas to relax his ass, let me tell you!"

"Fuck you, freak bitch. All this is enough for him." Butterfly smacked her fine ass. "And he's enough for me. He don't need X."

"Oh, he likes deep pussy, huh?" They all laughed and Butterfly had flipped Britney the finger. "I'm just playing, girl. He's really good for you. Since you've been with him you've been taking care of yourself and

# BUTTERFLY

looking superb and your confidence has went through the roof."

Buffy smacked her lips. "I wish I had a dick that could transport me," Buffy said.

"You got Ray Ray's stank ass," Britney said, trying to sound encouraging.

"Please!" Buffy said.

"He ain't no Mace," Butterfly added, smiling at her luck.

"But Butterfly, you have to worry about that pretty bitch he's going home to."

"Why you bringing that up, stank 'ho?" Britney asked the obvious.

"It's the truth, let me tell you. He's been with her a long time."

"And I hate it! But he's with me now, and he loves fucking me. That bitch will never be able to replicate what I do." Butterfly had a real attitude and a jealous streak.

"I know what you mean, gurgle-throat," Buffy said. They all laughed.

"Who told you that?" Butterfly was surprised.

"Love told me while I was sucking his dick. He told me that I don't gurgle in the back of my throat while he's busting a nut. I ain't never heard no shit like that, bitch. But I'll be sure to learn it, let me tell you."

"Gurgling in the back of your throat!" Britney said, as if hurt that Butterfly could hold such a technique to herself.

"Trade secrets, bitch. Gurgle in your ass," Buffy said, and they all laughed.

# MICHAEL A. ROBINSON

## Chapter Thirty-Seven |
*Down-Low Suspect*

In jail, whispers create rumors and rumors create
what prisoners take as hard core facts. When the
whispers started about Atwater and Butterfly
meeting every night at the automatic money machine,
and him accompanying her to pill line at times, and
that he was locked up with Butterfly in the chapel's
library during the morning hours, Atwater had come
under suspicion.

The suspicion first came from the Moors, which was
the organization he was not only a member of, but a
leading official. Then Craze-zo started to get a whiff of
it.

Atwater knew that he was weeks away from going
home, and he didn't like the fact that his reputation
was getting tarnished. But it was something that came
with the territory.

He knew that if he just put money on a number of
individuals' accounts, it would all be hush-hush. But
even when he tried to put money on Craze-zo's
account, Craze-zo had become even more suspicious.
And the rumors had finally surfaced, and that's when
Craze-zo brought the issue to him.

They were about to lift weights, and Craze-zo
couldn't put the thought behind him.

"Moor, cuz, I've been hearing some strange shit, and
I don't know if to believe them, or just take it as some
hating ass niggas that we need to holler at with some
straps. But niggas is saying that you fucking with that
punk, Butterfly." Craze-zo kept his eyes on Atwater

because he wanted to see his reaction. He had to read his partner, no matter what his partner said.

"Fucking with the punk . . ." Atwater looked his little partner straight in the face. "Like what?"

"Atwater, what you mean like what?" The shit was too much to grasp for young Craze-zo. And his nigga whom he would have rode to the depths of hell with, didn't give him an outright "no" answer. He couldn't believe that he could have fallen victim to some fag shit!

"Craze-zo, the shit is bigger than what you think. But trust me when I tell you that I ain't gonna ever do something that'd be on some punk shit."

"Come on, Atwater. Give me more than that. We're like fam'."

"Sit down." They were standing by the squat rack, and there was a bench at the side of it.

Atwater sat down and Craze-zo sat next to him. "I'm pimping the punk."

It took Craze-zo a minute to digest what he had just heard, and it was worse than what he'd thought. "Cuz, you're getting money to let fools run trains on him like what happened to him in 4B?"

"No, I ain't no sucker like that. I'm gonna let you in on what's going on, so you'll be on point. I got a list of millionaire punks that I got from the white boy who works in education. I put a couple of Butterfly's flicks on a social website and gave him the game. You know I work in the chapel with him, so I've been giving him the game. I've made $80k off him already." Atwater underestimated the money. If he had said the real amount, he knew Craze-zo wouldn't have believed his story.

# MICHAEL A. ROBINSON

It was a sigh of relief for Craze-zo. He didn't believe for one second that his partner had fallen victim, and now it was all confirmed. "I'm glad to hear that. They was saying it like you was fucking the punk or something."

"Never that. I can't take nothing home to wifey. That's my word!"

"I don't know why I ever doubted you in the first. You my nigga."

And that was how he had kept Craze-zo's respect and friendship with a lie. He knew that Craze-zo wouldn't be ready for the truth, and he knew the best thing would be to lie.

"And I'll show you how a real nigga do it. I'm going to have my partner send you a gee to show you how I'm living."

"A gee, my nigga!"

"Yeah, get some new shoes and send your son something."

They worked out, and after they had finished, they were about to leave when Old School called Atwater.

"Got a sec, Atwater?"

"Yeah. Craze, I'll be right back. Hold up a minute."

Atwater ran into the gym where Old School was sitting in the bleachers and a couple of guys were playing one-on-one.

When Atwater sat at his side, Old School said, "You know everybody's talking about you and that boy?"

"I ain't trippin', old timer. I'm getting money though. She's an investment to me, and I want these fools to know not to mess around with mine."

"I know you're sharp, Atwater, and I thank you for

# BUTTERFLY

the eight grand you put on my books."

"It's nothing, old timer."

"No, listen. I really appreciate that shit. And you're going to have to start feeding your wolves around here just in case some drama pops off."

"I already know, and I'm already over it. It feels good to be able to look out and have something put away for when I get out next week. And when I hit the streets, I'm gonna show you innovation. I'm taking my pimping to the next level. And I ain't like the fools that say they're gonna do something for you and never give back. Trust me. When I get out, I got you, Old School."

"You make me proud." They embraced.

"I'm about to continue on my journey," Atwater said.

Old School laughed, because he knew the obstacles that lay ahead of Atwater. And he knew it was going to be very difficult.

# MICHAEL A. ROBINSON

## Chapter Thirty-Eight |
### *The Day Was Naughty*

Atwater was too close to going home. He only had two more days, and the thought was killing him.

Butterfly, on the other hand, was getting her head together for being left in jail all alone. She knew it would be a challenge in itself, but one that she was willing to take. She had gone to work and she and Kathy were rearranging the chapel's library. They were trying to make more room for more religious apparatus that had come in.

Kathy wore tight slacks, doorknocker earrings, and a smart blouse. She looked like the kind of middle-aged white girl who'd be married to an NBA star. She had scaled a small ladder to put some books on the top shelf.

"Put this in the Catholic section. Can you reach it?" Butterfly asked.

"Yes, I got it. I'm not that short." Kathy's blouse loosened from her slacks and Butterfly could see the skin of her butt.

"Damn, girl, you got an ass of steel."

Kathy laughed. "Almost as big as yours." And she got down from the ladder.

"No, you got me," Butterfly joked. "Everybody on the compound says you got the phattest ass."

"I don't believe you. My hips are only thirty-six! Here, let me feel yours. Umph, it feels good." Kathy grabbed Butterfly's ass and held on to it.

"Okay, girl, let my ass go," Butterfly joked, looking

# BUTTERFLY

at her strangely.

"I don't really want to," Kathy said, giving Butterfly a weird look.

Butterfly had to be blunt with her. "Are you coming on to me?"

"You've never ever thought about being with a woman?"

This was the worst thing that Butterfly could have imagined possible. "Have a seat." After they sat, Butterfly broke it down to her. "You have to understand that I'm a woman that's trapped inside a man's body. If I were to even think about being with a woman, it would seem completely weird to me. I love men and men only.

"Plus, you're my girl and without you, I wouldn't have ever known this love that I have for Mace. And it goes beyond words, my appreciation for you."

"I don't know what I was thinking," Kathy said. "It's just that you have this strong sexual aura. And I want to tell you the honest truth. Lately, when I make love to my husband, all I can see is your face. I'm always turned on when I'm around you. You just seem so exotic and erotic. It's just a spell."

Kathy couldn't tell her the rest! She hadn't yet felt embarrassed to tell her what she already had, but if she had continued, she would have said how she thought Butterfly was so beautiful and how she wanted to see Butterfly get ravished by Atwater in front of her while she watched and played with a dildo at the same time. The thought was unnerving and she felt the moisture between her thighs fall, and she had to cross her legs. Kathy followed every word that came off Butterfly's lips, and she wanted to feel those fluffy, velvet lips kiss all over her body; starting from her perk tits, to her full mound between her legs! It was all stimulating and mesmerizing at the same time, but it was just shadows overcast over her sex life. She didn't know what she'd do, but the thought lingered, and it was one that had to be fulfilled.

She wished Lazy Eyes was still here so that she could tell him what she always wanted to tell him: that she wanted him to fuck her with raucous abandon while Butterfly fucked her in the ass. And it would amount to double penetration and double the orgasmic relief!

Butterfly smiled, full of herself. "Really?" Butterfly asked, thinking it was funny that even women were attracted to her.

Kathy shook her head, looking intoxicating, sultry, and her eyes were like a romantic evening sky. It was just that she was extremely horny, and hell had raised her temperature to the level of fever.

"Lock that door. I want to show you something."

Butterfly studied her for a minute. Seeing mischief behind Kathy's eyes, which she didn't trust, she hesitated to comply. But she had gotten up and put the 'Do Not Disturb' sign on the door and locked it.

"What you want to show me?" Butterfly asked suspiciously.

"Look how wet I am around you." Kathy unfastened her slacks, pulled them down, and stepped out of them. Her body was perfect.

She looked like a model from a *Curve's Magazine*. Butterfly couldn't help but be slightly turned on, and the thought was weird to her.

"You have a great body."

"Come here, Butterfly. I won't bite you. I want to

# BUTTERFLY

show you something."

It took Butterfly a moment to start moving her legs, but she moved closer to Kathy, who took her hand and placed it between her thighs. Her pussy was soaking wet and the moisture had seeped through her hot pink G-string.

"Girl, a woman's pussy gets wet like that?" It was Butterfly's first time ever touching a woman's pussy. She had never seen one except on TV.

"You've never touched a woman's pussy?" Kathy was shocked.

"Why would I?"

"Here, I'll show you more." Kathy pulled down her G-string. Then she took off her blouse and then her bra. There was no fat on her tanned body, and her pussy was plump and shaved.

"Kathy, girl, this shit is turning me on. Put your clothes back on." Butterfly, who always thought that women made her feel nauseated was feeling an urge that she had never felt before, and she didn't like it at all!

"Kiss me."

"I ain't kissing a woman!" Butterfly protested, but it was too late because Kathy had already kissed her.

At first Kathy's kiss felt weird, but Kathy tasted good. The kiss turned passionate and Kathy grabbed Butterfly's breasts and soft ass. The gesture relaxed Butterfly and she . . . she . . . she . . . didn't know exactly what gave her the urge to do something that had crossed her mind a number of times. But she went along with the urge, and she touched Kathy's pussy. It was clammy, soft, and wet like a bog, but it was wonderful to touch and get an immediate reaction from Kathy, who moaned

239

softly and grinded into her fingers. Butterfly slid one of her fingers into Kathy's pussy and it felt slick and tender, and she couldn't imagine how an ass could feel as good as a pussy for a man.

It awakened a new curiosity inside Butterfly to want to understand women better, because her body limited her in so many ways. She pulled Kathy down to the ground and kissed all over her short body until she made her way down to her pussy. She stuck her tongue into the pussy. It was slimy and gooey, but the reaction she got from Kathy made her want to continue. Kathy pulled her face against her pussy and fucked Butterfly's lips. Butterfly thought she would suffocate from how hard Kathy had grinded into her face, and then she felt Kathy's body shiver uncontrollably. Her pussy gushed out in anguish, and a stream of pussy juice shot in Butterfly's face. It was wet, murky, powerful, and it took all that Kathy had not to scream out loudly.

"Girl, what was that?"

"That's a woman's orgasm," Kathy responded as she panted for air.

"I'm talking about this stuff on my face."

Kathy laughed. "You hit my G-spot."

Kathy leaned up and licked her juices from Butterfly's lips, still turned on. Butterfly thought she was a nympho. Kathy went and turned the lights off and then started to undress Butterfly, who laughed because she was still embarrassed and thought this was all crazy.

"What are you doing, Kathy?"

"Just hush up," Kathy said playfully.

Butterfly lay on her back after she was completely

naked. Kathy trailed her fingers gently over Butterfly's skin and her goose bumps loosened. She kissed all over Butterfly's nipples, and she kissed the softest and fluffiest lips she'd ever kiss before. It was more than thought-provoking, that lips could be so powerful, soft, succulent and fluffy all at the same time. Kathy made her way down to Butterfly's teeny-tiny penis and rested it in her mouth. She ran her tongue under the head. It felt incredibly good!

"Girl . . ." Butterfly wasn't too sure of the feeling and the feeling was heightened when Kathy stuck three of her fingers in her ass and started to fuck her with them while she fondled one of Butterfly's breasts with her free hand.

Butterfly felt her whole body throbbing uncontrollably and she beat her thighs into the whirling of Kathy's tongue and her fingers that slammed into her ass. Butterfly couldn't contain it anymore. She shot a wad down Kathy's throat, and she bit down on her own clothes so that she wouldn't cry out! As Kathy's tongue lingered and whirled, she had Butterfly in the grips of a screeching orgasm three minutes later.

"Kathy, that was wonderful!" Butterfly said. Kathy spit out her cum in the trashcan, and then she lay at Butterfly's side trying to catch her breath, as well as Butterfly.

"I thought it would be. You know there's more," she said.

Butterfly thought there was no way in hell that she was going to fuck a girl. It was unlikely to happen anyways, because her dick was so terribly small.

"I'm fine with what we've just done."

"Damn, I needed that!" Kathy exclaimed. She

# MICHAEL A. ROBINSON

couldn't help but think how very tired she was of fucking her husband. She had been taken with having an excellent body, and she worked out and took supplements to achieve those results. Her husband, on the other hand, couldn't care less, and plus, Kathy had other needs. She had a hunger that was exciting, adventurous, and wild. She just wasn't able to tell him that she thought about Butterfly, Lazy Eyes, and now Atwater, when they had sex.

"You have a freak inside you, Kathy." Butterfly laughed so hard and full that it was impossible for her to stop laughing.

"You laugh like that's bad or something."

"It's not that at all. But I should've known something was up with you. You have that perfect body, and you can't keep it preserved like that for nothing."

"It is for nothing. I've tried to be honest with my husband one time, and I told him that maybe we should consider becoming swingers. And he went berserk."

Butterfly laughed. "What did you think he'd say?"

"I don't know. I didn't even think about it."

"I can't believe we just did that. But I can't lie, it was different."

"Different? Is that all?" Kathy was shocked and pleased as well.

"I don't think women are for me. I'm strictly-dickly." They laughed and Kathy sat up.

"How is it being with black guys?"

Butterfly couldn't believe the question. "You've never slept with a Black man?"

"You had never slept with a woman, so don't act surprised."

"That's fair. But it's different."

242

# BUTTERFLY

"Here we go with it's 'different' again." They laughed.

"Not like that, girl. I mean, my first love, Clayton was white. I've had sex with him a thousand times before. It's different with him and Black men because Black dick feels like fire's inside you." They laughed.

"How was Lonny?" Kathy's eyes said it all.

"Girl, don't tell me you were barking up that tree?"

"I can't lie, Bobby. I wanted him so bad! He had the sexiest eyes and smoothest voice. My god—I wanted him." They laughed.

"He was . . . I think he was the best ever." Butterfly wasn't lying. She could remember how he would slam dick into her without end. Damn she still missed him!

"Was he big?"

Butterfly shook her head wanly and smiled. "My— I'm missing out on life!"

Kathy was a true friend. She had shared such a wonderful and vivid experience with Butterfly that would never be forgotten, and she wanted to share something very special with Kathy in return.

"I have something for you . . ."

# Chapter Thirty-Nine |
*Naughty ... Again And Again ...*

The day was still young, and Atwater had to go on what the prison called a Merry-go-Round, which was when an inmate who was about to get released had to go to each department and have them sign him out. He also had to pack out all of his belongings and get everything ready so that he could leave.

He didn't have to go to work anymore, and he knew that even on the streets he'd miss Butterfly's sweet ass for however long they'd be apart, which wasn't that long, considering that she was about to get released in one month.

So he headed over to their honeycomb hideout. When he went to the door of the chapel's library, the 'Do Not Disturb' sign was on the door, and for a minute it threw him for a loop. Atwater placed his ear to the door, but he couldn't hear anything. So he lightly tapped on the door, and seconds later, he heard Butterfly whisper, "Mace, is that you?"

"Yeah."

Butterfly unlocked the door and pulled him in.

Once he was in, candles lit up the room and Butterfly and Kathy were butt naked. They lay on the floor! His jaw dropped in sheer disbelief.

Kathy had always been somebody who had a perfect body, and he had caught himself on a thousand occasions imagining having sex with her. And her body looked ten times better naked. She didn't have an ounce of body fat, and her body had curves in all the right

# BUTTERFLY

places.

"What are you all doing?"

Butterfly laughed and lay back down with Kathy. They kissed. Kathy pushed Butterfly onto her back and climbed on top of her while she grinded her hips against Butterfly. The mere scene made Atwater's penis stiffen in his pants, and he wanted in!

"Atwater, aren't you going to join us?" Kathy asked, wagging her ass as if it were a tail.

Butterfly laughed because she knew this would be the perfect present she could give the both of them.

"What?" he asked, still in disbelief.

Kathy got up and grabbed him. She didn't kiss him or anything, but she went straight for his pants and snatched his dick out before he could even protest.

"Your dick is gigantic!" she said and slammed it into her mouth.

Butterfly went around to indulge in a tasty bit of Kathy's sapping pussy, and the shit was so raw and savage to Atwater!

Kathy placed a condom on him and pushed him down into a chair and turned around to ride him reverse cowgirl. She guided his dick inside herself and rode him while she kissed Butterfly.

"Your dick is like fire!" She slammed her hips down faster into the pending tide. Her body lurched and twisted and she wrung herself of a blinding orgasm as she squeezed Butterfly.

Kathy was so drenched that she collapsed on the ground.

"You can't hang," Butterfly said. Atwater laughed.

Butterfly got on all fours, and after Atwater changed his condom, he kneeled behind her and slammed his dick in her. He fucked her fast and hard and the erotic grunts brought Kathy out of her fatigue. She was revived by the moans between the two.

Butterfly looked back at Atwater and gave it back to him as much as he had given to her. She was feral and savage.

Kathy played with her soaking wet pussy, and she wanted to feel Atwater's ramrod again, or feel Butterfly's fluffy lips! She lay down in front of Butterfly, and Butterfly feasted on her buffet.

Atwater felt the condom burst, and he stopped to put another one on. But while he was putting another one on, Butterfly and Kathy lathered his dick with kisses between the two of them . . . dick worship. He could have split both of their heads if he nutted in their faces, but Butterfly kept coaching Kathy to let Atwater fuck her in the ass. It was too much to think about getting his massive member inside her little asshole. But Butterfly wouldn't accept no, and after Atwater sat back down, Butterfly greased Kathy up and guided Atwater's dick into her ass.

Kathy had to sit up while holding the arm of the chair and resting her feet on Atwater's knees. At first she rode him slow, because his dick was just too big for her. But once Butterfly administered her tongue while Kathy was riding Atwater, Kathy loosened up more and bounced up and down on his dick as fast as she could while Butterfly sucked on her clit. When the contractions of a swift orgasm hit her this time, she gushed all over the place. While she came, Butterfly and Atwater hugged her between the two of them as they kissed. Kathy joined into their kiss, and all three of them were kissing and fucking and the day was naughty!

# BUTTERFLY

## *Don't Leave Him With Nothing...*

Atwater told Butterfly to come back to the chapel after lunch. They had much to talk about. He went back to the unit and thought about what had just happened, and it was an occasion to celebrate. But he had one more day to wait before then. And he had to keep something for Shonda when he went home. He couldn't go home and be shit-faced.

After lunch, he went back to the chapel, and it was just as he thought. Butterfly lay naked on the floor. He didn't have anything left after the earlier escapade that day, and he had much to talk to her about. But Butterfly wouldn't relent. She wanted to suck his dick for what seemed like endless hours, and he nutted two more times. Atwater didn't even know he could nut that much, but Butterfly knew a technique which didn't matter if he had just nutted; she'd use her tongue to tickle the sensitive part of his penis until it stiffened again. She'd keep this up for as long as she liked. He felt she could make him nut twenty or more times, even if nothing came out!

"Suck that big dick!" he coached her and nutted again. "Damn, you got my shit tender as fuck!" And he nutted again.

He had to pull her up because there was no end to her industry. And he needed more brains than wit because he had to talk to her.

"Damn, you ain't trying to leave nothing for Shonda?"

"Now why would I do that?" Butterfly didn't even look convincing.

247

# MICHAEL A. ROBINSON

"How did you get Mrs. Hoover in here?"

"She came on to me! You know I'm strictly-dickly. But did you like it with her?"

"Fuck yeah! She had some wet ass pussy, but her ass ain't like yours." They laughed.

"We have to concentrate. I go home tomorrow. And you'll go home on the 16th of August. I got some plans for you." Atwater snatched his dick out of Butterfly's hands. "Stop fucking with my dick! Stay focused for a minute."

"What!" Butterfly was mad because she wanted to get fucked again. She didn't want to hear of his endless plotting and planning. He was always scamming on something.

"Have you ever thought about being a pimp?"

Butterfly thought the question wasn't only crazy-funny, but she thought it was completely ridiculous! "Are you out of your mind?" she said as she laughed.

"Do I look like I'm laughing?" Atwater was dead fucking serious.

"Hell no, I haven't thought about being a pimp!"

"That's right, because I'm the muthafuckin' pimp, and you're going to be my bottom 'ho." Atwater was convinced. He wouldn't let his bitches plot or rebel or even think about bucking.

"Mace, I ain't 'hoing for you or nobody!" It was too much to think about Atwater wanting their relationship to end on such a horrid note.

"You still don't trust me? You still don't understand greatness when it's right in your face? You still don't know when you're amongst the stars? You still don't understand when the sun is shining on your pretty face? You still don't understand that I'm not going to put either

248

# BUTTERFLY

of us in harm's way? You still don't understand that I've taken you as the pupil of my eye, and tended to your every need? I've been your counselor, your spiritual adviser, your financial adviser and you'd still question me! You think I'm just made of dick and bubble gum? Everything I do is for power and prestige. I haven't done this eighteen year bit to return to the streets and be a fucking gnat on the wall. I'm including you in my endless hours of research and ruminating mind to get everything your heart could ever desire. And you're still questioning me?" Atwater was livid, or at least that's how he was acting. He had known Butterfly too well, and he knew what she'd say before he even asked her. He had silenced her and he knew he had her.

"I'm sorry. I didn't mean it like that."

"You meant it like that!" He got up and dressed as if he was going to leave.

"I'm sorry. Don't leave me! I'm sorry. I'll do it, Mace. I'll do anything you want. Anything!"

Atwater turned his back to Butterfly because it's exactly what he wanted to hear. It's exactly what he had plotted to hear and it fell right into his lap.

He turned around. "What did you say?"

"I said I'll do anything you want. I'm sorry, baby." Butterfly hugged him and held him close.

"You'll fuck a hundred men and will do it happily if I tell you?"

"I'll fuck a thousand men if you want me to."

Atwater studied her to see if there was any sincerity in what she said. The truth couldn't have been gleaned any easier. Butterfly was his bottom 'ho.

"You won't ever question me again? You'd walk naked in the bitter cold until your toes blistered and

# MICHAEL A. ROBINSON

bloodied and you would know that I have the map to the treasure; and you'd follow that map until we got that treasure?"

"I'd do it, Mace." Butterfly kissed him on his neck. "I swear to god I'd do it!"

"Good, because I have a plan."

An hour later, Atwater said goodbye to everybody on the compound who was his friends. He had hit a couple of laps with Craze-zo and told him that when he got out in one year, he could come and live with him and get money. Atwater then went to his brothers in faith and gave them things, and said his goodbyes. He was just anxious, weary, and sleepless. He couldn't wait to get out and prove his merit.

He only had one person who was above all others on the compound who he wanted to see and nobody else mattered. It was Old School. At 7:00 p.m. he had snuck up on Old School in the law library, who was reading the *Wall Street Journal.*

"I don't pray, I prey," Atwater said behind Old School's back, and Old School laughed.

"Prey on the weak, not the strong and the wise, because who else is going to rule the world."

Atwater hugged him and sat at his side. "I'm out tomorrow, Old School."

"Seems like you're going to be leaving me, little brother."

"But not for long. I have something for you. And I ain't like all these pussy ass, weak muthafuckas who say one thing, but when they get out, they do something else. Old School, with my hand over my heart and my hand to Allah, I'm going to get you out of here."

"Sounds like you're saluting an Amerikkkan flag."

250

# BUTTERFLY

"I'm saluting an American hero. I owe you everything. You developed me from nothing."

"The talent has always been there, Atwater. It's in all the brothers, the Hispanics, and all the other underprivileged, but there are those who'd want to keep them in place. Riddle me that."

Atwater smiled cleverly. "I'm going to get you out."

"The powers-that-be . . ."

Atwater interrupted him. "I'm gone, Old School, and I don't want to hear any bullshit defeatist shit. I got you, and you should know that's coming from a man's mouth. You taught me that a real man's words have magical properties to them that could make the impossible possible. Just know that I'm a real man, and it was you who birthed me. You gave me the real resurrection."

Old School had tears in his eyes, and he knew that Atwater was the son he'd never had.

Atwater got up to leave. "I'll see you on the streets."

And that was all that needed to be said. The rest was understood.

## Chapter Forty |
### *And It Was As If—As If, He Had Never Left*

A twater couldn't sleep the whole night. He had been so anxious that he tossed and turned in his bed. To kill some of the tension he was feeling, he had gotten out of the bed around dawn and did push-ups.

Morning had come, and he was out of the cell as soon as the doors popped. He made his rounds around the prison and said goodbye to everybody except Butterfly and Old School.

At 9:00 a.m. he dressed out in Ferragamo threads that Shonda had sent him. Atwater had been processed out of prison, and he stepped out into freedom!

Shonda had pulled up in a crispy white 2014 Mercedes Benz S550. She jumped out of the car and ran into his arms. She didn't even have time to remove her Prada Aviator sunglasses as she held on to him as if life had stopped moving for her.

"You're finally home!" She couldn't believe it.

"And they'll never take me again. Damn, you look good!"

He did a once-over, and she was fine to death. Her hair was pinned down to one side and cascaded over her shoulder in long, soft waves. She wore a black lace blouse that displayed her breasts with taste and a knee-length dress with black platform sandals, earrings, a heart pendant attached to a thin gold chain that hung to her belly, and an edgy and elegant perfume.

"You're going to get in trouble looking that good." Atwater spun her in a circle, but he was ready to get

# BUTTERFLY

away from the prison to make it all official. "Let's get out of here."

Once they got inside the car, he didn't know whose car it was because she drove an Escalade.

"Whose car is this?"

"Yours." She kissed him and they drove off, heading for DC, where they went to a restaurant and ate soul food. From there they went stepping at a small club in Adams Morgan. The DJ played old school R. Kelly, Maxwell, and Sade.

"This reminds me of when we were young," Shonda said as Atwater spun her.

"We still are young." They laughed.

"I'm going to show you in a minute. You just wait." He winked his eye, and he was ready to go to their Marriott Suite on Connecticut Avenue and get it on.

They were all over one another once they were in the elevator going to the suite. They couldn't even walk because they were kissing and fondling each other. Atwater took off each item of his clothes, until he was clad in only boxers. By the time they made it to their suite, a trail of their discarded clothes led to their room. Shonda laughed because it was indecent that they were damn near naked, but after eighteen years, she couldn't care less! Once he opened the door, he carried her across the threshold and took her straight to the king-sized bed and flung her down.

"Hold up, baby, just give me five minutes to look at you," Atwater said, trying to stop his heart from pounding so hard with lust-pumping adrenaline.

Shonda was beautiful under the dim-lit room that made her skin look golden. Her body was better than how he had remembered, because now she had the right thickness in all the right places; when they were younger, she was a lot thinner, but now she was well-proportioned in all the right places. And Atwater cherished the moment thinking that. But because of Shonda, he never had unprotected sex with Butterfly. Shonda wasn't only his children's mother; she was his best friend throughout the past eighteen years of his life. The thought he cherished most about her shot him in the chest with instant guilt. Damn, he had been fucking a boy and loving it!

At that moment he just wanted to curl up with Shonda and feel the heat of her body, hear her heart beat against his ears, and cherish the softness of a woman that nobody would ever be able to replace. But those thoughts were instantly gone as Shonda crawled on him and took his dick into her hands. He felt her small and soft hands running over the shaft of his penis. He smiled for having been so hard on himself.

Shit, eighteen years left a lot of room for trial and error, and growth and development. As Shonda kissed the tip of his erect dick, he made a mature and final peace with himself that he'd accept the past for the past and the future for the future. But for that moment in time and space, there was only one person aching in his heart, body, and soul . . . Shonda!

Atwater went straight to tasting her wet pussy, and he dragged his tongue from her toes to her thighs. She tried to get away from the impending stimulation, but he had a vice-grip on her, and he feasted till she gushed out rivulets of an explosive orgasm.

He climbed atop of her and slammed his dick into her; she was as tight as a virgin would be.

"My god, Mace!" she cried out as he went deep

inside.

He kissed her passionately, and they made love until the moon withered in the midnight sky beyond. And his incessant days with Butterfly.... Would have to be revisited—he knew. But tonight was all about his lovely Shonda.

**Back To Business...**

When Monday had come, they headed to St. Louis. The city was nothing like how he remembered, and he knew it would take him some time to get used to it. But he had bigger things to focus on. Atwater had plans, and he was focused. He couldn't let anything keep him from accomplishing them.

He went to his house in Baden, where Mason and Macy, his mother, his best friend Tyler, his sisters and brothers; his whole family were. They threw him a welcome home party, and he caught up on old times with everybody.

After the party had ended, he had taken Mason and Tyler for a spin in his new car.

"Thank you all for everything. This was good to come home to family and friends."

"Good to have you back, my nigga," Tyler said, who sat in the front seat. "I know you're about to do something big."

"That's right, and I'm going to need y'alls help. I got some big plans, and I'm trying to hit these streets running, if you understand what I mean."

"Dad, you're not going to sell drugs again, are you?"

Atwater had to look at his son in the rearview

# MICHAEL A. ROBINSON

mirror.

"No, fool. I have bigger plans, and I'm going to need you especially. You remember telling me about your friend Liam Val, who you said has an inside scoop on different people in politics and the gossip about them."

"Yes, I remember telling you. But why?"

"Wait till we get to a bar and all sit down and talk."

They went to a sports bar, and Atwater checked out the scene. Everybody was chatting and telling jokes and it was peaceful. He remembered all the days that he wished he was out and about and chilling with his family and now he had that. He didn't have to worry about the jail stuff anymore, and it made him feel good.

"What were you talking about, Dad?" Mason brought him out of his not-so distant reverie.

Atwater studied his son and Tyler. Tyler looked like the average dope dealer, and his son looked like he was being groomed to be a politician or something. But Atwater knew he had to take the reins on every one in his inner-circle, and he would have to let them in on his plans.

"I got something big I'm putting together, and your friend is going to be critical for me putting it together. Tell me more about him?"

"What do you want to know?"

Atwater had to take it slow with his son. His son was game conscious, but at the same time, going to all those private schools made him a little soft, or at least that's what he led one to believe.

"Is he for game?"

Mason couldn't believe that after his father had

done all that time, he would come back to the streets and want to sell drugs! It was contrary to all the stuff he spoke about strategizing success, and although Mason loved his fake uncle, Tyler, he always thought people could make money in all types of ways that didn't include selling drugs.

"Pops, you're talking about selling that stuff again?"

Even Tyler was shocked by Mason's insistence that Atwater wanted to sell drugs, but it was as if Atwater expected it.

"I'm not going to even entertain that question again. But I'm about to break it all down to y'all. We're going to use your friend to gather information on politicians, entertainers, law enforcement officials, you name it. We're going to use this information to barter power."

Tyler laughed. "Fool, you done lost your mind in there. You're trying to get a nigga killed!"

Atwater smirked, and his son saw that it was truly dangerous. "Pops, you tripping."

"Mason and Tyler, you muthafuckas betta not ever doubt me! I work off of trust and loyalty, and I don't need nobody under me who's scared or fearful. I'm about to get super rich and powerful and if you two are shortsighted and fearful, you can get up from this table right now.

"In this age of information, I want to be the one who, not only barters and sells it. I want to be the one who's manufacturing the shit."

Neither of them had left the table, and they sat feeling chastised. Tyler saw it then. Atwater still was the leader he had remembered, and he knew it wouldn't be long before he would gather a mob together that was stronger than the first one they had,

had. Plus, Atwater didn't want anybody to question his judgment. He wasn't a weak ass follower, a flunky, a yes-man.

"How can you manufacture information?" Tyler asked.

"Now you're ready . . ." Atwater looked at Tyler. "What did you do with the letter I sent you?"

Tyler took the letter out of his front pocket. "It's right here."

"Did you get me a crew that ain't tied into no drug shit, because that's the worst thing that could happen is for me to get on some ongoing investigation."

Tyler chuckled. "No, these fools ain't no hustlers like that. They street niggas though, that need plenty direction. They good niggas though."

Atwater looked over at his son. Fuck the food and the drinks, it was time to go. "Let's wrap this up. I want to meet them right now, and I want you to call Liam Val and tell him I want to meet him asap."

"Dad, we haven't eaten yet." Mason and Tyler looked at one another with confusion.

"Come on. Fuck that shit. I have catching up to do."

As soon as they got in the car both Mason and Tyler were making calls as Atwater had ordered them to do. They went to a nearby park where Atwater was supposed to meet his new crew. By now, the sun was setting, and it set a tangerine colored glow that enveloped the city. It was the first time since Atwater left that he finally felt at home.

He still felt messed up, realizing that so much had changed and he just wanted to keep himself busy with building his empire, so he wouldn't have to cry over all the years he had lost for a mistake Tyler had made.

# BUTTERFLY

When they drove up to the park, Atwater noticed about eight cars at the parking area. All the cars were painted nice and had expensive rims. When Atwater, Tyler, and Mason got out the car all the other guys exited their cars. There were eight cars and twelve people. Atwater only needed four or five.

Tyler greeted them by pounding their fist and giving them dap, as Atwater studied them calmly. Tyler came back and he began to introduce them. "That's Lil Rogg, Big Rogg's middle son—"

Atwater held up his hand, because he didn't need to know them all. He looked for something else that an introduction couldn't fully determine. He studied their eyes. When he looked into eyes that were too ambitious, he looked them over. If he saw envy or conceit, he looked them over. When he saw admiration with a hint of camaraderie, he knew he had his men.

"Let's go," Atwater said as everybody looked puzzled.

Tyler was tripping by now. He thought jail had messed up Atwater's head. He looked over at the crew he had assembled and told them he'd holler at them later. When Tyler got back into the car, Atwater pulled off. "You all right, Atwater?" Tyler asked, knowing Mason was quietly thinking the same thing.

"I only saw three I could use. I need the cat with the Saint Louis baseball cap, the cat with the Jesus cross chain, and the biggest one that was there."

"That's Biggie, Q, and Tre," Tyler said as he laughed. Atwater was still sharp.

"What's up with Liam?" Atwater asked.

"We can go over to his apartment right now," Mason said as he guided Atwater to the apartment complex.

Liam was Hawaiian with the red complexion of a Native American. His long hair was matted in dreadlocks. His body, although short, was chiseled with rock hard muscles that needed to be on display. When Atwater, Tyler, and Mason went into his apartment, Liam had on a wife beater, cargo pants, and sandals. He looked like he was dressed for far warmer climates than the muggy spring day that was approaching summer.

"Y'all smoke weed?" Liam asked, after they greeted each other.

"What you got?" Atwater asked.

"I got some granddad-purp."

"Blaze it up," Atwater said.

It was just what was needed to let the tension out of everybody. After being gone so long, people become a bit estranged, and it's only so much a visit and phone calls can do to compensate for being in person. Liam was playing Bob Marley over the sound system. He had *Popular Mechanics*, *Hacking*, *Scientific American*, and *Popular Science* magazines scattered on the coffee table in a stack in front of body building books.

"Mason tells me you have something I can make some money from," Liam said. He needed to pay his college tuition, and if he had anything left over, he wanted to buy a motorcycle.

Atwater felt so relaxed after the weed hit his system that he almost forgot all the pending business at hand.

"I need to find out certain information about people in high places," Atwater said.

Liam looked at Mason, and they both laughed.

"What kind of information?" Liam asked as Tyler studied Atwater cautiously.

"I need any information on anybody who's a sexual

deviant."

"Dad, that's impossible to find out," Mason said, who was on the edge of having a bout of giggles. But the more he looked at Liam, he wasn't so sure about that.

"I don't know. There may be a way." When Liam said that, everybody scooted to the edge of their seats as Liam went over to turn the sound system down. "Look, all the major companies in the world gather tons of information on people based on their buying habits, the things they read, and the websites they visit on the computer. Basically, it has a lot to do—"

"Edward Snowden, the WikiLeaks guy. All the stuff with the NSA," Mason interrupted.

"That's my boy," Liam added. "Basically, what I'm saying is that I could tap into certain porn industry databases, and get a profile on anybody they have a file on." Atwater and Tyler were tripping about what they were hearing.

If what Liam was saying was right, and he could do what he was proposing, Atwater could make a fortune far beyond anything he had ever expected. With a little ingenuity, he could lock himself in a monarch of, not only wealth, but power and influence. And power and influence were prized far more than wealth.

"So all I'd have to do is give you a list of the people in high places, and you could give me any info as to if they are sexual deviants?" Atwater asked, amazed at the power this kid, who was not even twenty-one years old, was about to give him.

"Pops," Liam said, "I'm not only going to be able to give you a 'yes or no' answer as to if they are sexual deevs, I'm going to be able to tell you exactly what gets them off, as if you were in their heads."

# MICHAEL A. ROBINSON

"That's bullshit!" Tyler said. Of course he couldn't understand why Atwater wanted to know that type of info, but he didn't believe info like that was held on people.

Atwater was already writing down names on the back of a sheet of paper that was on the coffee table. He already knew the names by memory from what he had planned from day one. He handed the paper to Liam, and Liam laughed at the twenty-six names he saw. "Fuck!"

"Watch your mouth," Atwater said to Liam. "We're going to make each other filthy rich."

"Yeah, and very dead in the process." Contrary to Liam's statement, he had sparkles of excitement in his eyes. This cloak and dagger shit was right up his alley—living on the edge with no brakes.

\* \* \* \* \* \*

After they left, Atwater drove home. Shonda and Macy had cleaned everything up, and they were waiting Atwater's arrival. Regardless of Atwater's excitement, he made it a point to spend time with his daughter. Around 8:30 p.m., he and Shonda got dressed and went to an elegant restaurant. When they returned home they had passionate sex.

Not too long after, he was glad to find out that Shonda was pregnant. It was the best news yet, because he'd get a chance to take part in raising his seed. But he had a more pressing matter; which was, building an empire, and the drama that lay ahead in doing it.

# Chapter Forty-One |
### *Together Again*

A fter Atwater left the jail, Butterfly had went through a deep depression. She knew she'd be with him in under a month, but the thought of him being away was killing her.

On more than one occasion, Kathy had tried to rekindle their lust-fun, but it could never be rekindled. Butterfly was just strictly-dickly, and the thought that she had been with Kathy disgusted her. But she kept it as friendly as possible.

Atwater had her head fucked up. He had all these dreams and goals of being wealthy and powerful, and she just didn't believe that she fit into any of it. She didn't believe she had what it took. She told Britney and Buffy the details and they laughed like crazy, but it did make sense.

Her release-date came like a blink of an eye, and she had an emotional farewell hug with Britney and Buffy and she knew she'd miss her support team. She was then processed through the slow and agitating release procedures, and she dressed out in her clothes.

Atwater had sent her a banging Akris gown that had a split on the side and Manolo Blahnik shoes, and she thought the shit was too fucking elegant to have to drive home in.

But after she dressed out, she felt a hundred times better, and when the COs saw her, they laughed. "Where the fuck you think you're going? To the Grammy's?"

"To none of your fucking business!" Butterfly was

like that! She had a little attitude, and she wasn't the scaredy cat she had come to jail as. Buffy and Britney had rubbed off on her. She didn't care what people thought of her, and she wouldn't be scared of getting her ass kicked anymore.

Butterfly was no longer the girl that Peyton had set up, or the detectives had frightened to snitch on Glen, or the girl that needed protection from Sosa, Black, or otherwise. She remembered how frightened she felt when Black had shoved her face into the wall and snatched down her pants, and she just believed that after being with Britney, who knew how to fight, and Buffy, who knew how to talk shit, she was a mix of the two.

Her true confidence told her that she could stand up to her father and tell his hateful ass to go fuck himself and take her brother with him. And she'd be woman enough to take the ass whipping that would probably come with it. But she felt the strongest confidence knowing that she had made her peace with her mother, Sandra, had a man that truly loved her for her, and that she'd told her uncle Kevin she never wanted to see him again.

Above all that, she was free!

When she saw Atwater, who pulled up in a rented drop-top red Ferrari, she dived into his arms. He was dressed like a Miami playboy, and he looked finer than ever.

"Damn, I missed you!" she said. She couldn't wait to get fucked tonight.

"Come on, we have a plane to catch."

"We're not going to drive?" Butterfly looked disappointed. She was going to give him head to the

# BUTTERFLY

earth's end. "You know I don't have to report to my probation officer till Monday."

"Just get your fine ass in the car." Atwater's dick was already hard. He'd been wanting to fuck Butterfly the whole time he'd been out. She was the only one on God's green earth that knew how to gurgle nut out of a man's dick.

Butterfly sauntered her buttery hips over to the passenger seat. When she got in, she saw that Atwater had real makeup for her to use in a toiletry bag. She made her face up, and she looked good to death. All she needed now was to whip her hair up, and she would have been the baddest bitch on the eastern seaboard.

"Where we going?" she asked as they sped down the highway. She had just finished putting her final touches on her makeup, and she leaned over to rub his cock that stiffened to the touch.

"Just shut up and enjoy the ride."

"You want me to shut up?" She had a mischievous smile on her face as she massaged his dick. He smiled unevenly. "I'll keep quiet." Butterfly unzipped his pants and gave him the mega head he loved.

They drove to Philadelphia where they caught a first-class flight to Florida, where he had reservations for a two-night cruise.

Carnival Cruise line boarded, but before they had embarked, Atwater took her to a beauty salon that whipped Butterfly's hair up with an expensive weave that they styled in big bows cascading down her back. She felt fresh, relieved, and free! Atwater was amazed at what a good weave could do, and he took her to the mall to get some clothes for the trip. While she was there, she got a pedicure and manicure.

265

# MICHAEL A. ROBINSON

Now they went on the high seas, headed for the Bahamas: Nassau and Freeport.

After dinner, they went to the dance floor. "Tender Love" by Force MDs was playing, and after the song they went back to their small cabin. They had wild and savage sex until they couldn't move anymore. Afterward, Atwater had to prepare her mind for what he needed next.

"I got everything lined up, and now I need you to get me some bitches that look like you."

"Not right now, Atwater. Damn, come back and get in the bed."

Atwater made himself a drink, and sleep was the last thing he needed. "I need you to focus. We'll relax soon enough, but right now I want you to get your ass up and grab a paper and pencil."

Butterfly fumed, but did as she was asked. She wrapped herself up in the bedsheets and came to Atwater's side as he sat on the edge of the bed with a laptop. He went to a website that had ads for transvestites, and he and Butterfly poured over different people until they wrote down the names of who they wanted to interview.

"You have qualities that I know I'm right about why I chose you to do this job. You're going to be able to relate to these girls, and they're going to look up to you for a lot of reasons."

After the two-day cruise, they went in separate directions. But Butterfly knew what she had to do.

*Recruitment...*

A month later, it had been exactly as Atwater had

# BUTTERFLY

said it would be. She didn't even know that she could have that much influence on other people. But she carried out his instructions to the tee, and she only recruited people who were classy and who were loyal to Atwater and her.

She just didn't know he was going to be so persistent, anal retentive, pressuring her about everything. And she thought that their weekend on the cruise ship would be spent full of wild sex, but all he wanted to do was tell her what she had to do! And the simple fact was, she loved him harder than ever, more than ever, and it paled the love she felt for him when they were in jail together. Now she'd ache if she wasn't with him, and she hated it. She hated that he was so different now.

Damn, he had turned into a drill sergeant overnight, and she felt like she was losing her identity in his. He told her how she would have to use pleasure to attain information, how they were going to use cameras and spyware to catch politicians, entertainers, and law enforcement officials in embarrassing and compromising positions. And he even went as far as to actually want to use truth serum drugs. She thought that wasn't only funny, but crazy!

Maybe she didn't see his ideas at all as being practical, and that's why he had been on her so hard. But she did do her part, and she recruited her fair share. Atwater's project was in its beginning stages and he was edgy. He'd fly back and forth from St. Louis to DC, or he'd do visual conference calls over Skype from his home office. But he took the shit as serious as a heart attack.

Butterfly had recruited ten people, one was a white girl who was no older than fifteen, but she looked the

267

part, and she was really sharp for a kid. Her name was Faith, and she was best friends with a transvestite who was nineteen, whose name was Lacy.

Lacy was most definitely the greatest asset to Atwater's project. He/she, which would better be indicated as a she, was a slender Dominican girl without blemish to her creamy and milky white skin, dashing features, and pink succulent lips that were as fluffy as Butterfly's. She was by far a clever talker, and her wit was beyond her years. But she was as sassy as any Latina.

And that's when it blew. Lacy had got a video of her fucking a mayor of a city in Maryland, and his name must be protected for obvious reasons. Although Lacy was a transvestite, she loved to dip, if you catch the drift. She gave the DVD to Butterfly, and Atwater did what he was best at.

He sent pictures of the video to the Mayor's office with a contact number, and within minutes Atwater was on the phone with him. He was able to negotiate a sum of $1 million to an offshore account to keep quiet. But it was a source of income that Atwater could always use.

The next big item scheme came in person of Faith, who had slept with a married pastor of a mega-church, and to keep the statutory rape issue hush-hush, he had paid Atwater $2 million, and the two schemes had been finalized within a week of one another.

Butterfly was busy doing the boring part of instructing everybody who she recruited on where to stash the equipment, how to attract the man, and how to conceal their identity, which included how they were supposed to wipe a place down of their fingerprints.

# BUTTERFLY

Their true identity would never be revealed, and whenever Atwater presented anything to the tricks he was scheming on, he would use the real identity of somebody else who fit the bill.

But nothing could compare to when Lacy had set up a Federal judge, and she had made a tape of her fucking him in the ass! It was their greatest achievement, and when Butterfly had called Atwater with the news, he had chartered a leer jet to fly him there immediately; he didn't want anybody to get a copy of the DVD.

Butterfly had just flown out of town with a Senator/trick, whom she was baiting, and she would be gone for two nights. Lacy and Faith were at the airport terminal awaiting Atwater's arrival.

When the private jet landed, he walked out into the glistening sky looking like a million bucks. With this DVD of the sex scandal, sky was the limit. He was about to put the DVD up somewhere safe in St. Louis.

It was the third time he had seen Lacy, and when he thought Butterfly was gorgeous, Lacy was fine to death! She wore a pink DKNY miniskirt and her tits were a bit smaller than Butterfly's, and she didn't have nearly as much ass. Faith trailed her, and they both were five star ladies: their hair had been whipped by hell!

He hugged them, and as he hugged Lacy, she slipped him the DVD. It wasn't long before they were above the clouds headed toward St. Louis.

Atwater put the DVD on. It was the best! The video had clarity and the judge's voice could be heard all too well. It was all he could hope for and much more. He couldn't help but reach over and kiss Lacy on the cheek.

"Ain't no looking back!" he said over and over again. And this time he knew it was the truth.

# MICHAEL A. ROBINSON

Faith was at a table in a corner making lines of cocaine. Atwater didn't know that Lacy or Faith were heavy users, and he didn't realize it until he got up to get a glass of champagne and saw her making perfect white lines. "What the fuck is this!" He was livid. He didn't want the pretty little bitch in the back of his privately charted jet getting high off that shit.

Faith didn't know what to say, and Lacy came to her rescue. "Papi, it's just for celebration. Don't have a heart attack. We've worked our vaginas off, and we're going to celebrate. All of us!"

Atwater eyed her for a second. That sassy ass Latin shit was mesmerizing. "Go ahead then. I need to take a piss." Atwater had popped the DVD out and placed it in his front pocket. He wasn't going to let it out of his sight for one second. When he came out of the bathroom, Lacy and Faith were snorting the long lines off the table. Their noses were white, and they laughed like little girls.

"This some good stuff. It has my pussy tingling," Faith said, leaning back in her chair. She was just too smart to be so damn young and fine. Her little body looked like sex on the beach and fuck on the ocean.

"Shut up, mami. Watch your tongue. Our boss is here."

Atwater laughed. "Quit with that boss shit, you pretty muthafucka."

"Papi, you're the one acting like you got something stuck up your ass." They all laughed. "Come over here and do a line and chill your uptight ass un poquito."

"I ain't doing that shit." Atwater sat at Faith's side. She was one of the finest white girls he'd ever seen, even though she was a bit on the slim side.

"Fine, papi. More for us."

# BUTTERFLY

"Butterfly told us about when you all were in jail,"
Faith said.

"She runs her mouth too much."

"She said you had a big dick," Lacy said, snorting
another line of cocaine.

Atwater laughed. He knew what they were trying to
do, and he wasn't having it. He thought it was just a
senseless game, but Faith reached over and caressed his
dick.

"What the fuck are you doing?" But she stroked his
dick, and the little bitch looked like she wanted to be
stuffed. The energy was so fucking erotic that he had to
stand up for a second. His dick was hard as hell and they
both saw it. "You never tried this shit before, Boss?"
Another stupid ass pestering question, but this time it
didn't sound so dumb and the shit didn't look so bad.

"Move the fuck out the way. Let me see what this
shit is working with." Atwater threw caution to the
wind, because he was so happy with the shit that was in
his front pocket that he knew he was going to celebrate
tonight anyway. He took a deep whiff of the white
powder, and it seemed like fire was being rammed in his
head. But his head instantly felt numb, and then a
feeling of extreme euphoria followed.

The girls didn't pay him any attention. Faith went
over to Lacy and they kissed passionately and groped
one another's breasts. The shit was so stimulating to
watch, that Atwater's dick was throbbing.

Lacy grabbed his dick, and he was fucked up
because he knew if Butterfly had found out, she'd go
berserk. But he was too far gone to say no, and his
altered state had no resistance. Lacy sucked his dick,
and the shit was the bomb. He fell back into a seat

behind him as she slurped his dick.

Lacy had heard so much about Atwater that from the first time she saw him, she was in love with him. He was more than Butterfly had described, and she and Faith would always talk about him behind Butterfly's back. They would say that they each would have his love, no matter what Butterfly thought. They worshipped him as much as Butterfly did, and when they started seeing the money come in that he had promised them, he was all that and then some.

Faith played with her pussy and Atwater watched her. Her pussy looked so clean and pure, and he knew he was going to fuck her young ass. His dick felt like it would explode, and Lacy grabbed KY jelly from her Louis Vuitton purse and greased her ass. She wanted the shit so much that she turned and slammed his dick in her ass as she rode him reverse cowgirl.

She fucked better than Butterfly, but her head could never compare. Atwater fucked her good, and she brought her head back to him and stuck her tongue in his mouth.

Faith's pussy was tingling and she wanted to get fucked too. She went over and kissed Lacy after she had yanked her face from Atwater. Faith straddled Lacy who was getting fucked from the back by Atwater, and Faith put Lacy's six-inch dick inside her.

The shit was wild! When Atwater thought the shit with Kathy and Butterfly was crazy—this shit was bananas! Faith leaned over and kissed Atwater as he slammed his dick into Lacy's ass and all three of them fucked one another.

Lacy sucked on Faith's perky tits and slid inside of her pussy as she felt Atwater ram his dick inside her.

# BUTTERFLY

She grinded down into his dick as Faith bounced up and down on top of her and they were all so coked up that they could fuck for hours.

Atwater motioned Faith to get up and she went on all fours and Lacy got behind her and fucked her. Atwater climbed on Lacy and fucked her from the back and Lacy and Faith were screaming with bliss!

Atwater couldn't nut for nothing because he was so high. But Lacy's ass was so good that he put in work on her.

Faith had seen Atwater's fat ten-inch dick and she had never been with a guy who'd had a dick over eight inches. She was scared, but she wanted him so bad that she begged him to fuck her.

Atwater lay on the ground and the young bitch slid down on his dick and it was some of the best pussy he'd ever had. The shit was tight and wet and she grinded back into his dick and screamed like he was killing her. Lacy didn't just stand and watch, she slid her dick into Faith's ass and they double penetrated her little pussy and ass until she was biting and scratching from heart shattering orgasms. It came, one after the other, and she had three orgasms, before either of them had one.

Atwater wanted some more of Lacy's ass, and Faith sat on his face while Lacy smothered his dick with her ass. His dick slid in and he almost fainted. The ass was better than any pussy he'd ever had, and she slammed back into his dick as Faith moaned and groaned and grinded her young pussy against his face. His dick flared and he exploded inside Lacy's ass and it was the hardest he had ever nutted before!

# Chapter Forty-Two |
*Fed Up*

What seemed to Butterfly like the other side of the world, was actually Seattle, and she was whisked off to a banquet by a Senator who patronized the escort service that Atwater had set up called: *Washington's Choice High-End Escort Service.* It was clear now that Atwater had somehow converted her into a high-class call girl, because she was encouraged to sleep with the past five clients they had gathered intel on. These clients would be extorted by the week's end.

The banquet was immaculate, but the ceremonies were boring with a lot of brownnosing and ass-kissing.

But the threads Butterfly wore made her look the nicest she thought she'd ever look. She wanted to fall asleep in the soft material and dream about the love of her life, Atwater.

Everything up until now was hard work, and she had to stay positive to keep up with this facade. She wanted him to herself, and she was tired of sharing him with Shonda. She had to go weeks without seeing him, and it made her crazy! And it was always the same excuse that Atwater had: "Shonda's pregnant, emotional, and she needs me right now."

She downed her glass of sparkling champagne, and it took everything in her power not to spunk the whole night and fly back to DC on a red eye flight. How much of this would she have to take!

Butterfly longed to feel Atwater inside her. She loved when she hadn't had sex in days, which allowed for her ass to get as tight as a vise-grip. Atwater would slam his dick in her, and she'd bite her bottom lip. It felt like he was ripping her in two parts, and it was the height of ecstasy. She would throw her hips back as he ripped further away, and he'd squeeze the breath out of her when he gushed a milky river inside of her. Her head would feel like it was going to pop as he rammed, jerked, squeeze and drained himself inside of her. His dick and his words were ten times better than any drug she had ever done, and she could lie in her bed alone all night and the hours would slip away as she thought about him. She had to re-cross her silky shaven legs because she felt her insides quiver at the thought of it all.

Butterfly was tired of this! She felt crazy without him and couldn't take the fact that he shared his life with somebody else that wasn't her . . . and . . . and . . . and . . . she wanted him to herself. Foolishly she was in love and nothing could change that. She only wanted all the money that was pouring in to help him manifest the dreams he held so dear to his heart.

Butterfly was twenty-one now, and her life up until that point had been something she hated. Everybody had judged her, and the more she thought about it, it was just because she had a dick! The hate she had for her dick made her certain that her past thoughts about getting a sex-change were etched in stone. It was something she'd do as early as next month.

### There Was Nothing Atwater Couldn't Do...

Two days after Atwater had got his hands on the tape of the federal judge, he had set up an appointment with one of the most powerful mob bosses out of Chicago.

# MICHAEL A. ROBINSON

Atwater, Tyler, and their crew had rented a private jet and had flown to Chicago where they were chauffeured to a mansion in the suburbs.

Atwater's party of ten was escorted to a conference room in the mansion where an Italian Boss, whose name was Joey Bispucci, sat behind a desk. He was strikingly handsome, but he had the eyes of a killer, which Atwater noticed immediately. He was surrounded by security guards, an attorney, and other wise guys who were all dressed in expensive suits.

Once Atwater was seated, Joey asked, "So you're saying you can help my uncle Pauli?" Joey's question was full of sarcasm, and if Atwater was bullshitting, none of his crew would leave alive. His uncle Pauli was serving a double life sentence at ADX, and if the highest paid attorneys in the nation couldn't get his uncle out, how could this fucking moolignon get him out?

Biggie, Atwater's bodyguard, tossed a manila envelope on the desk.

"What's this?" Joey opened the envelope to see a picture of the scandal.

"One of those faces should look familiar to you."

"What kind of friggin' homo shit is this?" was Joey's first reaction. But as he looked closer and closer, he noticed who Atwater was talking about. "Get the fuck out of here! That's Judge Snider! These are fucking impressive."

Atwater smirked because he knew he had him. "To say the least. Which one of these gentleman is your uncle's attorney?"

You asked for the attorney to be here; he's here," Joey said with his uncle's attorney standing at his side.

"I wanted to ask what stage Mr. Bispucci's

# BUTTERFLY

Subsection 2255 was at?" Atwater knew all the answers he asked, because of course, he did his homework before he made the appointment. He knew everything about the Bispucci family. He had found out all the in-and-outs, and he knew he had them by the balls.

The attorney was just as lavish and as snobbish as the bosses around him. "He's on his subsection 2255."

Atwater knew exactly what a U.S.C. Subsection 2255 was. It was a procedure that allowed somebody to appeal his conviction in front of the judge who originally sentenced him, and it all made more sense, because this was the same judge that they now had by the balls.

"Who has the final say-so in a subsection 2255?" Atwater enjoyed himself.

"Judge Snider." The attorney looked over at Joey with eyes that told him they had to pay whatever Atwater was asking. However, the attorney had yet to see the photos that Joey then handed to him.

"Oh my god!"

That was music to Atwater's ears. "You think you could score a favorable decision with those?"

"Without a doubt," the attorney said.

"What do you want?" Joey was tired of the beating around the bush.

"Considering that Bispucci Inc. has an estimated wealth of a quarter of a billion, and when he was arrested, the Feds seized a little over $20 million in cash and assets, which they'll have to cough over once his case is overturned. I'm thinking $30 million."

Joey was livid, and it took his bodyguards to calm him down. "Are you outta your fucking mind! What do

277

you think? We have $30 million just laying around in the house?" He'd have Atwater's head on a platter before he'd let this smart moolie with photos get that kind of money from his family!

Atwater was forever the esteemed gentleman. "I understand your frustration, and I truly sympathize with the whole shock of it all. But if you don't put this judge in your front pocket now, he's going to let the Feds take all of this." Atwater looked around the luxuriant mansion.

"Frankly, my friend. You don't have a choice."

That's when it dawned on Joey that Atwater had done his homework. He looked over at his attorney who could read his mind.

"Joey, I'll have to agree with him. The Feds are already closing in on the gambling operations, the overseas investments, the butcher shops, the restaurants—hell, everything. I advise you to take this as a major breakthrough and a major turning point. You can keep the Feds at bay now by simply controlling the judge."

"Get him the friggin' money," Joey spat.

"All of it?" his banker asked, who was a part of the Bispucci family.

"Get him the friggin' money already!"

### The Boss Is In The Building...

The breaking news aired on every station:

"Shocking news just in. The Bispucci crime family's head, Pauliano Bispucci, has been immediately released from ADX maximum security.

"His conviction was overturned when District Judge

# BUTTERFLY

Snider declared that his conviction was based on an illegal search and seizure, and his twenty-four-count indictment for the following crimes; money laundering, tax evasion, drug trafficking, and murder for hire, and a continuing criminal enterprise, were unconstitutionally attained."

The news showed Bispucci leaving the federal courthouse a free man. There was a crowd to welcome him and journalist were asking him questions and snapping pictures.

"How do you feel about the judge's decision?" a journalist asked Bispucci as he left the court building to get into a limo.

"Let our forefathers who drafted the US Constitution praise the judge's decision."

Atwater laughed. He was a new creature now. He was in a huge Jacuzzi that was built into the ground at the decked-out penthouse flat in DC that he shared with Butterfly. He was smoking a cigar and wore a gold necklace, a bracelet that shimmered with diamonds, and a Rolex which was just as dazzling.

"You like that, don't you?" Butterfly asked, who looked like a million and one bucks in her swanky pale silk robe and her expensive weave that fell to the fall of her back. Her diamond studded earrings and the perfect makeup on her face made her look more a movie star than just simply a model.

"Fuck yeah. Justice served. Fuck that judge. I did eighteen years because I didn't have nobody who was laced with game like me. We ain't even been out a year yet and we're multi-millionaires, and I have that sweet ass of yours to thank. I got a springboard on power."

It was now or never for Butterfly to speak her mind

as she slipped into the hot water with him once she disrobed.

"That's what I wanted to talk to you about. I'm tired of this. This was you're idea, and I only did it because I promised you I would. I'm not complaining, like I promised I wouldn't, but now that I got everything in line, I want to quit. I've been thinking about doing the surgery."

"Where the fuck is all this coming from?"

"I just want to be with you, Mace! I've stopped doing drugs because of you. I'm not even bipolar anymore. You always make me feel complete. I just want to be with you." Butterfly looked coy and sexy and Atwater truly loved her. When the matter of truth is questioned again, he truly, truly loved her! It was sheer ambition, hunger, and drive that made him desperate enough to turn her into a high-class call girl. Yet, out of all ten of his workers, Butterfly had only fucked about five clients, each one about twice, which was nothing in comparison to his other transvestites.

He could afford for her to quit. And the decision he was making was only because he did love her and wanted her to himself. He coveted her to such a degree that he made her and the rest of his workers take HIV tests monthly as an added incentive to his clients that the product was healthy and clean. But on Butterfly's account, he wanted it so he could have unprotected sex without having to worry about bringing anything home to Shonda.

"That's all I'm saying." She kissed his lips, and she didn't know that he had been doing lines of coke ever since he started fucking Lacy and Faith. His attitude had changed, but she attributed it to the money and power.

# BUTTERFLY

"If that's what you really want to do, we can make it happen. But you got to find somebody you trust to hand over your responsibility to."

Butterfly smacked her lips. That would be the easiest thing to do in the world. "Lacy can do it much better than me. It's like she's made for this stuff, and what's more important, she's loyal to you."

By now, Butterfly's hand was under the water caressing Atwater's dick. She straddled him and slid his dick inside her ass as she stuck her tongue down his throat and let him bust a mega nut inside her. Yes, he most definitely loved Butterfly! The love he had for her was some shit he didn't think possible. It made the years he had spent with Shonda seem like nothing, and it made Lacy's fire ass and Faith's pussy, pale in comparison. It was her heart he loved most and the chemistry that made everything else seem like nothing.

But Atwater could hardly think about his flailing love with her. He had the most exciting news of it all. Tomorrow was a really big day for him, and Butterfly would be at his side when he received it.

# MICHAEL A. ROBINSON

## Chapter Forty-Three|
### *Ain't Nothin' Like The Old School*

T he next day was a breeze and Atwater and Butterfly had traveled to a place that they thought they'd never see again. But when they arrived, the place seemed foreign to them, as if they had never been there before.

They were chauffeured in a limo from DC to Schuylkill, Pennsylvania, and they traveled the whole way with a fine girl who looked no older than twenty-one years old.

They were going there to pick up Old School!

Old School looked completely debonair in his Italian cut suit and his slick-back salt & pepper ponytail and Aviator sunglasses once he left out of the jail. He was being escorted by the DEA agent who had cracked him many years ago. Atwater had dug up so much shit on the DEA agent, until he knew all the agent's fetishes and quirks. He had found out that the agent was not only a married man who was a homosexual on the down-low, but he also liked to smoke meth. Butterfly had matched a guy up with the agent who worked for their service, and after the episode went according to plan, the agent was more than too happy to lie to Old School's prosecutor and say that Old School had given critical assistance that resulted in the arrest of a big time ecstasy ring out of Buffalo, New York. The prosecutor filed a motion to Old School's judge, asking for an immediate release for Old School's substantial assistance, as they styled it. It was too funny to believe that it was all a lie in the first place and Old School

# BUTTERFLY

would get out of jail because Atwater had set the DEA agent up! Imagine that.

Old School broke down when he walked into freedom. He had never thought he'd ever see the outside of the prison's gates, and now it had truly happened. He hugged Atwater, knowing this was the son he'd never had, and they were family for life.

When Old School got into the limo, he saw the young girl who Atwater had brought for him. She was a young tender, and Old School had to get used to affection because she was naturally all over him.

"What Craze-zo doing in there?" Atwater asked. He had spoken to him frequently and sent him money.

"He's still a fool." They laughed.

"And Buffy and Britney says you should write them, Butterfly."

Butterfly smiled. She'd get around to it, but it wasn't like she didn't send them any money. It wasn't that she didn't want to write them. Atwater had her doing so much stuff, and she couldn't think about anyone or anything else other than being with him.

They flew back to DC and Atwater showed Old School the sky blue Bentley Brooklyn he had bought for him and the penthouse suite that was across from the building where his penthouse suite was that he shared with Butterfly.

It was funny, but after Old School made love to the young girl, he felt like one of the tricks he had condemned all those years. The young girl's name was Michaela and her skin was golden, her hair blonde and wavy and she had green eyes. Damn was she fine!

Old School expired within minutes after he had given her mind-boggling orgasms and showed her tricks she

# MICHAEL A. ROBINSON

never knew existed. Then he lay there and tickled her brain with his strongest asset, his mind.

"Oh god," he exclaimed pleasurably, "I see a lot has changed since I've been gone."

"What's changed?" she said and her voice sounded sweet to his ears.

"When I was young, these kittens here walked on all four legs." He caressed her pussy gently. "Now they have wings that can fly."

"No they don't!" She laughed.

"Yes they do—I swear to God they do!"

"How does it feel when you're inside me?"

"Like I'm king in heaven." She laughed at Old School, and she thought he was the smartest man in the world and the best lover she'd ever meet. "Riddle me this: a man's mind or a woman's pussy? Where does the power lie?"

It didn't take much to think about how men ruled the world. "A man's mind?"

"You're very wrong, sweet thighs. A woman's pussy has the power of life, death, and influence.

"On the right bed, the whisper in the right ear can change the world. This is magic if you learn to use it. As long as you don't ever allow yourself to become like one of those women who forget that their power over men lies in their beauty and femininity. I can show you how to get the world at your door steps. Baby, you have all it takes and much more.

"If you can say what I'm about to say next, you can have it all."

"What? What is it? Tell me, I'll say it?"

Oh, was she beautiful. Old School was going to have to spend the rest of his day catching up on

# BUTTERFLY

endless fantasies.

"Say this: I don't pray, I prey."

"I don't pray, I prey." She laughed, and he lusted for her for it. She was the first girl he had sex with since the female CO he had a sexual affair with five years ago. Old School, unlike Atwater, had compromised over ten female COs, and he had never once been tempted to have sex with a boy.

"That's it. Now give me some more of that power of yours." He made love to her for hours until she fell asleep in his arms dreaming of one day owning the world.

Old School called Atwater on his iPhone that took him hours to figure out how it worked.

"Come and get me out of here, before this girl has me addled-brained."

Atwater laughed. "I'm on my way."

Atwater walked over to Old School's building, and they went back to Atwater's flat. All of the opulence, including the flat Atwater had gotten for him, was too much to be thrown back into.

It looked so clean, spotless, plush and luxuriant that it would take some getting used to.

They went into Atwater's lounge and Atwater poured them some Remy Martin and they sat down on the leather couches. Atwater drank two glasses of the Remy Martin, and Old School knew Atwater had something to say.

"What's going on, young blood?"

"Old School, I started using that stuff." When Atwater said 'that stuff', he implied cocaine.

"So what? Don't get a hang up over it. Look how you're living? You're driving fast cars, you have your

285

# MICHAEL A. ROBINSON

boy, millions, living in plush lofts. It's a rush, but you're going to get back into the groove." Old School already knew what 'that stuff' meant. The signs were there, and Atwater couldn't hide them, even if he wanted to.

"Damn, I love you Old School. That's exactly what it is! I feel like I'm out of control. Shit is just coming at me in high speeds. And it ain't only that: I've been fucking Lacy, who's a boy. The shit is getting bad to where I like fucking transvestites now. Old School, I'm losing my soul."

Old School laughed. "Young blood, if you had a soul, I wouldn't have dealt with you a long time ago. A man don't need a soul, he needs a brain and a high-IQ. When was the last time a person made millions or changed the world and he attributed it to his soul?

"You wanna know why nobody can ever judge you? There is no right or wrong. There ain't no good or evil. It's just how your computers programmed, and that's why I always tell you to think outside the box. All you have to do is get control of yourself again with these circumstances of having freedom. Just get control."

Atwater knew he could do it. He thought about what it would take, and it wasn't anything other than coming to grips with his new situation of having everything he wanted, when he wanted. Cocaine, he could stop or manage, along with his family life and his love affair with Butterfly. Everything was manageable, and he could hold it all in the palm of his hand. One thing was for certain, Old School gave him his poise back.

He ran everything down to Old School: how he had schemed, set people up, used cutting edge technology and spyware to get the evidence to ransom millions from politicians, entertainers, and law enforcement officers, and how he had negotiated over $30 million in proceeds. They sat up and talked all night, and now Atwater had his foundation and mental support back.

### *Done By Design...*

Months later, Lacy wore a pink Hugo Boss long sleeve looking robe, which was actually a minidress that exposed her flawless, long legs. It was loosely tied in the front and showed that she didn't have on a bra and showed off her flat, sexy stomach.

She and Faith were inseparable sex demons. Faith wore an Emilio Pucci Greek bleached printed scarf with tassel details over a fluid red dress and her perky breasts dangled erotically in the thin material. The both of them had just the right amount of wrong. They were in a fashion contest and both of their coifs were whipped by hell. They could only be topped by Butterfly, whose pinch of peach Gucci body-suit and flowery vest, and stilettos, could only be considered as the height of fashion. Her hair was pulled in a tight ponytail that hung to the bottom of her back. She had on doorknocker earrings, gold bangles that covered her forearms and a gold chain that hung past her belly button. Her vest was open to show her tasty collarbone and supple neck that Atwater had sucked on as he fucked her from dusk till the twilight of the next day.

They headed for Vegas, and Atwater knew he was pressing his luck, because he had been gone all week. Shonda was due any day now and she wanted him home at her side.

They spent the weekend in Las Vegas partying and

# MICHAEL A. ROBINSON

gambling, and Atwater had finally decided to hand the
reins over to Lacy, who had recruited many of her
friends and was running most of the operation. Through
Atwater's connect, Liam Val, whom she would never
meet, she had arranged for more than $100 million in
set-ups. They were bathing in cash!

Everything was good until, on their way back to DC,
Lacy rubbed Atwater's dick and Butterfly had seen it.
They were about to fight on the plane, and Atwater had
to break it up by slapping Lacy for the disrespect to his
girl, Butterfly, but it wasn't enough for Butterfly. By
now she had the idea that he had been fucking Lacy.

Atwater couldn't believe the clumsy move played
on the part of Lacy, and now he wasn't so sure the
move was clumsy. When they touched down,
Butterfly stormed off the plane, still in tears. Atwater
didn't have time for this shit! He headed back to St.
Louis to chill with his wife.

# BUTTERFLY

## Chapter Forty-Four |
*It's A Girl*

The following day, Butterfly was scheduled to fly to Miami to get the operation that would make her a woman. She had been doing the psychological evaluation to make sure it was what she wanted to do, and the evaluation took five months to do and the hell with it! She could live without a penis. It wasn't like she ever used it anyway, other than to piss, and it was disgusting for her that it was attached to her body, no matter how small and ridiculous it was.

When she arrived at the airport, she was whisked off to the doctor's office and once there, she was placed in a small room where she was given anesthesia. And two cosmetic surgeons went to work as the anesthesia worked on Butterfly.

*She, she, she—she was at the hospital and Atwater was standing there at her bedside. He was yelling for her to push, and the more she pushed the more pain Butterfly felt. And it was almost as if her body was being ripped in two. She felt sharp knives cutting on her, and she felt the blood pour from between her legs, and she pushed harder and harder.*

*Atwater grabbed her hand and sweat poured from her head as she pushed harder and harder.*

*The doctor was screaming for her to run—to run and never turn back! But Atwater was there, and she'd never run from him and the more she pushed, the harder he held her hand. And at that instant the doctors cried out*

289

*victoriously and celebrated as Atwater looked on in amusement and smoked a cigar.*

*"It's a girl!" they screamed*

*When the anesthesia had worn off, Butterfly came to. She was now a full-fledge woman, but what was more apparent from her dream: Shonda had had a baby girl.*

Butterfly flew back to DC three days later. It was the most amazing feeling that she was now complete. She had to heal fast so that she could lose her virginity to Atwater. She was still in pain, which made her temper quick and edgy.

She had called Atwater, and he didn't answer his phone. Somebody had stolen his phone and he had to get another number, but how could she have known? When he didn't answer his phone, Butterfly freaked out and called his house.

Shonda picked up the phone on the first ring.

"Is Mace in?"

"No. May I ask who's calling?"

What Butterfly said next was done on purpose. "Can you tell him Butterfly called?"

It took a minute for it to register in Shonda's hearing, but then it dawned on her instantly. "This wouldn't be the Butterfly he was in jail with?"

Butterfly knew she had taken it too far, and she hung up.

### Jail Talk Versus Street Talk...

That night, when Atwater came home, Shonda had leaned into him. She couldn't even finish making dinner, and the baby kept crying as if she knew what her mother was going through. Shonda was livid!

# BUTTERFLY

"Why the hell is that boy calling here? I heard you talking about him to Tyler, and I distinctly remember the way he looked at me during a visit when you were in jail."

Atwater had to play it cool, because this shit was not cool at all. "You're overreacting. I had her—"

"Her? What the hell do you mean *her*?" Shonda had heard it all! This was ridiculous!

"I put 'him' on the Internet, and we used him to get some tricks to get some money—that's the honest to God's truth."

Atwater had thought about those tricks, many of whom were heartbroken when Butterfly had gotten released from jail, and they'd never heard from her again. They tried to find her, but Butterfly had changed her name, and it was as if she were a ghost. The tricks felt scandalized, but what could they do now?

"You're lying, Mace!"

"What the hell you saying then? You saying I'm fucking a punk?" This was the hour of truth, and when Atwater leveled the question at her like that, it did sound impossible.

"I didn't say that, but why would he hang up when I asked him a simple question?"

"I don't know?"

"You think I'm stupid, don't you?" She was, she knew, because she'd never ever believe that Atwater would be one of those creeps who were on the down-low and leading a double life—fucking what she thought to be a punk! The thought was unnerving, impossible even! But she just couldn't let the idea go that easy, because it all made her feel ambivalent. "I remember how he looked at me during the visit, Mace!"

she screamed.

"I don't know. Maybe he thought you were cute."

"Damn it, Mace!" Shonda could have laughed or cried, because Atwater was making light of it. "That wasn't the look he gave me. It was a look like you all had something going on."

"You know what? You need to stop watching those talk shows. That shit is messing with your head."

"I'm going to get to the bottom of this!"

"Just keep your snooping ass out of my office."

"This is my house too!" Shonda was so mad with grief, her hands were shaking. Atwater had only been home ten months, and he had already begun to run the streets all in the name of 'I got to catch up!' She could almost spit the words back in his face, because now they had three beautiful kids together, and for at least one of them he could be there.

She never expected to get pregnant so soon, but his dick felt so good after all those unrighteous years of her forced celibacy, that she made sure she sexed him nightly. That only lasted a month, until he started flying all over the country and chasing a dream that consisted of power, influence, mansions, exotic cars, and money in the bank that would ensure their children's future.

But what was it with this Butterfly thing coming back into the picture? She remembered seeing that 'thing' and thinking that their lives were somehow tied in something she still could not understand. The thought of it was enough to get a gun and kill Atwater! Yet, she could never believe that her Mace, the father of their three beautiful children, could ever lay up with a thing like Butterfly.

# BUTTERFLY

But she would get to the bottom of it . . .

She was brought out of her grief when she heard their three-week-old daughter Nyla crying. As she gave her daughter a warm bottle of formula, and while she fed Nyla, she could see how she could forgive Atwater for even the gravest unpardonable sin if she had to.

### It Was The Girlie Thing To Do...

Atwater could kill Butterfly! He couldn't believe this imbecile-shit. And it was the least he'd ever expect coming from her! After all the shit he had explained to her while they were locked down, and she was trying to tear at the seams of his life.

He hopped on his chartered private jet and flew to DC immediately. He walked into the penthouse suite and slammed the door.

"Butterfly, what kind of idiot shit caused you to call my wife!"

Butterfly was in pain, and she could barely move her legs as she lay on the couch looking at the HDTV big screen. She was agitated, in love, lonely, and she just exploded. "I don't care! Fuck that bitch! Just leave her so it can be me and you."

"Was that your plan all along?"

"What the hell do you think? I've given the better part of myself to you! That bitch just rode the wave, and she's reaping the reward of my hard work."

Atwater couldn't believe what he just heard. He loved Butterfly more than life, but his life had order, and he wasn't willing to throw it all to the wind.

"You know this means I have to chill on you until

293

things calm down?"

"What do you mean? You said you'd never leave me!" Butterfly couldn't even stand. Atwater was about to start for the door and she couldn't stop him, because she wanted to run into his arms and tell him that she was sorry and everything was all right and would be all right and they would be together forever, and she would always have his love.

"That was before you tried to destroy my family! Yo, you're on your own!" Atwater started for the door, but Butterfly's piercing cries shredded his heart in two. He loved her. Honestly he did, but she had to learn this lesson well. There was no way she would be allowed to ruin his life. He turned around. "I did nothing but love you, and this is how you repay me?"

"Don't leave!" Butterfly cried as she tried to crawl toward him. "Don't leave! You said you'd never leave. You're my life!"

Atwater hesitated. He didn't feel so bad now that he saw her like that on the ground, and it was easier to forgive and forget. He wanted to pick her up and hold her in his arms. But she had to learn!

"I'm out." Atwater stormed out of the door and went to see Old School across the way.

But, but, Butterfly panicked. She went berserk and grabbed her phone and called Atwater over and over again and he didn't answer! She went crazy.

She thought she had arrived at the end of her life and all her beauty and youth could be summed up in two words. Those two words had haunted her forever, and she saw it every time her father and brother looked at her. It was so disturbing and confusing that she went to great lengths to cure how people viewed her.

# BUTTERFLY

It was two words that described why she had to find pleasure in a man slamming his dick up her ass, when it was on rare occasions that she could get her own pleasure. She hated to face the truth of it, but the same words came hurling back into her face and it felt like a sharp slap.

Butterfly wouldn't accept it, but somehow she already had. She had carved her body out, and divested it of its wholeness because of the words that so neatly described her. She had to say it to herself! She had to confess it, and she hollered out the words that were once leveled at her: "TWISTED FREAK!"

And it was those words that caused her great grief. She crawled to her wet bar and guzzled down liquor that poured down her silk robe. She just had to make it to her bathroom. She knew she'd never feel pain ever again.

Her stitches had torn and she was bleeding profusely. She hobbled to the bathroom, rummaged through her medicine cabinet, and took as many pills as she could. Butterfly took the lot of them all, and miraculously enough, the pain was deadened.

She floated and she floated and she floated . . . much like a butterfly. Her head felt numb and her heart slowed. Her mind played tricks on her and the floor under her moved and she tripped and fell to the ground.

Her father was on top of her pummeling her with his fists, and when she thought it to be her father, it was Clayton, and her father had Clayton's face and Clayton had her father's face.

Her heart sped up and it was beating too fast and she cried out for help. But when the help didn't come, she cried out, "Stop Daddy! I love you. I swear I do!

# MICHAEL A. ROBINSON

Please just stop beating me! I'm going to die, Daddy, and I love you-I love you! Please stop, Daddy. Please save me, Daddy! Please don't kill me!"

But it was Clayton who pounded away and threatened her. "I wish I never met you, faggot! You killed my mother, you faggot bitch! Die, sissy!"

"No I didn't! Please don't kill me, Clayton! I deserve to live!"

But then kids appeared and they danced in a circle around Butterfly and teased her. "You're a sissy, you're a fag—you're a girl and you're on your rag." And they repeated the song infinitely.

"I'm not-I'm not! Stop it! Shut up! Shut up! I'm not a fag or a sissy! I'm a human being! Why won't y'all just let me live!" Her cries went unheard as she imagined Peyton smacking her again and hearing Peyton's hateful words: "I hope you kill yourself, you TWISTED FREAK!"

Butterfly found the strength to make it to her feet, and the ground rocked under her. She hobbled to her penthouse balcony, looked over the lights of the city, and they were moving. Her mind was watery and she, she, she, she saw tall glades of grass and her arms brushed the grass as she ran into her favorite orchard that was filled with butterflies. She ran to catch one, but the butterfly floated beyond her reach. Butterfly tried to catch the butterfly because she was blinded by the butterfly's beauty. It flew so softly on the sun-drenched wind that Butterfly longed to have wings to fly. She stood on the banister of the balcony and when she felt the warm current of the wind, she thought that she could fly. And before she could leap, she slipped off the ledge and fell back into her penthouse suite.

# BUTTERFLY

Atwater had been across the street at Old School's penthouse suite, and Old School had the young girl by now eating out of the palm of his hand. Atwater spoke to Old School for about an hour, and Old School explained to him that you never, never, never, ever leave emotionally unstable people alone with the threat of you leaving their life forever. Especially after you have been the force that has enabled them to change. Old School's experience revealed to him that, that's how you turn a good girl bad.

Atwater, as always, agreed with Old School, and they walked across the street to the penthouse suite that Atwater shared with Butterfly.

"Butterfly, where the hell are you?" It was the third time Atwater had yelled her name, and now he had grown worried after Old School gave him an 'I told you so' look.

Atwater went to his bedroom, and saw the doors to his balcony wide open. When he walked over to shut them, he found Butterfly lying in a pool of blood.

"Old School, call 911! Hurry up and call 911!" Atwater's cries pierced through the silence of the night as he heard Old School dialing the number.

"Wake up, Butterfly!" Atwater screamed as he held her in his arms and checked her pulse. It was beating slow enough for her to be as good as dead! "Call 911, Old School!"

"They're on their way," Old School said as he returned to Atwater's side.

Moments later, the ambulance arrived, and they applied CPR as they rushed Butterfly to Howard University Hospital. The doctors had pumped her stomach and had lost her twice. She struggled for her life as Atwater sat with Old School in the waiting area.

Atwater's mind flashed on all the good times they had up until that point. For all it was worth, the love he had for her had to see past everything he was brought up to believe about people being different. He had taken her out of the context of being a social evil and realized she was a human being with fears, love, and aspirations like everybody else. But nothing was evil about Butterfly, and she was the best prettiest person he had ever met. And it made him think about when Old School told him there wasn't anything evil—it was the programming. People always programmed themselves to hate anything that was different. But his mind couldn't grasp why she would want to kill herself. Between tearful eyes, he asked Old School, "Why would she try and kill herself?"

Old School looked at him with knowing eyes, as he said, "It was the girlie thing to do."

The cruelty of realizing and understanding what Old School had said summed up Butterfly's whole existence—what she had always tried to make Atwater understand: she was a 100% black woman.

As those thoughts sunk in, the sun was rising in the distance, as Butterfly continued to fight for her life.

# BUTTERFLY

## Butterfly Reading Group Questions

1) How do you think readers who have been molested by close family members and those who were no relation to them could learn something from Butterfly's story?

2). Is there anything anybody in Butterfly's family could have done to keep her from using drugs or becoming a homosexual?

3). Do you think Butterfly should forgive her mother, possibly her father and brother, or her uncle for what they had done to her?

4). What do you believe the reader could take from the double life Butterfly's uncle led? Does it send the wrong message regarding prosperous pastors of mega-churches?

5). Do you think there are transgenders who can lead a successful modeling career and model in some of our most widely viewed magazines, movies, and clothing lines, as the opposite sex without anybody knowing?

6). Why does Old School and Atwater have so much ambition for being powerful? Do you believe their experiences with the judicial system, being incarcerated and their harsh sentences have anything to do with it?

7). Do you think that Atwater is gay? And if so, do you believe he should tell his wife Shonda and his children?

# MICHAEL A. ROBINSON

8). Do you think it's right for Atwater to set up politicians and judges to acquire wealth and power?

9). Do you think the politicians and judges will try and take revenge on Atwater because of the dirt he holds over them?

10). If there was one message in the book that Butterfly wanted to convey the most to the readers, what do you believe it would be?

# BUTTERFLY

## About the Author

Michael A. Robinson has always been described as having a gift for creating stories that make fictional stories mirror real life. He hails from Carson, California which is a city in the harbor area of Los Angeles County.

He grew up in an era in LA where people were trying to make their dreams reality, and he has persisted in this mindset by keeping true to his core beliefs of: reach one, teach one.

Growing up in a gang infested environment, having traveled extensively around the Nation, and having lived 2 years in Brazil as a fugitive, he has an aspect of life that is rare and jewel. All this is exemplified in his writing . . . a writing style that is fluid and natural, raw, yet real.

**Fan address:** Michael A. Robinson
#17572-074
USP Big Sandy
P.O. Box 2068
Inez, KY 41224

CPSIA information can be obtained at www.ICGtesting.com
Printed in the USA
LVOW04s1559290814

401516LV00018B/607/P

9 781936 649686